THE
Golem
OF
Rabbi Loew
Johnny Townsend

The Golem of Rabbi Loew

Jacob and Esau Cohen are the closest of brothers. In fact, they're lovers. A doctor tries to combine canine genes with those of Jews, to improve their chances of surviving a hostile world. A Talmudic scholar dates an escort. A scientist tries to develop the "God spot" in the brains of his patients in hopes of creating a messiah.

A Jew-by-Choice navigates Jewish/Muslim relations during Pesach. A gay Lubavitcher dating a Catholic is attacked and left for dead but becomes a police officer in response. The Golem of Prague is really Rabbi Loew's secret lover.

While some of the Jews in Townsend's book are Orthodox, this collection of Jewish stories most certainly is not.

Praise for Johnny Townsend

The Golem of Rabbi Loew will prompt "gasps of outrage from conservative readers…a strong collection."

Kirkus Reviews

"Pronouncing the Apostrophe," from *The Golem of Rabbi Loew*, is "quiet and revealing, an intriguing tale…"

Sima Rabinowitz, Literary Magazine Review, NewPages.com

"Johnny Townsend's…keen observations on the human condition come in many shapes and sizes…reflecting on both his Jewish and Mormon backgrounds as well as life in the vast and varied American gay community…His perspective is sometimes startling, sometimes hilarious, sometimes poignant, but always compassionate."

Gerald S. Argetsinger, Artistic Director of the Hill Cumorah Pageant (1990-96)

In *Zombies for Jesus*, "Townsend isn't writing satire, but deeply emotional and revealing portraits of people who are, with a few exceptions, quite lovable."

Kel Munger, *Sacramento News and Review*

In *Sex among the Saints,* "Townsend writes with a deadpan wit and a supple, realistic prose that's full of psychological empathy….he takes his protagonists' moral struggles seriously and invests them with real emotional resonance."

Kirkus Reviews

Inferno in the French Quarter: The UpStairs Lounge Fire is "a gripping account of all the horrors that transpired that night, as well as a respectful remembrance of the victims."

Terry Firma, Patheos

"Johnny Townsend's 'Partying with St. Roch' [in the anthology *Latter-Gay Saints*] tells a beautiful, haunting tale."

Kent Brintnall, Out in Print: Queer Book Reviews

Gayrabian Nights is "an allegorical tour de force…a hard-core emotional punch."

Gay. Guy. Reading and Friends

The Washing of Brains has "A lovely writing style, and each story [is] full of unique, engaging characters….immensely entertaining."

Rainbow Awards

The Golem of Rabbi Loew

Johnny Townsend

Contents

Tagging Along...9

A Life of Wind 19

Making the Messiah 36

Leather Jew..53

The Lizard of Oz 78

Jewish Dogs...97

Pronouncing the Apostrophe 111

Sue a Jew 158

The Tarot Reader..181

The Convert's Mezuzah 202

Vampires of the Blood Atonement..................240

The Golem of Rabbi Loew..............................264

Books by Johnny Townsend............................295

What Readers Have Said.................................305

Tagging Along

"Hello? May I speak with Mr. Cohen, please?" asked the male voice on the phone. It was obviously someone who didn't know us. Everyone at work knew who I lived with, and I'd known my friends long enough to tell them. Jacob never gave our number to his students, and he said his colleagues at the university knew about me, at least about my name.

"Which one?" I asked, covering the mouthpiece when I realized I was sighing. It was probably a salesman, but he didn't need anyone else to be rude to him today.

"Mr. Jacob Cohen."

"Just a minute."

I called Jacob to the phone and he strode over in his towel, his hair damp but neatly combed. He stood by the kitchen door to talk and I sat on the sofa and picked up the *T.V. Guide*, it being my night to choose the first program. I didn't look at the listings, though. Instead, I looked at Jacob.

He'd started working out at the Y seven months ago, and his arms and chest were becoming curved and firm. His legs were already muscled from all the running we both loved to do since we were kids. His stomach was not quite firm yet, but he was fast getting there. I thought I could even see one ripple in it now. I wished I'd had the nerve to join the Y when he had.

Not that he would have let me anyway. The whole reason he joined was to get some time away from me, even for just a few hours a week.

"We always do everything together," he complained. "I can't even go to the drugstore to pick up some aspirin without you tagging along."

Of course he'd say it that way. "Tagging along." I was three years younger than Jacob, and it seemed I'd been following him all my life. Mom dressed me in his hand-me-downs. I got all his old toys. Three years after he went to first grade, I had the same teacher. I learned the clarinet in middle school, just as he had. I collected the same Casper and Wendy comic books.

I became a bar mitzvah like he did. I took the same courses in high school, joined the same track team, dated sisters of the few girls he dated, did everything he did, just three years after he did. It had always seemed to please him as we were growing up.

Jacob did go away to college, though, while I stayed home to work. He ended up with a PhD in French and I became a produce supervisor at the grocery. But he'd had a chance to go to school and I didn't. Dad could only afford to help one of us, and I didn't want to be saddled with student loan debt the rest of my life.

Part of me always felt as if he'd been the one to inherit our father's blessing. Why our parents had named their two sons Jacob and Esau I'd never understand. Certainly not why they reversed the order of the names. They'd insisted we be the best of friends and prove that two brothers, even ones apparently set against each other from birth, could, through faith in the God of our fathers, make love the presiding force in their lives.

I looked at Jacob again. We'd been living together for three years. We had a lot of fun together, and I could always make him laugh. But he told me the other day he no longer felt right about us, that our sex life was getting stale, that he was tired of us never going out with friends.

Yet wasn't that his choice? He was the one who never wanted my friends from work to come over, and he never invited any of his own friends to the apartment. It was amazing we even had our own friends, as often as we did everything else together.

As far as sex went, however, maybe he was right. I always let him make the first move. He'd always taken the lead in everything as we were growing up. It was what he did. Take charge. Wasn't that the way it was supposed to be?

Jacob's back was turned to me now as he talked on the phone, giving instructions about some kind of exercise he did. Must be a friend from the Y.

Perhaps it was time for me to take some initiative, keep things interesting for Jacob. I sneaked over and knelt behind him and slowly reached up to put my hands on his hips.

"Oh!" Jacob jumped and looked down at me.

I put my finger to my lips and smiled. Then, motioning for him to continue with his conversation, I turned him so that he was facing me and pulled off his towel.

Jacob gave me a look which seemed half fear and half something else I couldn't figure out. But I had to show him I was growing up, that I could make some decisions on my own. I looked at his chest, taut and lightly hairy, and then took him in my mouth as he at first paused and then finished talking to his friend and hung up.

"Is that all you can think of?" he asked after he replaced the receiver. "Sex?" He pulled my head away from him.

I didn't say anything but stayed there on my knees, afraid to look up.

"Look, Esau, I've got to get over to the Y. This guy I met there is just starting out and doesn't know how to do anything yet. I'm going to go help him."

"How long—I mean, what time do you think you'll be back?"

"God! Why don't you install a time clock by the back door? I don't know. I'll be gone as long as it takes."

He was dressed in a couple of minutes and paused by the sofa just long enough to peck me on the lips. "Love you," he said. I nodded but pretended to be studying the *T.V. Guide* again. As soon as he was out the door, I tossed the magazine on the table and looked at Jacob's towel on the floor.

How could Jacob make friends so easily? I'd dated maybe four guys, two of them seriously, in the seven years Jacob was away at school. He said he'd dated a dozen men. Then again, he came out when he was eighteen, and I didn't come out until I was twenty. That plus our three-year age difference gave me only two years of dating to his seven, but there was more to it than that.

It wasn't that he was better looking. Well, he was now that he was working out, but we basically had the same body type and similar facial features, which was probably why we found each other attractive in the first place. He'd been the one to seduce me, a couple of months after he came back to town to teach.

I'd been over at his place to watch T.V. with him, and he started rubbing my feet, then my legs, and before long we made love for the first time. I knew right then that I wanted to spend the rest of my life with him, but it was Jacob who formally proposed to me three months later.

Our parents thought it was wonderful that we were so devoted to each other, that we wanted to live together, go out together, become close again as we'd been before Jacob moved away. We, of course, could never tell them we were lovers.

We did tell our gay friends, but we usually didn't tell them we were brothers. Instead, we either said we were cousins or that we both simply had the same last name. It was easier that way, and since none of my friends had ever met Jacob before, and none of his had ever met me, the lies weren't that hard to pull off, well worth the effort.

There might be less prejudice among gays than straights about sexuality, but how could we explain *our* situation to people? Always another closet to come out of.

I doubted if Jacob had said much about me to the friend he was going to see tonight. I knew Jacob had sex with other men. I didn't like it, and I'd never had sex with anyone else since we'd become lovers, but I never tried to make Jacob feel bad about it, either. I knew he needed his space, though I hoped this was a temporary phase.

I hadn't even been to a bar, with or without Jacob, in over two years. Before now, Jacob had never let other men come between us, so the self-imposed seclusion hadn't really been that hard to deal with. When Jacob's infidelity began to bother me, I just told myself that, being gay, I should be more understanding about non-traditional sexual behaviors.

I stood up and walked over to the bookshelves along the wall. I'd read most of the books already, even Jacob's French novels. I took two years of French in high school, as Jacob had, and after he went to college I studied more on my own, so I could write him letters while he was away. Since we'd been together, Jacob had taught me still more.

Every Tuesday we spoke only French to each other to stay in practice. I thought about getting a degree, but by now I no longer felt I had to do all the same things he did, and I liked having a different job than he had. Sometimes, Jacob would say, "You're wasting your mind," or "Maybe we're not as much alike as I thought," but I always refused to go to school when he offered to help.

Produce was no big thrill, however, and I did like French, but even a year ago, I could see that Jacob was growing tired of my "tagging along." "Do we have to watch every T.V. show together?" he'd ask.

But our taking turns to decide what to watch was just a formality. We always liked the same things, *The Discovery*

Channel, Nova, Fawlty Towers, Masterpiece Theatre, Star Trek: The Next Generation.

In the past seven months, though, I'd been watching a lot more on my own. We had cable, so of course we had Bravo and watched lots of foreign films. We also had a Spanish channel, and since I'd taught myself some Spanish over the years, I decided to use my time while Jacob was working out to become more fluent in a third language. A couple of my employees were Hispanic, and I practiced with them daily.

For some reason, I never wanted to tell Jacob about it, but in the past seven months I learned five more tenses and maybe a thousand more words, ten more each of the three evenings every week when Jacob was at the Y. It was kind of fun knowing something he didn't know.

Lately, there'd been a show on cable about the U.N. I used to wonder about translating, but the idea of interpreting seemed even more exciting, having to perform right on the spot. When I'd mentioned it to Jacob, he said interpreting would be boring, but it could hardly be more boring that packaging single bananas separated from the main bunch by shoppers.

Maybe I could take some political science courses at college, if Jacob was still willing to help me. If he wasn't, perhaps incurring some debt was something I'd simply have to do. I could learn a fourth language. I might have it in me to learn a dozen languages if I really tried. I'd never considered it before. I wanted to stay with Jacob forever, but I had to face the idea of living my own life without him if it came down to it.

I turned away from the bookshelves just as the phone rang again.

"Hello?"

"Hi, Esau. It's me, Jacob."

"Hi." I wanted to add "dear," as I usually did, but he'd probably see it as me being possessive. No need to antagonize him any more tonight.

"Look, I'm sorry about what I said earlier."

I couldn't reply and so said nothing.

"Anyway, there's this guy here who's just learning how to work out on the machines." He paused. "I got to thinking, since I'm explaining everything anyway, why couldn't you come over and learn, too? I—I do need time to myself, but I like being with you, too. I miss you when we're not together."

"I know, Jacob. It's okay." I paused. "I think I'd like that." I'd already started doing some sit-ups and push-ups at home, but not enough. I'd looked into another health club in town, but it cost more than the Y, and I was afraid of what Jacob would say if he found out. Besides, I liked learning my Spanish, too.

"Good." Jacob sounded relieved. "You want to come down then?"

I looked at the *T.V. Guide* and then at the bookshelves. "No," I said. "Not tonight. I can start coming next time if you want."

"Why not tonight?"

I shrugged even though I knew Jacob couldn't see. "I don't know. There's a movie at the theater I've been meaning to see. I figured tonight would be a good time."

"You're going out? By yourself?"

"I'll be back by 10:00."

"Oh. Well, I'll see you in a little while then."

"All right."

"Oh, and Esau?"

"Yes?"

"I liked what you did earlier when I was on the phone. I just wasn't expecting it was all."

I laughed. "There may be a few more surprises in store for you. I hope you don't mind."

"You can do anything you want, as long as you still love me."

"I do, Jacob."

We were both quiet a moment, but I finally managed to say goodbye, and we hung up.

I picked up the towel and threw it over the rack in the shower. I thought about changing but saw no need and so went straight to the newspaper. A 7:30 showing. I could make that easily.

I opened my wallet to make sure I had at least a ten. I knew Jacob would be hurt I'd turned him down, but maybe on my way home, I could pick up the latest copy of *Blue Boy* or *Honcho* for him. Maybe I could think of a way to respond differently in bed tonight or perhaps even initiate something myself for a change.

Putting my wallet back in my pocket, I took a deep breath and walked out the door, singing a song I remembered hearing the night before on one of Jacob's CDs. It was a French folk song about a little boy. Or was it two little boys? How did that go now? I couldn't remember. I shrugged and began humming a Spanish tune instead.

A Life of Wind

"So what do you want to do?" Chris asked.

"I don't know," said Baruch. "Something different."

"But you've got a free apartment now, plus a reasonable salary. Why do you want to quit?"

"I've been manager of this Bed and Breakfast for ten years, ever since I came to New Orleans. There has to be something more out there for me."

"Well, don't slit your own throat. You shouldn't quit till you find something better."

"But Chris, there's no room for you here. The eight years I was with David, we lived apart. That's not going to happen again."

Chris didn't say anything, and Baruch didn't push it. Baruch had mentioned moving in together several times, and Chris always remained silent when the subject came up. But Baruch was forty-two now. He was tired of hiding who he was from the neighbors or people at work. Chris, who was only thirty-five, lived in Lake Charles and worked offshore on an oil rig. He was afraid of what might happen if his co-workers found out he was gay, but that was no worse than what might happen if Baruch's Lubavitcher community discovered he was gay. Well, maybe it could be worse. They could push Chris into the Gulf of Mexico.

"You going to look for a new job here or in Lake Charles?"

Baruch didn't want to scare Chris, but Chris had to accept that they were partners or there was no point in being with him. "Lake Charles," he said. "I can't get over there, so I'll just have to look for something by computer."

"I've got to get going. I'll see you again next Tuesday." They kissed, and then Chris walked across the garden patio and out through the iron gates to Esplanade Avenue. Baruch worked in the Tremé neighborhood, right next to the French Quarter. It was a poor area with lots of crime, so Baruch followed Chris to the gate and watched him walk to his car, parked almost a block away.

Baruch waited until he saw the car drive off before heading back to the hotel. He liked to go in and relieve Kim, the other employee, for half an hour on days after Chris left. Though he didn't get paid for it, it made Kim happy and made Baruch feel less alone after Chris drove away.

Chris came to see him once a week on Baruch's Tuesday off, if it coincided with Chris's time off. Chris worked two weeks on the rig and then had two weeks off. Baruch didn't have a car, so Chris drove in from Lake Charles on Monday evening and was waiting in the apartment when Baruch got off work.

They'd make passionate love to each other and then spend a couple of hours catching up on the news of the last few days. Since they emailed constantly, most of the news was repetitious, but they always saved some little tidbit to tell in person.

They didn't do anything all that incredible really. They played Scrabble, and listened to Rob Thomas songs, and watched Israeli movies. They drove up to City Park and walked along Bayou St. John. Once, they went to the art museum in the park, and Baruch then spent several weeks painting a reasonably decent portrait of Chris's mother from a photo he'd brought from Lake Charles.

Baruch of course had never attempted representational art before, since it was forbidden. Still, he knew Chris loved his mother, and he wanted to acknowledge that in some way. Chris was genuinely touched and said he loved the painting. Chris wrote him poems almost every week, and, although they were atrocious, Baruch kept them all in a binder, in plastic page protectors. Chris also ordered Jewish books online that he hoped Baruch would like.

Baruch in turn started learning French, so he could talk with Chris's mother if he ever finally met her. She spoke English, too, though Cajun French was her first language, and he wanted to show some respect. Baruch also watched every episode of *Soap*, an old 1970s sitcom Chris loved, cuddled in Chris's arms. And he wrote Chris long emails about growing up in India where his father had been a rabbi, little episodes that were his own version of Isaac Bashevis Singer's *In My Father's Court*.

The phone rang at the front desk, and Baruch answered. It was a young couple from a town called Windy Creek in Alaska who wanted to book a room for three days, a month and a half from now, for their honeymoon. It was a slow time of year, so Baruch told them they could get a fourth night at 75% off if they wanted. The young woman making the reservation asked her fiancé, and they took Baruch up on the offer. "We may as well make the most of our honeymoon," she said. "You only live once."

Baruch thought about her words after hanging up the phone. He'd lived two lives so far, maybe three, and felt very lucky. He couldn't believe he'd found Chris and was still luxuriating in his company. How could he be so fortunate as to have found two soulmates? He'd met his other soulmate, David, his very first day in New Orleans, not long after stepping off the plane from Israel.

After Baruch's wife and two young children had been killed by a drunk driver, Baruch simply had to get away from Jerusalem. His father didn't want him to leave for America, but Baruch had always wanted to live in the States and knew it was time. Since there was a Lubavitcher community in New Orleans, he decided to try there.

There'd been a lot of turbulence at the beginning of the flight, but Baruch prayed, and soon the sky was calm. Baruch knew it was a sign he'd made the right choice.

After arriving in New Orleans, he rented a room in a Bed and Breakfast on Esplanade and then took a walk through the Quarter that first evening. Sitting on the levee, watching the ships and ferries go by on the Mississippi, he noticed an attractive young man with long, dark hair walking by. Baruch nodded at him, and the man nodded back. The man walked a little further and then turned back.

"I noticed the side curls and the skullcap. You're Jewish?"

Baruch nodded.

"My name's David. I'm Jewish, too. Not Orthodox, though."

"I'm a Hasid."

David looked confused. "You're a hussy?"

"A Hasid."

They sat and talked for three hours that evening on the levee. David hadn't attended synagogue in fifteen years but was still intrigued by Baruch. Baruch, for his part, felt he had nothing to lose and told David of his upbringing in India, and then of his family's move to Jerusalem after Baruch's mother died of pneumonia. He explained how his brother Chayim had always loved art but had been afraid of studying anything outside of the yeshiva.

Then after Chayim was killed when his legs were blown off in a bus bombing, Baruch decided he'd take an art class himself, in addition to his own yeshiva studies, because he'd always liked art as well. He especially loved designing ketubot. Baruch talked of his marriage to Leah a couple of years later, and of his family's recent deaths. Then he blurted out something that surprised even himself. "I loved her, but I think I could love you even more."

David leaned over then and kissed him, and Baruch took him back to his room, where he made love to a man for the first time. It was faster than a whirlwind romance. He and David were lovers from that night on.

The next morning, Baruch discovered that the Bed and Breakfast where he was staying needed a full-time manager. He asked for the job and got it. He'd been living there ever since. Hashem had a way of opening just the right door at the right time.

David had wanted them to live together, but Baruch didn't want any other Hasidim to discover he was gay. Strangely, now that he realized for sure what he'd long suspected about himself, he didn't feel the least bit guilty, yet he still knew he needed to keep it a secret. Though David wasn't happy about it, he accepted the arrangement.

They'd been surprisingly content together for eight years before David developed stomach cancer. At that point, Baruch took David in, not exactly "coming out," but not caring what anyone else thought, either. He'd cared for him those last few miserable months.

And then he was alone again.

Baruch had been angry with the Lubavitchers for making him feel he shouldn't love another man and making him miss out on seven years of living with David. So he'd cut off his payot and started attending Beth Israel, the Orthodox congregation on the Lakefront. They wouldn't like his being gay, either, so he still had to stay closeted among them, but orthodoxy was as far to the left as Baruch could bear to go just yet.

He was forty then and felt that life was over. He continued to perform his managerial duties, and he said his prayers, and worked out at the gym until he was too winded to go on, and that was the extent of his life for a very long time.

Until one day when Chris stayed overnight in one of the rooms at the hotel.

Their eyes locked when Chris was checking in, and the next day when he was leaving, Chris gave Baruch his phone number in Lake Charles and said, "Call me sometime." Then he left the first of his awful poems.

Baruch did call, and soon they were emailing regularly. When Chris came to visit again in New Orleans, he stayed in Baruch's apartment instead of one of the hotel rooms. It turned out, however, that Chris was Catholic. Even worse, he was uncircumcised. But Baruch liked him, so they kept seeing each other. And after a few months, Baruch accepted the idea of marrying outside his faith.

It was too rare finding someone you really loved. You couldn't pass on the opportunity just because of their religion. You had to go where the wind carried you.

Somehow, though, dating Chris made him unhappy with his job. It wasn't just that Chris made twice as much money as he did. Money had never been important to him. It was more a sense of confinement. He was always at the hotel, even on his days off, and he never got two days off in a row.

He'd never once been able to visit Chris's house, and Chris could visit just once a week, and then only for two weeks a month. It simply wasn't enough. Baruch knew he'd have to move to Lake Charles, where he could see Chris more often.

After Kim came back to the desk, Baruch piddled around in the garden surrounding the patio that separated the main house from his quarters. Being manager meant he worked the front desk, cleaned the seven rooms in the Bed and Breakfast, and took care of the grounds. Though this was still technically his day off, he liked puttering around with the flowers and plants, watching the wind rustle through the leaves. If he worked in the garden today, that would be one less thing he had to do tomorrow.

He thought about landscaping as a career, but a few hours a week was one thing, while 40 hours a week might be too strenuous. He was in good shape but not getting any younger.

After working in the garden for an hour, Baruch went inside and took a shower. Then he sat on the sofa in his bathrobe, reading Maimonides. He never tired of reading Jewish books, and his father had hoped he'd become a rabbi one day, but now his father wouldn't even speak to him anymore. When Baruch told him that David had moved in, that they were married, his father had sat shiva for him.

He'd known how his father would react yet still felt compelled to tell him, though he didn't really know why. It wasn't as if he'd told anyone from the shul, because he knew their friendship would disappear like fog in the wind. Still, he'd felt his father ought to know the truth. Though telling the man had made Baruch an orphan, with Chris, he wasn't alone in the world anymore. He read until the phone rang at 10:00. It was Chris.

"Just wanted to let you know I made it home okay."

"I miss you already."

"I miss you, too."

Baruch had thought about getting a job offshore with Chris, but even if they were assigned to the same rig, he knew it would be too awkward trying to act straight all the time in front of all the other guys. He'd want to touch Chris at some point.

"What do you have planned for tomorrow?" Baruch asked.

"I'm seeing my mom." She was the only other person who knew Chris was gay. Baruch hoped she was the kind of mother who'd want her son to be happily married, even if it was to another man, and not a woman who would keep her son all to herself. He didn't know yet which was the case. Chris was vague on the subject, and Baruch didn't know if Chris's reluctance to commit was his own doing or his mother's influence.

Baruch was glad to have come out to his father in Israel, even if it resulted in cutting him off from the rest of his family. It felt like one of the few real things he'd ever done. He still remembered the sensation he'd experienced when he got off the phone with his father, as if he was breathing fresh air for the first time.

Baruch and Chris chatted for another half hour. They didn't talk every day, just a couple of times a week by phone, though they emailed daily. But that wasn't going to be enough to satisfy Baruch for long. He'd already wasted too much of his life being respectable. It was more important to be with the person he loved.

The next morning, Baruch was back on duty at the front desk. Two people were checking out this morning, which meant he had to call cabs for them. It also meant he was able to get an early start on cleaning those rooms. One other room was unoccupied, and the others he'd clean after the guests left for the day. While the towels and linens were in the dryer, Baruch worked again in the garden.

Once all the rooms were clean, and with no new arrivals expected until evening, Baruch began feeling antsy. He left the hotel and took a walk through the French Quarter. He simply had to get out, get away for just a few minutes, and there was a pleasant breeze today.

He walked up Burgundy to St. Ann, then walked back down Dauphine to Esplanade, and then up Bourbon to St. Ann again. On the corner, Baruch stood outside between the Hurricane and Oz, two of the most popular gay bars in the Quarter. He'd been out only a handful of times after David died and before he met Chris, but he knew where all the bars were. On an impulse, he went into the Hurricane.

"What can I get you?" the bartender asked, a slim man about his age, with a bushy handlebar moustache.

"Are you hiring?" asked Baruch. Maybe if he got some heavy-duty experience in a French Quarter bar for a few months, he could find a bartending job in Lake Charles more easily. It would be a place he wouldn't need to worry about people "finding out" and might help him make some gay friends there. He'd have to start socializing away from the Jewish community at least a little. Exclusively loving people who would hate him if they really knew him was too painful.

"You have any experience?"

"No, but I have two days off a week. I can come in and train for free on those two days till you think I'm ready." He wasn't sure if bartending would be condoning drunk driving, though he could always refuse to serve anyone who looked even moderately impaired.

"Let me get you an application." The bartender left for a moment and came back with a piece of paper. He handed it to Baruch and said, "You willing to blow me to get this job?" He smiled, but Baruch couldn't tell if he was serious or not.

"I have a boyfriend."

"You didn't answer my question."

"No, I'm afraid not."

"You believe in playing by the rules?" The bartender laughed.

"My whole life is filled with rules." In fact, he'd have to get back to the hotel soon for his 3:00 prayers.

"Maybe you should be a Meter Maid instead of a bartender."

Baruch shrugged and walked out the door. A gust of wind slapped a flier against his chest, and he turned it over. Someone was advertising their services as a dog walker. Baruch considered the possibility but then shook his head. There had to be a right job somewhere out there for him.

There probably wasn't much call for Hebrew teachers in Lake Charles. Or for portrait painters, either. He'd always liked meteorology, since storms had fascinated him from boyhood, but being a weatherman would also mean going back to school.

Just before 7:00, a guest arrived at the hotel. Baruch checked him in and carried the man's bags to his room. Then around 7:30, a young, straight couple checked into another room, and Baruch carried their bags as well. Now he mostly needed to stay at the desk to call cabs or direct people to local restaurants, Port of Call and La Peniche for the low brow, and Antoine's and Galatoire's for the high brow, always warning those who were walking to be careful of muggers.

The owner didn't like that Baruch scared the guests, but Baruch couldn't forget the rule, "Don't do to others what you don't want them to do to you." He'd want to be warned, so he warned others.

There was a computer at the desk, and Baruch filled out a resumé on Monster.com and another with the City of Lake Charles. Then he submitted applications to four different jobs in Lake Charles. Next, he emailed Chris to let him know what he'd done.

Chris was apparently online because he wrote back a few minutes later. "If you find a job here, you can stay with me a couple of weeks while you look for an apartment." Baruch guessed that let him know clearly enough that Chris didn't want them to live together permanently.

It had taken Baruch eight years to come around with David, though. He understood how it felt to be scared of discovery, to jump every time the wind blew or the doorbell rang, so he wouldn't insist. Not right away at any rate.

Over the next few days, Baruch applied to three more jobs in Lake Charles by computer. Monday afternoon, he started getting excited. Chris would be over around 7:00 to spend the night and then most of Baruch's Tuesday off. He was even looking forward to reading another of Chris's terrible poems.

Baruch especially liked working in the garden right before Chris arrived. He liked getting sweaty and dirty and then taking a shower and feeling perfectly clean when Chris came through the door.

Smiling, Baruch stooped down and began plucking weeds from a flower bed. A moment later, he heard a thump and turned to see two men coming over the fence near the back of the property. Baruch dropped his spade and started to run for the hotel but stopped when one of the men pointed a gun at him.

"Give it up," said the man with the gun. They came up to him, and Baruch took his wallet out of his pocket.

The unarmed man grabbed it, and the other man swung his gun and hit Baruch against the side of his head as hard as he could. Baruch fell to the ground, and both men started kicking him. This was it, Baruch realized. This was it.

"Sh'ma Yisrael," he began. Then he was kicked so hard in the stomach the wind was knocked out of him and he couldn't go on.

Baruch looked up and saw one of the men leaning over him with a knife. He felt a slice across his throat and a strong kick to the head. Then everything went black.

When he woke, it took Baruch a moment to figure out where he was. He heard a humming, like a box fan, in his ears. He opened his eyes carefully and looked around. There was an I.V. in his left hand. He was in the hospital. He tried to turn his head, but it hurt to move.

"You're awake!" said a voice beside him. "Thank God!"

It was Chris.

"What happened?" Baruch whispered, afraid to talk out loud.

"One of the hotel guests found you on the patio bleeding and called an ambulance. I got there just as the ambulance was leaving, and the woman from the hotel told me you'd been beaten, that your throat was slit." He choked out the last word.

Baruch felt oddly detached from the news. "At least they didn't cut my windpipe, or I'd be dead."

"They cut deep enough." Chris grabbed Baruch's right hand. "You're quitting that job right now, and you're coming to live with me. I'll take care of you till you're ready to go back to work."

"And then you'll help me find an apartment?"

Chris shook his head. "No apartment. You're staying with me forever."

Baruch smiled, but it made him feel sad, too. Why did people always wait for something horrible to happen before they decided to live life the way it should be lived? Why had *he* waited so long?

"We'll figure out something for you to do in Lake Charles. You can always get a job as a waiter until something better comes along."

"Oh, I know exactly what job I want," Baruch said quietly.

"What's that?"

"I'm going to be a police officer."

Chris was silent for a moment. Then he shook his head. "An openly gay cop in Lake Charles?"

"I'm never going back in the closet again. At work, or at shul, either. People are just going to have to deal with it."

"You don't want to spit into the wind."

"They're going to have to deal with it," Baruch repeated. "*We're* going to have to deal with it."

"And every day I'll deal with worrying about you getting killed at work, too?"

"Oil rigs aren't the safest places in the world, either."

Chris was silent another moment. "I just want to be with you. Nothing else really matters, does it?"

Baruch smiled and squeezed Chris's hand. "We're going to be okay," he said softly.

A few minutes later, a nurse walked over from her desk at the end of the ward. "Visiting hours are over. You'll have to come back tomorrow."

"No, I'm staying the night," Chris told her. "I'm staying till he's discharged, and then he's coming with me."

The nurse looked at him a moment, then shrugged and walked off. Chris smiled at Baruch, and Baruch squeezed his hand again.

Baruch was getting married once more. It had ended disastrously the last two times, but Hashem wouldn't take Chris away, too. Not even Job, whose life was "a life of wind," had been tested that much. Yet for all Baruch knew, Chris might fall off the rig and be eaten by a shark next week. Or get caught in a storm in the Gulf. All he had for sure was right now. So right now would be enough. Still holding Chris's hand, he closed his eyes and relaxed.

Chris hummed softly for a few moments and then began singing gently, "Mi sheibeirach…"

Baruch opened his eyes. "What's that?"

Chris laughed. "I ordered a CD with some Jewish music. I wanted to surprise you sometime."

"I can take only so much excitement in one day." Baruch laughed, too. It hurt his throat but felt good at the same time.

"I'll make sure every day is filled with excitement from now on. One way or another. Try to get some rest now."

Baruch closed his eyes again, and Chris continued singing. Baruch wanted to pay attention, but he was so very tired. He wondered what life would be like in Lake Charles. Every chapter of his life had brought something completely different. He didn't know what to expect.

Hashem had always been there for him, though, through everything, and Baruch knew He would be there again. Hashem had given him love, and life, and Baruch wasn't going to waste it this time. Chris blew him a kiss and sat back, holding his hand, which he clearly planned to hold onto all night. Baruch smiled and, despite the pain he felt across his body, closed his eyes again and gently fell asleep.

Making the Messiah

Victor Frankenstein wanted to create a man. David Himmelstein wanted to do more than that. He wanted to create a prophet. He was tired of waiting for the Messiah. There'd been so many false messiahs over the centuries. Jews had been exiled and killed for ages, and even now, back in their own country, there was so much dissent within their ranks, not to mention the deadly assaults from Palestinians and other Arabs. It was time for divine intervention. Maybe David couldn't create a messiah, but he could certainly create a prophet, and that's what he was going to do.

"Damnation!" he said, looking at his latest test results. It was so difficult to get the cells to differentiate exactly the way he wanted.

"Do another culture, Sarah," he growled. His senior lab assistant had blond hair, a slim waist, the loveliest green eyes, and perfectly perky breasts. She wasn't unlike the rabbi's wife, Hadassah. David was on the Board of Directors for his synagogue, and it was almost a full-time job keeping the rabbi in line, making him into the rabbi the congregation needed.

Attending services was made a little easier, though, by having the opportunity to look at Hadassah. It would be a sin to fantasize about her, but being around young women always made David smile, even at times like this. Looking at Sarah now, David did smile. It was a good day to be a man.

Yet he was still irritated. "Ben, come with me."

Ben was David's friend from synagogue. They'd met at the bar mitzvah of David's son, Isaac, three years ago. That was when the idea burst forth, in a casual conversation over rugelach.

"You have a fine-looking son there," Ben had said. "You must have good sperm."

"Excuse me?"

"I'm sorry. Always talking shop. I'm a fertility doctor."

David had nodded.

"We get so many losers in to donate sperm. I'd like to get some quality stuff in sometime. We need to create a better class of Jews."

"Eugenics. Now there's a topic to warm a Jewish heart."

Ben had shrugged. "Don't we do it already? We marry our daughters to the smartest scholar, marry our son to a girl with a successful, go-getter father."

David looked over at Isaac, a good-looking kid, but one who spent far too many hours on video games. David had read that doing so actually rerouted neurons. His son was a different person for choosing electronic games over reading books. There was no reason to assume that Isaac's choice had hurt his brain any, but Jews had flourished for millennia because of their love of reading.

Still, all that reading had never produced a messiah. Maybe it could only happen when new technologies like computer gaming changed their very bodies. While it was hard for David not to feel a little disgust when he watched Isaac play games, maybe David just needed to find the right game for his son to play. He'd tried giving him toy guns and toy trucks when he was a child, to make the boy appropriately masculine, but though Isaac was fit enough, there was always something a little offputting about him.

"Our kids marry someone beautiful or athletic," Ben continued. "The right height or the right body weight. Don't you think all those traits are genetic?"

"Well, I'm not a geneticist. I do stem cell research. The genes are already there by the time I get involved."

Ben nodded again. "Still," he said slowly, "you could develop good cells to put in embryos, couldn't you?"

"Not necessarily good or bad. Just dedicated cells. Cells committed to become certain structures."

"Just structures, huh? You couldn't get cells dedicated to making someone righteous or obedient, could you?" He laughed. "My kids hate being observant."

David had thought about that conversation for days. Something about it intrigued him. It suggested a possibility he couldn't quite put his finger on. Then one day, he was talking to Nathan, a neurologist who worked with soldiers and others suffering brain injuries.

"If only there was some way to repair neurons," Nathan had complained. "People are working on regrowing myelin, but making connections only helps if you have good cells to connect to each other."

David thought of the movie *Lorenzo's Oil* which he'd watched with his family a few weeks back. His wife, Anna, had been impressed with the dedication of Lorenzo's mother, Isaac had been appalled at the child being forced to live as a vegetable, but David had been fascinated by the ending, when the boy refused to have his mother read a children's story to him.

Lorenzo had been afflicted with his disease at a young age and had lost his ability to speak, but his brain had continued working. He simply had no motor control. He was still able to think like anyone else. And as the years passed, he matured and no longer wanted to hear children's stories.

David had looked over at Isaac, who still spent all his free time playing. This poor invalid was more of an adult than his own son. He almost wished some disaster would befall Isaac and *make* him into a man.

That was when David had his idea. If he could get stem cells to differentiate into cells designated for very specific parts of the brain, maybe he could affect not only intelligence and mobility but also personality.

In particular, David wondered if he could affect the areas of the brain dedicated to religious feeling or communion with God. There was no one "God spot," he'd learned from his studies, but part of the temporal lobe, part of the frontal lobe of the cortex, part of the parietal lobes, even part of the inferior temporal gyrus, all affected a person's ability to relate to God, to *believe* in God, to have religious and spiritual experiences.

What if he could take just a few cells programmed to develop into these specific areas and insert them into people's brains so those people could develop hyperabilities? Maybe the prophets of old simply had enhanced parietal lobes. Perhaps David could create a new generation of prophets to help Israel and the whole world in these troubled times. He already voted for laws which would make Israelis into good Jews, but it wasn't enough.

The idea simply had to be pursued.

"Ben," David said as they sat down now across the desk from each other in David's office. "Another flubbed test. This is taking way too long. I'd like to see some results in my lifetime."

"You know as well as I do that perfecting new techniques takes time. Three of our 'special' embryos miscarried. We have one baby born so far that appears to be completely normal, too early to tell yet if he'll have any special abilities, and three more pregnancies halfway along, one of which is still touch and go."

"It's maddening."

"Well, I can't risk doing any more for a while. If I get too many negative outcomes, I'll lose my license. We need to go slowly. The Jews have waited 4000 years for a messiah. We can wait a few more."

"I'm only after a prophet," David corrected.

"Even that's been 2000 years."

"Why is that?" asked David. "We had prophets before, no matter what else was happening with the Jews. And we've kept our identity throughout the last two millennia. So why no more prophets? Did we lose a gene that codes for the ability to receive revelation back when a million Jews were killed by the Romans?"

"We've had this discussion before."

David tapped his fingers on the desk absentmindedly. "I wonder if we're still a viable religion if we have no more direct contact with God." He closed his eyes. "We *need* a new prophet." David had tried praying in the wilderness himself a couple of times, to no avail. He'd asked Isaac once to take a drive into the desert with him so they could "commune with God," but the boy had looked at him as if he were crazy.

Ben shrugged. "We're doing the best we can. Even if the brains of these babies develop the way we'd like, it'll be twenty or thirty more years before we see the results we want."

"I'm forty already."

"Well, even if we don't live to see the outcome we're hoping for, if it does finally happen at all, it will change the world. It's a worthy pursuit."

"Do you know any other fertility doctors I could ask?"

Ben shook his head. "If we take too many chances, get too many people involved, we may lose everything. Better to be slow and sure. Rome wasn't built in a day."

"*Must* you use that phrase?"

"I'm just saying, it took centuries to develop the Talmud. Something that's going to galvanize Jews can't be rushed."

David nodded but had no intention of waiting very long. "I've almost got a cell line for the inferior temporal gyrus. If I can insert that into an embryo soon, we'll try that. It'll probably be a month."

Ben sighed. "If there was only some way we could know how these cells will develop once we let them out in the world."

David shook his head. It was almost like having children. You hoped for the best. You prepared for the best. But maybe your kid would turn out to be an uninspired blob of humanity that stayed in his room all day and contributed nothing meaningful to the world. "Most of the parts of the brain we're focusing on don't have corollaries in other species, so we're stuck with human experimentation."

"It's awkward is all I'm saying."

"We'll either win the Nobel prize or be put in prison."

"It's definitely awkward," Ben repeated.

David dismissed Ben, who came by regularly once a week so the two could update each other. David stayed in his office a little longer, though, brooding. It was great to have the education and power to do something. He just wasn't sure he had the intelligence and skill.

There were so few people in a position to change the world. Naturally, there were political leaders, but they were as likely to be a Stalin or a Hitler as a Gandhi or a Golda Meir. Of course, the real power was in science.

That affected everyone in every country around the world. The telephone, the steam engine, electricity, airplanes, the internet, the cell phone. But there was also gunpowder, the cross bow, the repeating rifle, mustard gas, atomic bombs. Yet whether good or evil, all these things affected *everyone*. And David's contribution wasn't going to be a repeat of Nobel's dynamite but of his peace prize.

David walked back to his lab and started working again, glancing now and again at Sarah, who was working busily. He was getting good results this afternoon, notwithstanding the earlier setback. It was a good day to be a scientist.

David was home by 6:30, and Anna had dinner waiting. It had taken the first several years of their marriage for David to turn Anna into the wife she needed to be. He had to provide cooking lessons, train her to keep up the house, even force her to read books on how to be sexually pleasing.

She'd resisted at first, but now she was exactly the kind of wife she was supposed to be. David almost felt an artistic satisfaction when he thought of it. Shaping her hadn't been unlike sculpting Michelangelo's David. Not that anyone should ever try to create representational images. Creating the real thing was what God wanted of his people.

You had to create yourself by working hard, but you had to help make each other into obedient servants, too. God *wanted* them to be co-creators with Him. That's why He'd given them the commandments.

Anna served the meal tonight with a smile, and David smiled in return and nodded. Isaac was belligerently silent throughout the meal, despite both David's and Anna's attempts at conversation.

"The Palestinians blew up another bus today," Anna said casually.

"I don't understand how people can let their religion turn them into monsters," David said.

"Are you okay with taking the bus to school tomorrow?" asked Anna.

"Whatever," said Isaac.

"I can take you the next couple of days if you like."

"Whatever."

"Apparently, hormones turn people into monsters, too," David observed. "Speak civilly to your mother."

Isaac stared in disgust at his father. David felt an impulse to slap the boy. Just last week, David had gone out of his way to buy a book for him, to show that he was a loving father, and Isaac was still ungrateful.

"Well, the military captured another terrorist cell today," Anna said, trying to bring the conversation back. "Arrested four terrorists."

"It's a good day to be an Israeli," said David. Isaac said nothing.

After dinner, David read a couple of articles in his study, surprised when there was a knock on the door. "Yes?"

Isaac pushed the door open slowly and looked in.

"You can come." Perhaps his son was there to offer an apology. David would be an adult and accept it. Maybe Isaac was finally becoming a man, three years after the official ceremony.

The boy trudged into the room and plopped down in a chair. "We need to talk."

David raised an eyebrow. That was the kind of thing Anna usually said, when David had forgotten a birthday or anniversary or even just to run an errand she'd requested of him. She hadn't given up trying to make him the husband he should be, either.

"Sure. What's up?" The two didn't often have real conversations, but David was willing if Isaac was. He simply could never figure out what was going on inside that brain.

"I don't want to go to college."

David raised his eyebrow again. Apparently, *nothing* was going on inside his son's brain. "That's still a couple of years away. We need to talk about that now?" Was there some kind of computer game that would inspire the boy to learn? To make something of himself?

"I want to quit school and join a dance academy."

David put his article down and looked at his son. What was this all about? The boy so often seemed to *try* finding ways to annoy him. He had to know that taking dance lessons would upset him. Was he asking in order to receive permission, or just to get David's adrenalin flowing? He wanted to tell his son to leave the room. But perhaps he'd agree to let Isaac take lessons after school, acting unconcerned, and see how that worked.

He frowned. Or maybe he should resist at the beginning and act like he was finally surrendering reluctantly a few days later on the idea of after-school dance lessons, to make Isaac feel he'd won a big victory. Or only agree to the lessons if Isaac could memorize a long passage from the Talmud each week, or even something from a biology book.

It was a fine line to balance being tough with being loving. Despite the awkward subject matter, David found that it was nice to finally be talking with his son, after weeks of silence. Maybe there was still some way to direct the boy toward a productive life. He felt his paternal instincts kicking in. It was a good day to be a father.

"You do realize that the life of a dancer is pretty rough?"

Isaac shrugged. "I want to make a difference in the world. You can only really do that through art."

"You think *West Side Story* made the world a better place?"

"I don't know. But *Fiddler on the Roof* did."

David nodded slowly. "Maybe."

"There's something else."

David looked up. There was an unpleasant tone in the boy's voice. "Yes, son?"

"I'm in love."

David was wary now. He felt Isaac was too young at sixteen to date, but he might agree to let his son double date if the girl's family seemed sound. He missed the early years when he could read stories about the golem or Hanukkah miracles to Isaac. But the boy was making an effort. So many kids his age kept everything from their parents. Sometimes, David wished he had a different son, one who was always obedient. But you had to work with the materials at hand. God gave parents trials to purify them. He wanted steel, not slag, out of His people.

"What's her name?"

There was a pause. "His name is Ari."

David paused as well. Then he said carefully, "Are you serious?"

Isaac nodded.

David nodded, too, sighed heavily, and then reached up and tore his shirt. Fatherhood was over. His had just been turned into a childless marriage. "You're dead to me," he said simply. "Get out of the house."

"But—"

"You're dead."

Isaac stood, his fists clenched. "You think that reading the Torah every day makes you holy. That fucking a woman makes you righteous."

"The commandment is for the child to honor his parents, not for the parents to condone their children committing abominations." He pointed to the door. Part of him had suspected this for some time. Probably part of the reason he worked so hard all the time was to avoid having to experience this very conversation. Thinking of Isaac made him sick. But if he'd failed as a father, he simply had to succeed as a scientist. It was time to get back to work.

Isaac glared a moment longer and then marched out.

David finished reading his article. After he heard the front door slam, he went out to tell Anna they needed to cover their mirrors. The world was becoming so wicked. He and Anna had created a monstrosity. It was clear the Jews needed a prophet this very minute. They needed someone to bring forth the Messiah immediately. They needed the Messiah himself.

David was outwardly hoping to create a prophet, but deep inside, he was truly hoping to create the actual Messiah. The world was so awful, he simply had to succeed. David felt a lump in his throat and had to pinch himself hard to keep from crying. He'd study for the rest of the evening to see if he could learn some new useful technique he could start using right away.

The next day, David met Nathan for lunch. "What's new?" Nathan asked.

"We need to do more surgeries. I've got several cell lines ready to go."

"David, we've done over a dozen surgeries. We've accidentally created two lethal brain tumors, and the other patients, well, who knows? The problem with neurotheology is that in order to get a chance at accessing the brains of patients, there has to be something wrong with their brains to begin with."

"What about that one guy, Joel?"

Nathan shrugged. "He did go from being secular to joining a yeshiva. But all he does is study and pray all day. We still don't know if that's a reaction to the bomb that injured him or to the cells we introduced. And I'm not sure he's any more insightful or powerfully spiritual than he was before. He never leaves the yeshiva. He never *does* anything."

"It's a start."

"I suppose. But can you imagine a whole nation of men who do no work other than study and pray? The country would come to a halt."

"There'd be no more war."

"Only if you could gain access to the enemy, too."

A thought was forming in David's mind, but he couldn't formulate it.

"Don't we really have to change DNA itself rather than just add extra brain power to the God spots? I mean, Christians who enforced the Inquisition weren't lacking in religious feeling. They were fiends *because* of it."

"I'm developing cells for the part of the ventromedial prefrontal cortex that creates empathy, too. I can only do so much at one time."

"What we need is a perfectly healthy patient, not someone who—"

David snapped his fingers. "We have one!"

"What?"

"A patient with no brain damage or brain disease."

"What do you mean?"

"I'm going to bring my son in. You diagnose him with something, anything, and then you do surgery on his brain. You can put the God cells in for the parietal lobe, the frontal lobe, and the temporal lobe."

"Three areas? That's awfully risky, David. He might not survive the surgery."

David waved as if swatting at a fly. "He's dead already." David related the conversation of the previous evening. Nathan looked uncomfortable but finally agreed.

Later, as David was returning to his lab after lunch, he called Isaac on his cell. Isaac didn't pick up, but David left a message. "I'm sorry about last night, son. I hope you'll forgive me. Come home for dinner tonight. I'll have your mother cook your favorite meal. We still love you."

David felt a tingling in his spine. What if he was able to turn his apostate son into a prophet? He'd be responsible for his son's creation two times over. David could save the boy's soul and through him the souls of the whole nation. Perhaps he could talk to other parents with wayward children and get those teens "diagnosed" with problems that required surgery as well. David needed to start actively recruiting participants for prophet-making.

He stopped short. If he could turn sinners into tzaddikim, maybe David was actually the Messiah *himself*. He was ushering in a new age of righteousness. He already had two followers in Ben and Nathan, both powerful men. Maybe he should try enlisting a third follower, despite Ben's concerns.

David smiled. It was a good day to be a Jew.

What David needed was to add a geneticist to his list of co-conspirators in redemption. He needed to tackle the problem on all fronts.

One step at a time, but he'd get there. He'd introduce the world to lasting peace.

When he walked back into the lab, Sarah looked like she was preparing to leave. "What's up?"

"My mother was hurt in a bombing at the market today."

"Those demons."

"She's in the hospital in a coma. I need to get right over."

David's brows furrowed. "How old is your mother?" he asked slowly.

"Forty-five." Sarah put some papers away and buttoned her coat.

"Has she gone through menopause yet?"

"What? No, I guess not. Does it matter?" Sarah sounded irritated.

"Oh, no. No. Just thinking. Take all the time you need with your mother."

Sarah walked out. She was David's best assistant, but he had others if she needed to be gone for several days. The work would still go on. He picked up the phone and called Ben. "Yes?"

"I have a comatose woman who needs an embryo implant."

"What?"

"We need to start branching out."

Comatose women, women of childbearing age under anesthesia for almost any surgery, women undergoing pelvic exams. Lesbians.

David spent the next several minutes organizing a plan of attack with Ben and then hung up satisfied. He remembered the day he and Anna had brought Isaac home from the hospital, how they'd been filled with hope and awe at this life God had put in their hands. He remembered the day when Isaac was six, and the boy had given one of his toys to a Palestinian child, and the look that other boy had on his face.

Then David thought back to the time when he was a child himself, and he'd invited a Palestinian boy he'd met on the street home to play with him, and how his father had beaten him so badly that David couldn't sit for a week and had to sleep on his stomach.

David stared intently at the paperweight on his desk for a long moment, lost in thought. Then he took a deep breath and forced himself to smile. He brushed the hair off his forehead, pushed his glasses further up his nose, and walked back into the lab, humming happily.

It was a good day to be a Messiah.

Leather Jew

It had not been much of a trick. I'd met Kevin last night at the Phoenix here in my Marigny neighborhood playing pool. He'd cruised me openly, a cute guy, about thirty, so even though he was a bit drunk, I took him home. When I started playing with his butt, however, I discovered he wasn't clean and made him take a shower.

After he dried off, he lay face down on my bed, and I started playing again, but within a minute, he'd fallen asleep. I was no longer in the mood and so didn't mind. I went to sleep, too.

In the middle of the night, I noticed he was sweating an awful lot and pulled over to the edge of the bed. HIV meds were much better these days, so he shouldn't be having such terrible night sweats, but we hadn't even had a chance to discuss HIV status. The problem might not even be related. Finally, morning arrived, and I got up to drink an Ensure and read while waiting for Kevin to wake up.

A half hour later, he came to the bedroom door. "You must hate me," he said.

"It's no problem," I returned. Not having sex wasn't the end of the world.

He went to the bathroom, dressed, and headed out. I didn't mind seeing him leave and thought maybe I'd go back and nap a while. But when I went back in the bedroom, I stopped short.

A huge wet spot covered the bed, six feet by three feet across. Kevin wasn't sweating last night. He'd urinated.

I put the sheets in the washer, sprayed the bed with Lysol and Febreze, and turned the ceiling fan on. No more drunks for me. I didn't smoke or drink myself. It wasn't like I was looking for Mr. Right yesterday evening, but I'd at least hoped for someone I could stand for eight hours on a Saturday night.

I picked up the book I'd begun the day before, *The Path of the Upright*, by Moshe Hayyim Luzzatto, and lay on the sofa reading.

An hour later, the phone rang. "Tim? It's Fred. How are you?"

I knew instantly he was one of my clients, because Samuel was my real name. Tim was my escort name. I'd used up all my student loan money earning my biology degree and had no other way to pay for nursing school except to put an ad in the local gay paper. Fred was a regular, one of the ones I liked.

"You busy this morning?"

"Nope. Just reading."

"Can I come over in thirty minutes?"

"Sure."

Fred was fifty, bald on top, about eighty pounds overweight, with a plain face. He'd never had a partner but as a single parent had adopted four sons and put them all through college, one through medical school and another through law school. He'd founded a charity for unwed teen mothers, helping to get them through pregnancy and then back into school, paying for medical costs and childcare.

I thought him a truly sweet man, and I regretted my shallowness in knowing I'd never even consider someone like him for a lover because of his looks. I was thirty-nine and weighed 155, a good fifteen pounds too heavy myself, and often marveled that people would actually pay me for sex, but they did and I was glad.

Fred came over and we talked a while before getting started, which he always liked. "Nursing school going okay?"

"We learned physical assessment this week. How to do pulse and breathing rate and skin turgor and bowel sounds and everything."

"Doesn't sound too bad."

"Technically, we're supposed to do a thorough exam, especially on people in the nursing home who can't always tell us if anything's wrong, but unless we give them a bed bath, we don't usually bother with the private parts."

After nearly an hour of chatting, seeing that Fred wasn't going to make a move, I took his hand and led him to the bedroom. I massaged him a while, fucked him, and then sucked him off.

"Oh, Tim, you are simply too good to an old man."

I only charged $100 an hour, though most of the other escorts in New Orleans charged $150. I didn't feel that with my age, and being a little flabby, I deserved as much as they did. But Fred always paid extra, so that was another reason to enjoy his company.

We hugged as he left, and I went back to reading. I'd read close to a hundred Jewish books since I'd converted five years earlier and was only now beginning to feel like a real Jew. I doubted that being an escort would be looked upon too kindly by other Jews, but in a way, I felt I was performing a mitzvah, a good deed, a commandment.

My first boyfriend twelve years ago when I came out had a handsome face but had otherwise been somewhat malformed, with a slight hunchback, missing one arm, with the remaining arm smaller than usual. He'd pointed out that he had as much right to sexual expression and sexual satisfaction as anyone else, and often he was only able to achieve that through prostitution. When he told me about a friend of his who put himself through a doctorate program by escorting, it changed my mind about the sinfulness of the act.

I'd entertained the idea of escorting for years but only this past year when finances became desperate did I decide to try. I was a complete slut anyway, so the leap didn't seem very big. I'd even encouraged a friend struggling along on Disability to try, and he now called me his "pimp rabbi."

Sunday afternoon, I ate lunch at La Peniche with Alan, a friend in his sixties. Since we ate there every week, we were friendly with the wait staff, which made the meal pleasant. They knew what we liked to drink, tea for Alan and water for me, and brought it as soon as we sat at the table.

"Did you go out last night?" Alan picked up the menu.

"Lost two games of pool."

"Meet Mr. Naugahyde?"

I shook my head. "Not yet." Because I liked to wear my leather chaps and vest with my army boots, Alan used to tease me about finding Mr. Leather. But I'd pointed out that I wasn't *really* leather since I wasn't into S&M. So he'd amended it to Mr. Naugahyde.

I decided not to tell Alan about Kevin. Alan had at one point been infatuated with me, and I was still afraid of making him feel jealous or uncomfortable. I rarely told him about anyone I brought home. I certainly didn't tell him about my escorting. In some ways, however, even our relationship was "professional."

He paid for the meal whenever we ate out, paid for the movie twice a month when we went to the theater, and paid for our trips to New York and San Francisco. He'd told me right at the beginning he didn't feel it fair for him to miss out on my company just because I was poor. I was never convinced that my company was particularly worth having, but we'd been good friends for three years now. The fact that he paid for everything didn't mean I didn't truly like him.

"Did you find Mr. Date Guy?" I asked.

"No. I went to the Corner Pocket. They had fifteen dancers, but not one of them was worth tipping."

Alan went on to describe his week, picking up mail for his neighbor on vacation, calling a friend in Baton Rouge, his trip to the grocery, business with his condo association, watching a recent episode of *Survivor*, and everything else he'd done since we'd last talked.

He could go into agonizing detail, but it made him feel good to talk, so I listened. I wasn't much of a talker to begin with and kept back half the things I might find interesting in my own life to spare him hurt feelings. It was good he could carry a conversation by himself.

Many people who saw us together thought we were a couple, but that had never been much of a possibility. Both my previous partners had been a good twelve or fourteen years older than I was, but Alan was twenty-four years older, a month older even than my father. He also didn't like sex, and we only jacked off together maybe twice a year. According to his detailed accounts, he never did much of anything sexual with anyone else, except once with an escort in New York and another time with an escort in San Francisco. He liked to watch them shower.

And though my previous two relationships had been monogamous, I didn't want the next one to be, and Alan would've had a problem with that. He and his lover of twenty-three years had been monogamous, and their relationship only ended when his lover died of cancer. While I liked Alan well enough as a friend, I wanted someone with a more open-minded personality. I kind of hoped I might find a Jewish man. It wasn't a requirement, but it would be nice.

As we finished our meal, Alan looked over at me and sighed dreamily. "I love being with you. You're so good looking."

He told me that every time we were together. Sometimes, he'd say it two or three times during one encounter. I appreciated the compliment, but it always made me feel that if he didn't like my looks, we'd never have become friends.

So while I never felt cheap with my clients, I sometimes did with Alan. He was sweet and only trying to make me feel good, but I still felt I was trading my body for his company, which didn't feel so different from trading sex for money.

I'd never had a very good self-image, so hearing Alan's compliments was therapeutic, especially when he paid a photographer $200 to take two rolls of pictures. But when the photographer, a cute, flirtatious guy, arranged a second meeting at no cost to take photos of me in my leather, and I voluntarily removed my pants while keeping on my chaps, Alan had been horrified to see the resulting photos. I was instead glad to have evidence that at least at one time in my life I was reasonably good-looking and sexy.

Alan and I left the restaurant and walked together several blocks until our paths home diverged. We kissed and went our own ways. I sat on my stoop reading my pharmacology notes until the sun went down. That way, I could study and cruise at the same time.

My school schedule was Basics in Nursing on Monday from 10:30 to 12:15, followed by Pharmacology from 12:30 to 1:30. Tuesdays was lab from 8:00 till 2:00, Wednesdays were free, Thursdays was Basics again from 10:00 till 2:00, and Fridays was Pharmacology again from 10:30 till 12:30. It was a super easy schedule and the material surprisingly simple.

I'd originally taught college English for ten years but had gone back to school to study biology so I could go to medical school. I was terrified of the responsibility but fascinated by the knowledge. Because of my constant self-doubts, I wasn't at all sure I could make it. After interviewing unsuccessfully with medical schools for four years despite a GPA of 3.75 and an MCAT score of 29, I decided to go into nursing.

These courses were a hundred times easier than biochemistry, immunology, and endocrinology. My first semester was breezing by. As a result, I could afford to go out to the bars sometimes during the week in addition to weekends.

A few days after the bedwetting incident, I returned to the Phoenix. There was a regular group that played pool, and I felt more comfortable playing during the week, when there were fewer witnesses. I played for fun, didn't win a lot, and only hoped not to still have five balls on the table when the other guy finished.

I played Minister Dan and Tight Jimmy tonight. I often gave people nicknames which I only used in my journal. I found that when I read my journal a few years after recording an entry, I could sometimes no longer remember who people were, so now I added appellations to jog my memory. Dan had once been a Baptist minister, so he was Minister Dan. Jimmy, the first time he met me, had offered, "I give good head and I'm tight," so he became Tight Jimmy.

I lost both games I played tonight and was sitting at the bar watching Jimmy and Dan play another when I turned and saw an incredibly sexy man walk in with two lesbians. He was my height, maybe 5' 10", with dark hair and a moustache. I had a beard myself and liked facial hair. The man smiled and stood at the bar beside me.

"Hey," he said.

"Hey," I replied. "I'm Samuel."

"Randy." We shook hands. "You're cute."

"So are you."

He ordered a drink and remained standing beside me, watching the pool game. When the other two players finished and didn't want to play anymore, Randy said, "You up?"

"Sure." I had to resist grabbing his butt as he leaned over to rack up the balls. He offered to let me break, but I didn't want to ruin all chance of going home with him by revealing my pathetic breaking skills, so I let him do it.

He got one ball in on the break and two more before he missed. I got one in on my turn, thank goodness, before I missed. Then he got two more in. I missed on my next turn, and he got one in on his next turn. So there we were, him with one ball left on the table and me with six. And even with all those balls, I still didn't have any easy shots, happy when I managed to get one in before missing the next one.

Randy missed his last ball, so I had a chance to get another before his next turn. He missed again, and I again got one ball in. So now I had three left, but this time, he got his last ball in and went for the eight. He missed, and I got two in a row this time. And now Randy finished the game by sinking the eight ball.

"Good game," he said.

"Thanks for going easy on me," I replied. It was obvious he'd deliberately missed several of his shots.

"Oh, no, you were good," he repeated.

"You play a lot?"

"I'm in the High Heel Tournament." He motioned for me to rack the balls up again. "You know, all the bars have teams and play to raise money for AIDS hospices. I'm on Sanctuary's team. I'm the bartender there."

I'd have never started flirting if I'd known he was a bartender, because I assumed cute bartenders were always being hit on. But he seemed interested, so I decided I'd keep myself open.

"You have high heels?" I asked.

"Fabulous ones." He smiled. "They actually give you a couple of extra inches when you need to stretch over the table for some of those difficult shots."

We played another game, and while I played better this time, Randy still easily beat me. He bought me a drink, a diet Coke, and after we chatted several more minutes, I invited him home.

"I'd love to," he said, "but first I have to tell you I have a partner."

"Okay." I nodded. "I don't have a problem with that if your partner doesn't."

"Nope."

Randy and I walked to my place. He weighed about 140, slim and firm, with strong legs and a hairy chest. He was balding slightly on top, which I found kind of sexy. He was exactly my type physically. Too bad he wasn't available for more than a fling. But at least a fling was something.

I sucked him for a good while as he lay there. He didn't come, and after a while I grew tired. I thought he might reciprocate for a bit, but instead he asked if he could fuck me. He put on a condom and entered me with a little difficulty, not able to get quite hard enough. He fucked me for a while, got too soft to stay in, and slipped out.

We got dressed, and he gave me his card, telling me I could call him either at home or at the bar. Then he kissed me and left.

I was disappointed he hadn't come, but that could happen to anybody. I was more disappointed he hadn't so much as touched my dick. I expected that behavior from clients but not from dates. I got back in bed and beat off thinking about Bartender Randy, wondering if I'd really find another partner one day, if I even wanted that, and then fell asleep.

The next day was a gym day. I tried to go to the Club on Toulouse three times a week. I could never manage to work out for much longer than thirty minutes, but even that made me feel better. I did seven exercises for my arms and chest and three for my legs, which fortunately even without work looked pretty good. I unfortunately did no abdomen exercises. I kept trying to psyche myself up for that.

After the exercises, I sat in the hot tub alone. Within minutes, the heat became too much to handle. I took a shower and then headed up to the cubicles on the fourth floor in my towel. There were a few other people going in and out of the rooms, watching porn on the TV or peeking through glory holes into the next cubicle. One fat man kept following me, but I was after a cute man about my age. Of course, he totally ignored me. The baths were theoretically easy sex, but quality sex was rare, and as usual, I got dressed and went home without hooking up at all.

I hadn't been home thirty minutes when Fat, Hairy, Ugly Jay called. He was a regular, a married man from Slidell who came into town twice a month to meet "Tim." He was pleasant enough, so I didn't mean any disrespect with his nickname. It was simply a description tag like the ones I used at the bars.

Father McKenzie was the tag I gave to my client who'd formerly been a priest, so roly poly I used the name of a local bakery to identify him. Pisser Paul liked to piss on me in the tub. And Dreadlocks Ty was the name I gave to the cute, young, closeted black man who came to see me once a month. He liked to be fucked slowly.

Jay and I did our usual thing. I massaged his extremely hairy back for thirty-five minutes, a task incredibly tedious and boring. Then I lay down on his back and pressed my dick against his ass for several minutes. Next, I got some lubricant and fingered his ass for several more minutes.

Then, when he was sufficiently aroused, Jay turned over so I could suck him off. He almost always took exactly an hour. Today was sixty-one minutes from start to finish. He then dressed, put a hundred dollar bill on my bed, and headed out.

The next week at school was our first scary skill—injections. We had to give subcutaneous, shallow intramuscular, and deep intramuscular. We needed to know which size needles to use and the exact landmarks on the body for the different injections to avoid things like major nerves.

Then in lab we had to "check off," show that we could perform. We were given a hypothetical drug, drew it up in the appropriate syringe, changed to a new needle, so the one we used to inject the patient with would still be sharp, after looking up the drug to find if there were any tricks to be aware of.

For instance, for some sub Q injections, you had a preferred site at the stomach. For another injection, you might need to keep the tissue compressed with your fingers the whole time. For some, you massaged the site afterward. For others, you couldn't. And so on.

We demonstrated our new skills on some rubber dummies and then had to be ready to do the real thing on patients, who we'd start seeing the following week. I knew this was basic nursing, but it was still nerve-racking. I wondered if a medical career was right for me, after all. I didn't know if I could handle being scared all the time.

Saturday night, I headed back to the Phoenix. Two men kissed in the corner by the pool table, the players maneuvering around them to make their shots.

Then a man with a big box came through the door. If his package could cast such an impressive shadow in this dim light, he was worth a smile and a nod. The guy was short and squat, with strawberry blond hair, balding on top, and sported a heavy moustache. He looked like a young, thinner Wilford Brimley.

Every time he took a sip of his beer, several drops lingered on his moustache. I watched as he carefully licked them up.

"Can I help you with that?" I motioned to his moustache. He nodded, I leaned forward to lick off the beer, and he latched onto my mouth like a larval Alien.

We'd only been kissing a couple of minutes when he pulled back. "So when are we going to fuck?"

Damien took me home and fucked me so hard I had to beg him to stop.

"Well, we tried, didn't we?" he said with a shrug. "You okay if we still kiss when we run into each other at the bar?"

"You bet."

Tuesday was the big day, our first working with patients at Charity hospital. On Monday, we'd been given our assignments and gone over to decipher the illegible charts written by the doctors. Then we'd interviewed our patients before going to the library to research their health issues and the drugs they were on.

Today, we were in charge of giving the 10:00 meds. I checked at the drug box as soon as I arrived to make sure my patient's drugs were all in his drawer, as well as the appropriate hypodermics and needles. Then I checked the chart to see if any new medications had been prescribed since last night. No, thank goodness. Then it was time to do a physical assessment, check the patient for hydration and mental status and mobility and range of motion and everything else.

My patient was a seventy-five-year-old man who'd fallen off his roof while smoking pot and broken his arm. He also had diabetes, so I had to do finger sticks and give him his insulin, too. But the day went well, the worst part the detailed documentation.

Though I knew I'd had an easy assignment, I still felt overwhelmed by the experience. I also felt it was remotely possible I'd succeed. Even as a nurse, I'd feel like a failure for not going to medical school, but at least I'd be doing something useful, and maybe when I finished nursing school, I could give medical school one more chance. They'd see I was dedicated and maybe reconsider. It was enough of a possibility to keep me going. Of course, that would be even scarier, but it still pulled me.

Tuesday night, Cowpokes had country and western dance lessons, and I often headed over to watch. I didn't have any cowboy boots and never danced, but tonight I felt like getting out to relax. No one cared that I wasn't coordinated. They were all too concerned about being watched themselves.

I came close to getting the "barn dance" right. There were only six steps, repeated over and over two dozen times as we went around in a circle, one row of partners going clockwise and the other counterclockwise.

There was one man, about 5' 5", with a moustache and dark sandy hair, who I'd seen on a couple of other dance nights. Tonight, I approached him while he sipped his drink, sitting at a high, small, round table.

"You dance pretty well," I said.

"I've been doing it for years."

I sat next to him. "My name's Samuel."

"Matt."

We shook hands.

After chatting a few more minutes, Matt asked me what I did. "I'm in nursing school," I replied.

"I'm a high school Spanish teacher."

"That sounds nice, too. I wanted to get an Italian degree but couldn't get one in New Orleans. It never occurred to me to go somewhere else."

"You speak Italian?"

I nodded.

"So do I. And French. Where'd you study?"

"I lived in Italy for two years."

"Studying?"

"I was a Mormon missionary." I laughed. "You can imagine how many Roman Catholics in Rome were interested in Mormonism."

"So you're a Mormon?"

I shook my head. "I was excommunicated when I came out. Converted to Judaism several years ago."

"Io non ci credo in nessuna religione."

"I'm not sure I really believe very much, either," I said, also in Italian, "but there's a culture of education and ethics among Jews that I like."

We continued speaking Italian for several more minutes, and finally Matt asked me to come home with him. He also lived in the Marigny just a few blocks away, so we walked together to his place. He was uncut and just the right size, too big to get all the way in my mouth, but manageable if I used my hand as an extension.

I blew him for a bit and then asked for a condom. He opened a drawer in his bedside table, and I quickly pulled on a condom and lubricated myself. I lifted his legs and entered. As usual with a new man, I came faster than I wanted to. Then I went back to sucking him. Before long, he'd shot a load into my mouth, always a lovely experience.

"Damn, you're good," Matt said. "You could do that professionally."

"I do."

He laughed but then saw I was serious. "Not really?"

"Sure," I said. "There aren't many jobs I can fit around my school schedule. Certainly none that pay as well."

"I think that's disgusting." He started getting dressed, so I did, too. "And to think I was happy to meet someone who spoke Italian. I was hoping we could go out again, but I don't date whores."

I almost said, "But you do let them fuck you." Instead, I continued dressing in silence. I realized I probably shouldn't have said anything so controversial right away, but it wasn't something you wanted to have come out six months after you'd started dating, either. Matt didn't say anything as he led me to the door and ushered me out, not even a goodbye.

I shrugged and walked on home. It was stupid to start thinking of marriage right away, but when he'd seemed nice and spoke Italian, I'd put him in the "possible" category. Now after only an hour, he was in the "no way" category.

I needed to unwind and picked up *In My Father's Court* by Isaac Bashevis Singer, reading for half an hour before going to bed.

The following morning I was back at the hospital. We no longer had Wednesdays off now that we were doing clinicals. We were assigned the same patients as the day before. The only incident of note today was my patient's comment when I came to give him an injection. "At least your hands aren't shaking like they were yesterday." I could feel my face flush. I just smiled and gave him his injection.

The following Saturday, my older friend Alan and I went to see a movie and have dinner afterwards. I told him about school and the hospital but edited my account of meeting Matt. "Mr. Naugahyde?" asked Alan.

"He didn't seem interested. I must not speak enough languages."

"I'm going to the Corner Pocket later. It's 'fresh meat' night, so there'll be new dancers. I love tipping good looking guys."

"Have fun."

Back home, I had a few hours to kill before time to head for the Phoenix. I read some of *The Shavuot Anthology* and then lay in bed and listened to a music tape of some of my favorite songs. I turned out the light and closed my eyes as I listened to "It Must Have Been Love" by Roxette, "To Make You Feel My Love" by Garth Brooks, "Amazed" by Lone Star, "Smooth" by Santana, and "That's the Way It Is" by Celine Dion.

Sometimes, I merely listened, but at other times, I couldn't help but sing along. It was a shame that bars only played dance mix crap, and always so loudly. Music could be pretty if you let it be.

I wore my leather that night when I went out at 10:00, though it was really getting too warm for it. No one seemed interested. Tight Jimmy and I played a game of pool, and I talked to some other friends. I always rubbed Bed and Breakfast Rick's back every Saturday night. It was a ritual.

I debated whether to finally approach Bondage Ron, a beautiful man who always carried a length of rope in his left seat pocket, but I'd never been tied up and wasn't sure I'd like it, so I put it off for at least another week. I was more and more tempted each week. No S & M for me, but maybe a little bondage. Just once. We'd see. I cruised one real cute guy in a leather vest, but he never looked twice at me.

Around 12:30, I finally went home. I'd missed a call for Tim two hours earlier. That was always a risk when I went out, since I didn't have a cell phone, but I had to live while I was alive and accepted the loss.

But the following night, I got a call from a hotel in the Quarter and went to suck off a gay couple, both average looking, in town for the weekend. Even though it was two guys, it was still just one hour, so I only charged $100, and the couple said they'd call again next time they were in town. I had yet to meet a single client who tried to make me feel bad for what I did, the way Mean Matt had. Most seemed genuinely grateful.

The next Tuesday at the hospital, my patient was a man who'd been shot in the chest during a drug deal. His girlfriend sat at his bedside most of the day. As part of my assignment, I had to do a patient interview, asking about his medical history but also about his job, his relationships with family and friends, his ways of dealing with stress, his religious views, his usual eating habits, his bowel movements, and on and on.

Whenever I asked a question he didn't like, the man would pretend to fall asleep, and his girlfriend would feign napping, too. Then when I asked another question, if that one didn't bother them, they'd "wake up." But if I asked something else they didn't want to answer, they'd both "fall asleep" again. At first, I was too amazed to know how to react. But as I continued asking questions and they continued falling asleep, it was all I could do not to laugh.

"I know I'm only a nursing student," I told the nurse in charge of the ward, "but I've diagnosed a new disease."

"Yes?" Her eyebrows lifted.

"Synchronized narcolepsy."

Despite the lack of cooperation, the day went better than last Tuesday had. Still, I wanted to go out and celebrate my survival. Instead of Cowpokes this week, I went to my usual haunt of the Phoenix. I played a game of pool with Minister Dan, losing but only by one ball. Then I saw Aerobics Lee, the exercise instructor, at the bar talking to an attractive man around forty in leather pants. The pants had buckles all down the front. The man had a shaved head and a goatee, and he was slim and firm.

I felt more courageous than usual—leather will do that— and walked right up to him. "I haven't seen you here before."

"I come out on Tuesday nights sometimes. Wednesday is my day off."

The man had a slight accent, but I couldn't quite place it. It unfortunately wasn't Italian. "Where are you from?"

He paused a moment. "Israel."

I probably looked as shocked as I felt, but I finally managed to blurt out, "Ma nishmah?"

Now it was his turn to look shocked. After a moment, he replied, "Hakol b'seder." Then he added, "Who are you?"

"Samuel," I said, "and that's about all the Hebrew I know. I only studied one semester."

"I'm Elii." He offered his hand. "I never expected to meet another Jew here at the Phoenix."

"And you're a leather Jew," I said. "How wonderful."

"You like leather?"

I nodded. "Those pants look great on you."

"I look better without them."

Aerobics Lee now joined in. "You're made for each other. Now go away and leave me alone."

I realized I'd been ignoring Lee and reached over to give him a hug. It turned out that Lee and Eli had known each other for several months. It also turned out that Eli had been married to a woman in Israel and had three children, now being raised by Eli's parents in Tel Aviv since his wife had died of cancer and Eli moved to America.

Eli had been a Chasid and hadn't gone out with guys till after his wife's death. Even then, he'd been closeted until he broke up with his partner of eight years almost a year ago. Then he cut his sidelocks, shaved his head, and bought a leather vest.

We played a couple of games of pool, fun because he played as poorly as I did. It was almost 11:00 by this time, and I had to leave the house at 6:45 the next morning to get down to Charity by 7:30. Eli could see me debating whether to invite him home and made the decision for me.

"I never go home with someone until I've had a real date first," he explained. "You want to come over tomorrow night? Maybe we could watch a video." He laughed. "Or study Talmud."

"I've got a Tractate Ketubot," I said. "Is that all right?"

"Are you serious? You really have Talmud?"

I nodded. "But I've never studied it before. I'm afraid I'd be like a five-year-old studying with a college student if we did it."

"I'd love to study Talmud with you." His eyes practically glowed, a lovely vision. "Can you come by around 7:00? We won't overdo it. We'll study just a little and then watch a movie. Have you seen *Shallow Hal*?"

We exchanged phone numbers and addresses, and I walked home feeling happy. Eli was definitely on my "possible" list. I'd been in bed maybe ten minutes when I got a call for Tim.

It was for an in-call, and the man showed up fifteen minutes later. Dan was seventy and not too heavy. He wanted to kiss a lot, which was unpleasant because he tasted funny.

Was that Fixodent? Maybe I'd label him Denture Cream Dan if he became a regular.

The next day at the hospital went by surprisingly quickly considering how anxious I was for the evening. My patient had his staples removed and moaned loudly the whole time. The doctor was mystified, saying that the removal wasn't supposed to hurt. The patient, after sending his girlfriend away, finally admitted it didn't.

Because he was discharged shortly after that, I had to pick up another patient and was given a thirty-year-old black man who'd been shot in the head during a mugging. The bullet had entered near the temple and gone straight across, missing his brain but destroying both eyes. One eye was swollen to twice its normal size, so the eyelid wouldn't close over it. I had to apply ointment to the blind eye staring dully out at me. His other eye had been removed.

"I gave him my wallet," the man told me, "but he shot me anyway." His face made an awful, haunting image, but the man calmly discussed the Braille class his mother had signed him up for, and how he was on a list to get a seeing-eye dog.

I realized for the first time the helplessness I knew I'd continue to feel no matter how skilled a healthcare worker I became. But I was still glad to be there, scared or not. It was a mitzvah I could manage.

Thinking of mitzvot, I knew that escorting was one, too. With both jobs I was truly helping people, and that gave me satisfaction. I might not keep up the escorting forever, but for now, helping people sexually was just as rewarding as helping people medically.

I thought of something my next-door neighbor, Bicycle Jeff, had once said, "I have a lot to be ashamed of, and I'm proud of it."

After I got home, I went to the gym and had a good work out, doing a few abdominal exercises this time. At home, I studied a while and finished up more of my paperwork due tomorrow. Then, after a light supper, I made my way over to Eli's apartment. He was wearing the same leather pants he'd had on the night before.

"I knew you liked them," he said, "and I wanted to please you."

He was definitely on my "possible" list. I couldn't wait to press my face against the leather and inhale, then inhale again at what lay underneath. I gave Eli a kiss on the lips. He hugged me and continued to kiss me back for a full minute. Then we stood in his doorway looking at one another.

I was infatuated, a pleasant feeling, but I hoped we could become closer and move beyond that stage. I could really see myself falling for this guy. Being with him. How many leather Jews could there be in New Orleans? I wanted to find out what Eli was all about.

"I've got to tell you a few things," I said, wanting to be clear from the start so as not to disappoint him later. "I'm promiscuous, and I'm an escort."

He nodded. "I have HIV," he told me. "And I'm a terrible housekeeper."

I nodded.

"Now let's get started on that Talmud," he said, leading the way into his living room. I sat down beside him with a smile.

The Lizard of Oz

Oz Sagiv had always loved his penis. He started masturbating when he was six, though naturally it had been years before his dick would "spit," as he called it then. On circle jerks with his friends in Jerusalem, he was always the envy of the other boys because he could shoot the farthest.

He'd been raised observant but flagrantly started having sex with girls when he was fifteen, so his parents had been happy to send him to America for college. He wasn't exactly dead to them, but it became obvious there was no need to keep him in the promised land. It seemed less of a sin for him to stray if he was far away. Oz had earned his doctorate in chemistry in Chicago and was now an assistant professor of organic chemistry and biochemistry in Lincoln, Nebraska.

He'd gone through all the Jewish girls there quickly enough and started in on the shiksas. He enjoyed exploring a woman's body, but he enjoyed even more just having a woman devote herself to his penis. A couple of women had told him he was selfish, but he didn't really believe that was true. He did research for pain medication, didn't he?

Oz raised poison dart frogs and did studies on epibatidine. It turned out that poison dart frogs didn't produce toxins in captivity, but he could still extract a substance that was two hundred times more powerful than morphine and yet wasn't an opioid. It was unfortunately still too toxic to use as a painkiller, so Oz and many other researchers around the world kept trying to find ways to make it more useful to suffering people.

That was selfless, wasn't it?

Or did the fact that he wanted money and recognition for it make that self-centered, too?

After a couple of hours in front of class today, and several hours in the lab, Oz sat at his computer back in his apartment to send an email to his parents. They got along well enough despite Oz's worldliness. It didn't mean Oz didn't think they were great parents. Or even that he didn't appreciate Judaism. He simply disagreed that he needed to suppress his sexuality. God had given him this gift, and he was grateful enough to enjoy it.

When Oz turned the monitor to its screen saver, he sat looking at a close-up of his erect penis. It was beautiful. How could anyone not feel gratitude for such a thing?

He sat gazing at it a moment longer. The head was exactly the right size, and the venation and slight curvature of the 7 ¾ inch organ were perfect. And yet...and yet...something was missing. He couldn't tell just what. But slightly imperfect though his penis might be, Oz felt sincerely and deeply happy every time he looked at it, held it in his hands, or slid it into an appropriate orifice.

There were plenty of appropriate orifices.

It was Friday evening. Oz went to services, and after a nice Shabbat meal, he showered to get ready for the bars. He liked lathering his dick and masturbating a few moments in the shower, not to bring himself to climax but to tease himself for the fun ahead.

Tonight, he was going to a bar called the Rainbow Club to hear a band called Crocodile Tears. Oz wasn't sure why the club had such a New Age name when it catered mostly to a pierced clientele. Oz had rings in both nipples and his left eyebrow. He didn't like earrings, was not particularly inspired by other facial piercings, and was appalled at the idea of a Prince Albert. A cock ring didn't seem like quite enough adornment for such a special part of the body, but a Prince Albert was way too much.

Oz grabbed a beer and stood off to the side to watch the band. The lead singer was kind of cool, a slight woman with a red Mohawk, and a thin row on either side which looked blue in this light. Oz wondered what it would be like to rub his dick through her hair. Or to shoot off across all three bands.

A man bumped up against him. "Excuse me," the guy said.

Oz looked at him and nodded. "I like the arm," he told the man.

On the guy's left arm, he had four spikes about an inch apart protruding from the skin, some kind of implanted piercing. Worth considering.

"We put the devil in hell," the mohawked woman was singing as she and a male band member simulated intercourse on stage. "Devil—in—hell." The woman punctuated each word with a new thrust by the other band member.

"And you look like a devil to me," she sang, pointing out into the audience at random. When she pointed in Oz's direction, their eyes locked for a moment.

Oz felt a shock of electricity pass through him. He'd never been a groupie, but that girl was hot.

Oz flirted with a couple of other girls throughout the evening and picked up one phone number, but he was determined to wait until the end of the concert. When the group disbanded for a break, Oz made his way over to the woman as she sipped a drink.

"Yeah?" she said, looking at him a little critically.

"I'm a Jew."

She raised a pierced eyebrow. "So?"

"It's a blessing to have sex on the Sabbath."

The woman looked at him and laughed. "Oh, my god. I haven't heard that line since rabbinical school."

"What?"

"I'm a cantor. Graduated from school in Cincinnati. But there's not much demand for radical women cantors. So I sing in a band."

"Well, you sing like an angel when you sing of the devil."

"Oh, my god. Are you for real?"

"My tongue isn't my best feature," Oz admitted.

"Mine is." The woman stuck out her tongue. The tip was split in two for about an inch or so, like the tongue of a reptile.

"That's fabulous. It doesn't affect your singing?"

"Oh, it took a little adjusting. You got anything interesting going on?"

Oz suddenly felt very pedestrian. "I'm afraid not."

"Pity. I was getting interested in meeting your dybbuk."

"Would a tattooed dybbuk interest you?"

The woman considered. "Maybe," she said slowly. "What kind of tattoo?"

Oz thought quickly. Perhaps a tattoo really was what he needed to make his penis extra special. If it could be any more special than it already was. But a tattoo of what?

"Well?"

Oz thought about the woman's vagina, getting hard as he envisioned her bush covering the entrance, fantasizing about it being a cave. What would go into a cave to hide, to take refuge?

"My dick has a tattoo of a dragon."

"Really. I'm impressed. You seemed a little vanilla."

"Chocolate chip. It's mostly vanilla, with just a little pizzazz."

The woman held out her hand. "I'm Shira," she said.

"Oz."

"I've got to get back for my next set."

"I'm going to need to go. Can I get your number?"

Shira smiled and wrote something down on a napkin and handed it to him. "Call me Sunday. In the afternoon when I'm awake."

Oz grinned and then nodded as he turned to go. But in the street, he let out a sigh. Had he just committed himself to something he'd regret?

He began walking slowly down the sidewalk. All along the street in this neighborhood, there were clubs and cigarette shops and used CD stores, a sex shop, and a Taco Bell with grungy kids begging out front. But there was also a tattoo parlor a couple of blocks down.

Oz stood in front of the window and stared at the artist working on a young woman in a dental chair. He'd drill for a few moments, dab away the blood, and keep needling.

Oz's penis was sensitive. That's what he liked about it. He assumed he was more sensitive than the average guy or every other guy would be out fucking and beating off as much as he was. How would it be to have two thousand needle punctures? Just to impress a girl he'd probably only fuck twice?

Through the window, Oz looked at some of the photographs on the wall. There were some truly lovely pieces of art on those folks. Maybe—

Oz gasped. It was impossible as a Jew not to consider the possibility of another Holocaust, and as petty as it seemed, Oz worried about the death of his penis as much as his own death. But now he remembered the grisly stories he'd heard as a kid, how the Nazis had preserved any Jewish skin covered with tattoos, to keep as artwork. If he had his entire dick tattooed, his penis might live on forever.

He set his jaw and walked into the shop.

Unfortunately, the job had to be done in stages and took hours. The nipple rings had hurt for mere seconds. This involved significantly more pain over a significantly longer time. But it was for a good cause, so Oz just kept fantasizing about having sex with Shira onstage as she grunted "devil—in—hell."

He didn't want to have sex with her, however, until the work was complete and his dick had healed, so it was a few weeks before Oz made his move. He'd called her that initial Sunday as he'd promised, but on their first three dates, Oz simply requested to hear Shira sing Jewish songs. She seemed impressed he didn't grope her the first time they were alone.

For his part, it was new territory for Oz to get to know a girl even a little before having her go down on him. Listening to Shira sing, "A Price Above Rubies," Oz had to admit that maybe this particular girl was worth knowing.

Finally, it was time for Oz to act. He'd waited so long, though, that now he was nervous. It was easier if you had nothing invested. He tried scratching near his groin a couple of times to see if he could get Shira to look at his crotch. He stood up to sniff a vase of poppies on the table as an excuse to rub up against Shira ever so slightly. When that produced no response, he yawned and feigned sleepiness, hoping she'd yawn, too, and he could suggest a nap.

Nothing.

Oz sat on the sofa, staring at the flowers.

"Coward," said Shira.

"Huh?"

"Just ask."

Now Oz felt like a complete idiot. But he'd do it. "Wanna suck my dick?" he said.

"Charming. A service request."

"Well, you said ask."

"Ask if you can do something for *me*. Or at least for us. Not just for you."

"You don't enjoy sucking a beautiful dick?" Oz was surprised. The idea had never occurred to him.

"Have you no brain? Appeal to the woman, not to yourself."

"Well, let's just fuck then." Oz was a little peeved. "You like that, don't you?"

Shira raised an eyebrow. "That line work with most girls?"

"I've never had a problem before."

"You'd probably better go."

Oz felt a flash of irritation. "Witch," he said. "You're such a prick tease." He stood up.

"And you're a pussy tease. I really thought you were going to turn out okay."

Oz walked out of the apartment without another word, slamming the door behind him. He drove home, his hands clenched tightly around the steering wheel. He was so distracted he almost missed the turn for Amarillo Road. When he pulled up to his apartment, he sat in his car and stared at the dashboard.

Shira had hurt him. Oz felt emasculated, and he didn't like the feeling.

It was just after 5:00 in the afternoon, but the sky was dark with clouds, and Oz glared up at them. He'd tattooed his penis for this heartless woman, and she'd made fun of him without even offering herself at all.

It was Sunday evening. Damn. There was never any good bar action in Lincoln on a Sunday evening. Oz went into his apartment and picked up some of the wingless fruit flies he grew and dropped them into the frog bins. Staring at the frogs' beautiful skin, he started to feel better. A thing of beauty could be so deadly, he realized. But it didn't stop it from being beautiful. If he could only get some of the toxins out of Shira.

The week went poorly. Oz lost his train of thought in class twice and looked like a moron. He almost ran over a dwarf he didn't see in the crosswalk. He screwed up one of his experiments and had to stay late one night to repeat it. He accidentally deleted a long email to his parents before hitting Send. Worst of all, he'd lost his interest in masturbation.

Oz felt he'd lost a friend. How could this one girl affect him so? And how in the world could he get her to like him? He sat staring at his frogs one night, and suddenly a new idea struck him.

He should do something nice for Shira, regardless of whether she responded in kind.

Saturday after services, Oz went shopping. It seemed a little insulting to think he could buy Shira's love. But it wasn't a matter of love. It was a matter of doing something she might benefit from.

Women liked jewelry. Yet Shira was not an average girl. How could he presume to know her tastes? Oz wanted something nice but also something distinctive. Those didn't always go hand in hand. He looked for hours in store after store for something unique. Maybe he ought to just apologize and see how that worked.

Then suddenly, miraculously, Oz saw what he wanted. "Could I look at that piece?" he asked.

It was an emerald crocodile head with a single diamond teardrop.

"The broach is on sale," the salesgirl encouraged hopefully.

"Not a popular design?"

"It seems to send the wrong message."

"Well, I like it."

"Thank God," said the girl. "Look, I'll give you a little discount on something else, too, just for taking it off my hands."

"Oh, that isn't necessary."

"My boss has been on my ass for weeks to sell it." She looked appraisingly at Oz and then whispered, "Would *you* like to be on my ass?"

There. That was the way it was supposed to be. Easy.

Oz couldn't see Shira till Sunday afternoon in any event, so he took the girl's number and went to her apartment after dinner. Tammy had invited him for dinner, too, which Oz had declined. He didn't want to get involved. He'd already tried that. He was sticking to sex.

Tammy started fondling him on the sofa through his jeans, and while he got hard quickly enough, he also started feeling bored almost immediately. Was his diminished sexual interest still a problem, even with a willing girl? Oz tried to get more in the mood. He tried to think how her soft, wet flesh would feel around his penis.

Tammy unzipped his jeans and reached in to pull out his dick. Soon her mouth would be on him, and he'd be over Shira's spell. Maybe not over Shira herself, but Oz would have his perspective back.

"Oh my god. You're a freak!"

"Huh?"

Tammy was staring in horror at Oz's cock. It looked wonderful to him. Did he have a herpes lesion without realizing he'd been infected? A discharge? He hadn't had sex in a month. He shouldn't have any diseases.

"What's wrong?"

"I should have realized you were a weirdo when you wanted that broach. You'd better leave."

Oz zipped up and walked slowly out of the apartment. He wasn't mad, only mystified. Two girls in a row had turned him down. Was he past his prime already? He was only twenty-seven. He certainly hadn't squandered any opportunities, but were they all used up this soon?

In a way, that wouldn't be the worst thing in the world, though he'd have thought so a month ago. He'd had every girl he ever wanted.

Except Shira. If he could just have her, he'd be satisfied for life.

Oz drove home and picked up a flier for Crocodile Tears. He stood over the photo and masturbated, his first time in a week. He needed Shira.

It was all Oz could do not to go to the bar where Shira was singing that night. He wrote a card and wrapped his gift and slept fitfully. In the morning, he exercised and took a long walk and read a couple of research articles.

Then he headed over to Shira's place unannounced. He would show her his devotion and ask forgiveness. They'd pick up where they left off. He was going to have this girl.

Oz knocked at the door. He could see movement behind the peep hole and hear shuffling. She was clearly home. Was she not even going to open the door?

Finally, after an eternity, the door opened a crack. Shira stood with her hand on her hip, looking slightly irritated.

"Pilpul," Oz began singing. "People who need pilpul…are the luckiest people in the shul."

He smiled and handed Shira the card and box. She read the card without a word and then opened the box. When she saw the broach, she put her hand to her mouth and started crying.

"It's not *that* nice," Oz said.

"The band is breaking up," Shira explained. "Jack's going to Chicago and Bert's going to Los Angeles. I want to go to New York and sing in the clubs there, but I don't have enough money for a ticket, much less rent, so I'm stuck here in Lincoln."

Oz smiled grimly. "I've been a dick," he said softly, "but I'll try to make Lincoln so it's not so bad for you."

Shira took his hand and pulled him into the apartment. She led him to the bedroom without another word, and soon her forked tongue was licking both his balls, and then alternately tickling his left nipple.

"I want you to put the devil in hell," she said, lying in bed, discarding her clothes. "I wrote that song, by the way, so I get to keep singing it if I ever get another band together." She started humming.

Oz was just about to enter her when he noticed something. "You have warts?" he asked.

"Oh, yeah. Guess I kissed a toad at some point. You want a condom?"

Though warts on a dragon wouldn't be awful, he supposed, Oz did not want to mar the beauty of his cock with them. He also didn't want Shira to feel bad. What should he do?

Just at that moment, Oz saw the curtain that served as a closet door move just a little, and he jumped.

"What the—?"

"Don't pay attention to that guy. Ray, you can go ahead and leave." She smiled at Oz. "I'm here with you now."

The other man came out from behind the curtain and quickly dressed and left. Oz wasn't sure what to think. He'd been with another girl just last night, so he couldn't hold it against Shira.

"Come inside me, Oz."

Oz looked at his dick and then looked at Shira. "Let's get together again next Sunday," he said, reaching for his pants. He'd had an HPV vaccination ages ago, but it felt like tempting fate to rub up directly against a wart.

"You're not mad, are you?"

"I'm hardly an STD virgin." Oz smiled and leaned down to kiss her. "Though I'm clean right now. I'll see you next Sunday."

The following day between classes, Oz went to the campus clinic to see if he could get an HPV booster. He couldn't. While there, he decided to go ahead and get his semi-annual HIV test. He already had vaccinations for hepatitis A and B, so there wasn't much else he could do today.

The rest of the week went marvelously, though. Oz taught quite well, found two good articles he needed for his work, and developed a new theory he could begin testing that looked promising.

Friday, Oz was humming "Devil in Hell" and looking forward to services that evening. He made a quick stop at the clinic to hear his test results before going home. His penis was in that semi-erect state where he could feel it pressing slightly against his pants. It made him thoroughly aware of his blessings.

Shira wasn't performing tonight, he thought. Oz might give Shira a call and try for some Sabbath sex.

"Mr. Sagiv," said the nurse, "I'm afraid you've tested positive for HIV."

"Wait. What?"

"You'll want an infectious disease specialist and need to start thinking about treatment."

Oz stared at the woman. He felt as if someone had just dropped a house on him.

"You're going to be okay. Really. It's not a death sentence."

Oz nodded absently and walked out of the office in a daze.

Oz did not call Shira that evening. He did not go see her on Sunday. He did not go in to work the entire following week.

He was pretty much moving about in a fog, but he was in fact moving, keeping himself very busy the entire time.

Oz had missed services last weekend, but he attended this weekend. He didn't go to the bars, and he was afraid to masturbate. He spent Saturday afternoon and evening reading *A Night of Watching*, about the Danes saving their Jews during World War II.

Comforting after reading an article about early Zionists in Palestine turning away Hungarian Jews trying to escape the Holocaust.

But on Sunday afternoon in the middle of a heavy rain, Oz took a deep breath and headed over to Shira's place.

"You're pretty cold-blooded," she said as she opened her door.

"I know. I'm a prick."

Shira sighed. "Well, the tornado watch is almost over, but you better come on in."

Oz went inside and sat next to Shira on the couch. He couldn't look at her, staring at her red tennis shoes instead.

"So?"

"I got you a gift."

"Another one? I'd rather you were nice to me to begin with instead of continually trying to make up."

He handed her an envelope, and she opened it wearily.

"It's a ticket to New York," she said slowly. "But…what…?"

Oz handed her another envelope. "What's this?" She opened the second envelope carefully and pulled out some papers, staring at them for a long while.

"The apartment's in Brooklyn," Oz said. "I couldn't afford Manhattan. But it's only a block from the subway. I paid three months' rent. It's all I could manage. The lease is in my name, of course, but if you like the place, you can have it put in your name instead. The ticket's in two weeks. I figured I needed to give you a little time to prepare. But I thought you ought to go to New York. You're someone who can fulfill your dreams, and you should."

"I don't understand."

Oz shrugged. "I've been a cock most of my life. Just once, I wanted to do something that wasn't about me." He laughed. "But I guess if I did it to make myself feel better, it still is about me, isn't it?"

"This kind of selfishness I can deal with." She looked at the lease again and then back at Oz. "So are you…coming?"

Oz shook his head.

"Then why such an extravagant gift? We didn't even sleep together."

Oz shrugged again. "I just tested positive for HIV. It puts things in perspective."

Shira shook her head. "I've known lots of guys with HIV. Most of them biblically. And they were still dickheads."

"Then maybe it's just you," he said softly. "I do want to be with you. But even more than that, I want what's best for you."

Shira took his hand, and they sat on the sofa in silence for a very long while. Then suddenly, Shira withdrew her hand and sat up straight. "You have to leave now."

Oz nodded. He'd never known the pain of unrequited love before. Or the pain of any kind of love. It hurt, but there was a sweetness to it as well. He realized the nurse was right. He was going to be okay.

He stood up and headed for the door.

"Give me a call Tuesday night."

"Huh?"

"If we only have two weeks before I leave, we can't wait till next Sunday. But I've got to write now. I just thought of a new song. It's called 'Angel in Hell.' Get out. Get out."

She shooed him toward the door but got up to kiss him before he left. He'd only gone a few feet down the hall when the door opened again and Shira stuck her head out. "You might think of applying for a position at Yeshiva University," she said. "Or CUNY or something." Then she shut the door.

Oz smiled and cocked his head. Maybe New York wasn't such a bad idea. Even if things didn't work out with Shira, there were plenty of other girls to go through there. He'd get his dick back in gear before long. And if there were any groundbreaking clinical trials, it would be in the northeast.

He walked out to his car, looking up at the clearing sky. There was half a rainbow off in the distance. Oz drove home and sat on the edge of his bed, his eyes closed as he pictured Shira onstage, his hand gently caressing his penis. He teased himself slowly, letting the inner tickling grow gradually.

Then he stopped. He was going to save it all for Shira. Not because he had to or was supposed to, but just because it was what he wanted.

Oz got up and fed his frogs and then started working on his paper. Having another publication wouldn't hurt his chances for a job in New York. He wrote a few paragraphs, including data from his latest experiment, and then moved over to the window. Late afternoon sunlight was streaming in.

The phone rang, and Oz looked at the caller ID. It was Shira. He picked up the phone with one hand, held himself with the other, and smiled.

Jewish Dogs

It was just ten minutes after 6:00 when I heard the first shot. I hardly noticed it and only saw a couple of other heads turn to acknowledge the sound. The shot was outside, a single pop as our security guard was killed. I thought perhaps it was a rock hitting the window or someone dropping a can on the sidewalk. Inside the chapel, we continued the v'ahavta, which was always my favorite part of the Friday night services. We had a good cantor, and I loved to hear her voice as she led us in the chanting.

Only a moment later, a man rushed into the chapel shouting, "Jewish dogs!" There was no screaming until he started firing into the crowd of about thirty-five worshippers, and then pandemonium began.

There was no side exit. The only way to escape was the way the man had come in. I dropped down between the pews for cover and heard the sound of the gunfire coming slowly closer and closer. Around me there were shouts of fear and screams of pain.

I was scared, too, but I was also a fatalist. My great-grandparents had been killed in the Holocaust. My mother had been shot two years ago at Jewish Family Services when a gunman had forced his way inside. One woman had been killed in the building and four others wounded. Three of them had not even been Jews.

I remembered thinking at the time that as awful as it must feel to be martyred for your faith, it must feel even worse to be martyred for someone else's. My mother had eventually recovered, but it was impossible as a Jew not to be aware at every moment that a day like this might finally arrive.

As the shooter came closer, my fear began to turn into anger. I felt the overwhelming injustice of knowing my people were being killed. I knew I was going to die, but I decided the least I could do was try to prevent any more deaths.

I'd been sitting near the rear of the chapel, so it didn't take the attacker long to reach my pew. As soon as I saw his feet reach my aisle, I leaped up and rushed him. I could feel the bullets entering me, could feel the way the blows forced my body to pause, yet I was so angry I kept moving forward anyway.

There was still screaming all around me, and I was screaming as well, though in rage. I grabbed the man's arm, kicked him in the groin, head-butted him, and finally wrenched the weapon from his grasp. I gritted my teeth and immediately turned the gun on him.

Even after he was down, I continued shooting into his body for a full fifteen seconds.

I dropped the gun then and collapsed onto a pew, my adrenalin flowing so freely that my heart hurt. After a moment, I realized the rest of me was hurting, too. I'd been hit in the chest and one lung had collapsed. I'd been hit in the abdomen a couple of times as well. I worried about my liver and spleen and about peritonitis from intestinal damage.

But mostly, I just felt happy that I'd killed the bastard.

I looked about at people running out of the chapel now or lying in pools of blood. I clearly hadn't acted quickly enough. If I managed to survive, I'd have to live with that the rest of my life.

I tried to stay conscious as long as I could but was starting to fade by the time emergency personnel arrived. "Him!" I heard a teenage girl shout. "He saved us! I caught the whole thing on my phone. You have to help him!"

I remember thinking I wanted the other wounded to be carried away first. There was no point in "helping" if the rest died waiting for their turn.

But I passed out then and don't know exactly what happened next.

I did wake up briefly in the hospital later. A woman was looking down at me with a mixture of tenderness and detachment. "I'm Dr. Hirsch," she said. "We're going to take good care of you."

I smiled. "You're pretty," I said weakly. The woman was about thirty and blond, with a dimple in her right cheek. I think I winked at her. Then I felt like a fool. I was twenty-eight and single, but I wasn't a dog. I didn't know why I'd said such a thing. I closed my eyes.

"We'll date later," she said curtly. "Just concentrate on hanging on."

I couldn't manage to open my eyes again. I felt myself being jostled, and all I wanted to do was sleep.

When I woke up at what seemed a much, much later time, the first thing I noticed was how much better I felt. There were still several dull aches all over my body, though they weren't sharp as they'd been before. I saw an I.V. in one hand, and I felt a bandage on my head. I frowned. What was wrong with my head?

"Oh, Jason, you're okay!" My mother rushed over to my bedside and grabbed my hand.

"How many?" I asked.

She looked at the floor. "Nine dead," she said softly.

A wave of depression came over me, but I felt Mom squeeze my fingers. "There's no telling how many you saved," she went on. "That girl has her phone video all over the news showing you fighting the terrorist. We couldn't be prouder. Your father, too. He'll fly in later today."

I nodded, and I asked for names. One of the other congregants who went to Torah study with me was among those killed. I was glad my mother preferred Saturday services to Friday. How many shootings could one person survive? I remembered the Holocaust survivor who'd ended up being gunned down in the Virginia Tech killings.

An hour later, Dr. Hirsch came into the room and asked my mother to step out for a moment. The doctor stood next to my bed and put her hand on my arm gently. "It was touch and go for a while, but I think you're going to be fine."

"Until the next time, I suppose. It was my mother two years ago."

Dr. Hirsch nodded grimly. "Yes, I did some research. I'm glad she's all right."

"It's too bad Jews aren't really a separate race," I said. "We could use some special features, like a tortoise shell across our backs, or a triceratops shield over our heads." I smiled weakly.

Dr. Hirsch stared at me. "What in the world would make you say such a thing?"

"Drugs?" I tried to joke, but she kept staring.

I shrugged against my pillow. "People already see us as a different species altogether. The least we could do is have different protective genes or something. Not just Tay-Sachs." I smiled again. "I'm a geneticist," I explained.

"Is that so?" Dr. Hirsch breathed slowly.

"Well, all I really do is work in a lab. PCR mostly."

"And you want to manipulate the human genome?" She raised an eyebrow. "Are you sure you aren't just another Mengele?"

"It wouldn't be the first time the victim became the criminal." I remembered Magneto from the X-Men.

Dr. Hirsch sighed. "As it happens, genetics is a personal interest of mine as well."

"Really?"

"So maybe we *should* go on that date sometime." She laughed, but it wasn't a light sound. "When you're no longer my patient, of course."

"Of course." Though now I was starting to fantasize about something completely inappropriate. I hoped she didn't notice the accompanying changes in blood flow.

Dr. Hirsch pretended to check the I.V. in my hand, but I saw her eyes track toward my midline. I really was stupid.

"You made quite an impression on me," she said. "The paramedic told me you single-handedly stopped the shooter."

"A little late, I'm afraid."

"But you did it. I—I was intrigued." She squeezed my arm.

"Dr. Hirsch, aren't you behaving just a little unprofessionally?" I hoped she could hear the smile in my voice. Deflection and misdirection. Survival skills for the socially inept.

I had a vision of us sitting at a café drinking coffee and chatting, but within seconds, the image turned to one of us doing it doggy-style. I shook my head to clear it and felt a twinge of pain.

"It wouldn't be the first time I was accused of being unprofessional." She frowned and adjusted the bandage on my head. "Not that I've ever dated a patient," she clarified. "It's just—oh, never mind."

I was in the hospital another week, and there were a couple of follow-up visits over the next few months. I was soon back at work, and back at synagogue, back hanging out with friends and going to Jewish Singles activities. I began jogging again early in the morning, always looking out for muggers, and planting hybrid lupine and foxglove in my yard on Sundays. I read more Holocaust literature, began going to a gun range, and started lifting weights.

I went to a couple of bars, too sensitive about my scars to ask anyone home, but I watched online porn, feeling an animal lust I couldn't repress forever. I remembered that one of the Andes plane crash survivors had become extremely sexually active after being rescued, wanting to live life to the fullest.

I'd almost asked Dr. Hirsch out during my last office visit and then chickened out. I no longer had a medical need to see her, though, and decided I needed to focus more on the Jewish Singles group. I went to one dance and picked up a young woman a few years older than me.

The sex wasn't great, but it did make me feel whole again. Still, after a near death experience, I somehow felt I needed to be *more* than whole, more than just a mere man. I called Dr. Hirsch to see if she could recommend a psychiatrist I could talk to about what I was feeling. She was too busy to see me as a patient any longer and referred me to a colleague. I said I didn't want to see *her*, that I wanted to see a psychiatrist, but she told me to call Dr. Chen and hung up. So much for fantasizing about Dr. Hirsch.

At synagogue, the cantor tried to sing happy songs, beautiful songs, and the rabbi gave energetic, upbeat sermons. Mom and I had dinner once a week, and we made a point of talking about accomplishments various famous Jews were making in the world today. A bit reductionist, but you did what you had to to cope. I began to put the entire awful episode behind me.

It was at a potluck dinner six months after the shooting where I ran into Dr. Hirsch again. It was awkward, as I couldn't help but notice that she looked especially attractive. When she glanced in my direction, I felt my skin flush.

Why was it that in other animals, it was the female who usually went "in heat," while for humans, the male seemed perpetually excited?

"How're you feeling?" Dr. Hirsch asked with a glass of wine in one hand.

"That's a professional question, not a flirtatious one, Doctor," I chided. "And I thought you were too busy to ask."

Still socially inept.

"It's Rebecca," she said, holding out her free hand. "I wasn't too busy to ask your mother where I might run into you socially."

I raised an eyebrow. "Aren't you sweet?"

"We'll see about that."

We sat together and, after a little more awkwardness, began talking about ourselves. I told her of my time at Jewish camp, and how I'd wanted to become a cantor. I told her of trying to write popular new tunes for traditional Jewish songs. I couldn't sing, but I'd sent my music to other performers and sold two arrangements so far. Once I opened up, talking to the doctor seemed quite natural. She didn't feel like Dr. Hirsch anymore.

Rebecca told me how her uncle had immigrated to Israel years ago and been killed serving in the army there. She told me about her great-aunt who'd been in the camps and had broken glass sewn under her skin to see how her body would react.

I tried to lighten the conversation by talking of my boyhood dog, Avi, and vacations at our family cabin in the woods. Rebecca told me of her trip to Tel Aviv as a teenager and seeing the bus in front of hers explode.

"You're no Groucho Marx," I said with a smile.

"Sorry. I guess I feel compelled to tell you why I got into medicine. What made you interested in genetics?"

"My best friend growing up had hemophilia. I remember what a breakthrough it was to start getting factor VIII from recombinant DNA instead of from people."

"You're interested in recombinant DNA?" Rebecca asked slowly.

"Oh, do you know much about it?"

"I know we have transgenic mice and chickens and fish and sheep and goats and pigs."

"And plants."

"Oh, of course, and plants, too," she said absentmindedly.

"I used to want to work with yeast or bacteria to create new products like insulin or human growth hormone."

"And now?"

"Well, I only have a Masters. I was weeded out of my doctorate program. Too stupid. So now I just do routine work that the smart guys tell me to do. Not much in the way of original research."

"Fascinating."

I laughed. "I wish. I'd have liked to do gene therapy or something really useful."

"I hear gene therapy has only been done in non-reproductive cells."

I looked at her. Physicians knew so much that I didn't, but they often didn't have a clue about even fundamental academic research. "People are afraid to allow transmittance to the next generation," I said. "Germ line gene therapy is quite controversial."

"Do you know Dr. Zachary?"

I looked at her again. "Yes," I said. "He's at another institution, but everyone's heard of him."

"He's a good friend of mine."

"So why aren't you dating *him*?" I teased. "He's a better catch than I am."

"You've no idea."

I laughed at her willingness to insult me. I didn't feel offended.

"He's working on a project," Rebecca began before stopping and shaking her head. "No, I'd better not say."

"The only way to keep a secret is never to tell anyone." I batted my eyes.

"He's working on creating chimeric DNA," she blurted. "Composites of different animal species."

That was great, I thought, but hardly reason for secrecy. It had been done before. We'd already talked about the sheep and mice and chickens, hadn't we?

"In humans," she said quietly, making sure no one else heard.

I froze.

"In germ lines."

My mouth fell open. She looked at me in silence, and finally I was able to speak. "Rebecca, that's criminal."

Her eyes narrowed and her nostrils flared a little. "Wouldn't you like to have a dog's ability to smell fear? You could tell when a stranger was about to attack. Or how about a dog's ability to hear a wider range of pitches? Or how about a dog's tapetum lucidum, so you could see clearly in light five times dimmer than you can see now?"

"Rebecca…"

"You said you wished Jews could have a shell or some other protection. Wouldn't having more acute senses help make us better able to survive all the attacks we face?"

"Who wants a wet, black nose?" I tried to laugh, to change the subject, to escape this dangerous discussion.

"Everything is done subtly. You'd see the reflection of the tapetum, naturally, but everything else would look normal."

"You're not serious."

"Oh, Jason, you're not *really* against it, are you? Not really?" She looked at me anxiously.

I thought for a moment. It was outrageous, of course, but then Jews faced outrageous hatred every day, didn't we? Maybe we did need something extra in our genome. A genetic arsenal. If it worked, maybe it was something we should never even go public with, just have a kind of underground network to spread the DNA among our own people. This would be better than the Protocols.

"Well, I *suppose*—"

Rebecca reached over and gave me a kiss. Two people near us giggled. "I've been hoping ever since I saw your dick…"

"Excuse me?"

"Never mind."

I took a deep breath. "So are you going to get Dr. Zachary to hire me at a better salary?" I tried to look stern.

Rebecca laughed. "Maybe." She took my hand. "Come on, let's go to my place." We stood and started for the door.

"It's late."

"You can stay the night."

I smiled. "If getting shot nets me a Jewish doctor, perhaps it was worth it."

Once outside, we headed for our cars. "I'm not inviting you home because you were shot," she said. "I'm inviting you because of the injections."

I stopped. "Injections?"

Rebecca turned to me but looked at the ground. "I was so upset about the shooting. Dr. Zachary already had me looking for a viable candidate, but I couldn't bear to risk experimenting on someone healthy. When I saw you, though, I thought, 'He'll probably die anyway. If he lives, he'll be so happy he won't mind if we've succeeded.'"

"Succeeded with what?" I felt adrenalin pumping through my system.

"I made several injections into your testicles. Not all the sperm you produce will be transgenic, but lots of it will. You of course won't personally have any of the traits we're working for, but your children will have an edge. They'll have a better chance at survival. It seemed a fair thing to give a man who'd been shot five times."

"Oh, my god."

"And the fact that you're a geneticist. Well, it all just seems...cosmic, preordained." She shrugged. "I was never very good at gematria or the kabbalah."

I stared at her for a long, long moment.

"Are you going to report me? Are you angry? Do you still want to come over? Do you think I'm a bitch?"

I swallowed, and the adrenalin slowly faded away. I wondered if Dr. Zachary could get a couple of good germ lines going in Israel. Then have the guys donate to sperm clinics. I wondered what I could do here in my own country. "When we have sex tonight," I said carefully, "you do realize I won't wear a condom?"

Rebecca smiled. "I'm counting on that."

We started walking toward our cars again. "You sure the home movies of our kids won't play on late night TV right after *The Island of Dr. Moreau*?"

She rolled her eyes, and I wondered if there were genes to correct for social ineptitude.

"Our kids," she said, "will grow up to be great people." She paused. "The key is that they *will* grow up. Our kids are going to be survivors."

We'd just reached Rebecca's car, and she was opening the door when a man walked up to us. "Is this the house where the Jewish Singles are meeting?"

"Yes," Rebecca said, "you can—"

A shot rang out, and Rebecca fell to the ground.

"Jewish dogs," the man spit out.

Then he aimed the gun at me and fired again.

Pronouncing the Apostrophe

After the salt water and horseradish and Dayenu, we sat around the table eating the meal. It was fun to come to Steven and Marty's metal house near City Park, not far from the cemeteries at the end of Canal Street in New Orleans. There was an "I Love Lucy" magnet on the metal hallway paneling, a gargoyle magnet on the metal kitchen wall, and a David magnet with assorted firefighter and doctor magnet clothes on the metal bathroom door.

A mezuzah was attached by a magnet to the front door frame. Steven, Marty's lover of six years, was Buddhist but the one who'd prepared the seder.

"So there we were on the bus in Paris and these Muslims saw my Israeli army T-shirt and came up to me and said, 'We *fuck* Israelis.'" Marty calmly took another sip of wine. "So I just smiled and said, 'Some Israelis like that.' They didn't know what to say."

I smiled and spooned another matzah ball out of my soup. I was relieved to be at a seder tonight. The last four years, my partner, David, and I had gone to seders with a family in the congregation he was close to before we met. The family liked me, but they certainly weren't going to invite me this year after my breakup with David, and I wasn't up to a seder of my own yet.

David had been so sick the four years we were together that we hardly ever socialized, but after we broke up a few months ago, I began trying to reestablish connections I'd made in the past. After I'd dated Marty a few times eight years earlier, he and I had become friends, except when David's misery made it impossible for us to have contact with anyone outside of the HIV clinic.

"Let's not talk about Palestinians tonight," suggested Marty's mother, Joyce. "I want to believe we do have a homeland we can call our own."

"We're going to have to give up part of it," said Leon, Marty's father, "if—"

"No politics tonight," Joyce repeated. She turned to Marty and put her hand on his arm. "I saw termites swarming the other day. It seems a little early."

"Did you turn off your lights?" Marty asked, and she nodded.

"I guess y'all are okay here," I said.

"The addition is wood," said Steven, "and it's built right on the ground, so it's our Achilles heel."

"And the Gaza strip is Israel's. We don't need a two state solution but a country where everyone has rights."

"Leon, I said no more politics." Joyce turned to Marty again and then reached toward one of the bowls on the table. "This is excellent matzah ball soup. I think I'll get some more."

"Steven made it."

"It was the only way to get y'all to have a seder," Steven said. "I swear, y'all are a pathetic bunch of Jews, making the only goy among you prepare the meal."

"I couldn't cook as a goy," I said, "and I can't cook now."

"The rabbi accepted your conversion without making you learn even one recipe for kugel?" Marty asked.

"He only made me promise to raise my kids as Jews."

"Easy promise."

"Well, we did name our cats Sarah and Akiva."

"Close enough."

"David won custody."

"Are you going to marry another Jew?" asked Joyce.

I smiled. "That's what the rabbi asked me. But I'm not at all sure I'm going to get married again to anyone."

"What did your family think of you converting?" Joyce offered the salt but I shook my head.

"You mean the ones who know?"

"You didn't tell them?" asked Leon.

"My aunt knows. She doesn't have a problem with it. But when I broke up with David, my grandmother said, 'Now you won't have to go to that Jewish church anymore.' I told her I liked going, and she seemed worried. So I don't think she can handle it yet."

"She can handle your being gay, but not your being a Jew?" Marty laughed.

"Apparently, there are levels of apostasy."

"Seems like you're hiding to me," Steven said. "My family knows I'm Buddhist. They just have to live with it."

I shrugged. "Religion has given me a lot of pain. I'm not going to use religion to justify causing unnecessary pain to someone I love. She knows I still go to synagogue. That's enough."

"I notice you haven't drunk any wine tonight," Steven added. "Are you still Mormon underneath the kipa?"

I took another sip of grape juice. "My life began thirty-six years ago, and all of it is a part of me, including the good parts of Mormonism. But the reason I don't drink is because I never have. Drinking moderately would be fine, but I don't know if I can be a moderate drinker. There may be some terrible flaw in my genes or personality I can't realize is there until it's too late. It isn't worth the risk to me. If I never drink that first glass, I'll never become an alcoholic. Life is hard enough without adding another obstacle. I can't afford any more vulnerable spots in my life."

"But wine is a part of Judaism," Steven pointed out.

"He doesn't have to drink," said Leon. "He doesn't need to wear a yarmulke either. He just needs to live ethically."

"But it wouldn't hurt me to learn how to make challah. Maybe I could ask one of you to teach me sometime."

"Not any time this week," said Joyce. "But you can call me next week."

"I went to a Reconstructionist seder once," Marty said. "They had breadsticks."

"Breadsticks!" Leon looked more surprised than he had at his son's response to the taunts on the bus.

"Why didn't you wear your yarmulke tonight?" asked Marty. "I thought you liked it."

"Well, I'm Touro, and you're Sinai," I said, naming the two Uptown Reform congregations in New Orleans to which we belonged. "I didn't want to come overdressed." Sinai was "more" Reform than Touro.

"Is it uncomfortable still going to Touro after breaking up with David?" Steven asked.

"David could hardly ever go, anyway, so people are used to seeing me without him. I need to try Gates of Prayer and Chevra Thilim and maybe some of the others. I went to the mikvah at Beth Israel in Lakeview when I converted, but I don't want to go to an Orthodox congregation."

Joyce and Leon began talking of the changes they'd seen at Sinai over the years, the differences each new rabbi made, and some of the different things they'd seen at different seders. I couldn't help but think about how no matter where in the world I'd gone to a Latter-day Saint meeting, here in New Orleans, or when visiting friends in South Carolina or Los Angeles or Salt Lake, and even when living in Belgium for two years as a missionary, the meetings had been all but identical.

That seemed like a good thing at the time, but now I liked the idea that people were allowed to evolve. Mormons did it, too, but it had to be an across-the-board evolution mandated by the president of the Church. Mormons would cringe at the wide diversity of thought allowed in Judaism, considering divergence an automatic sign of corruption, but I'd seen for myself that Mormon theology could be corrupt even when everyone believed the exact same thing.

When the rabbi interviewed me before my conversion, I'd asked, "What will I be expected to believe?" He'd laughed and said, "You don't even have to believe in God. No one is going to tell you what you need to believe here." It seemed like cheating, after the rigid rules I was used to, but I could have that again with the Orthodox if I wanted it, and I definitely didn't want it. I wanted to believe what made sense to me, whatever little that might be.

"These haggadahs are quite different from the ones I've used the last few years," I said, knowing I had the plural form wrong. Was it haggadot? "I like them." I picked up the book still lying next to my plate and looked at the date of publication in the back. 1923. There were some beautiful engravings throughout.

"We've had them in the family since I was a girl," Joyce said, "though every year we seem to have one less."

"What's the biggest difference in this one?" Marty asked me.

"It's Ashkenazi and not Sephardic," I replied.

"Most of us are, really."

We continued to talk for another hour or so, and as I stood to leave, Steven asked me to call them so we could have Shabbat dinner sometime, or to call so Marty and I could go to summer services together. Services rotated among three synagogues in the summer, and I'd told them I usually chickened out going to new places by myself. I thanked Marty and Steven for the seder and felt relieved to find Marty still willing to accept me though I'd ignored him and everyone else for the last four years.

"I went to a couple of Lambda Chai meetings," I said at the door as Marty and Steven kissed me goodbye. I hadn't much liked those gay Jewish meetings, finding most of the men too cynical and bitchy, and nothing terribly Jewish about the meetings, but one man, who painted portraits on Jackson Square in front of the St. Louis cathedral in the Quarter, had seemed nice. "There's a guy who'd been studying to become a Baptist minister before he converted. He has a Buddhist lover. I'll have to get their number and give it to you. How many gay Jewish-Buddhist couples can there be in New Orleans?"

They laughed, and then I climbed into my car and chanted the Haftarah prayers as I drove back home. It was the first truly nice evening I'd had since David and I broke up. It felt good. Maybe things would turn out okay after all. I wondered if a thank-you note was appropriate after a seder. I'd send one anyway. I felt so weak compared to other Jews who all seemed to know what to do, even if they were secular.

I always felt I was trying to catch up. With my tape of prayers and Hebrew songs in the car, I could go through much of a Shabbat service every day, but there were still

1500 services I'd missed while growing up in another religion. Listening to only one service over and over would never make up for that. It didn't really need to, but I found it irritating to be all set in synagogue for one version of "Lecha Dodi" only to hear another version I couldn't sing along with. There was no music to read, only words, so even my years in the Gay Men's Chorus didn't help. I just sat in the chapel feeling alien and hoping the feeling would one day end.

I drove up beside my apartment in the Marigny, the neighborhood next to the French Quarter, and hurried to the door, looking about to make sure no potential muggers were on the street. At least once a week, there was a mugging or a house burglary in the neighborhood. Looking over my shoulder had become second nature. I darted in quickly and shut the door.

It was late, and I was tired, so I undressed as soon as I was inside and went to bed, saying one of my own prayers before falling asleep. My prayers at night consisted of pointing out to God that I was aware of at least ten specific, good things that had happened that day. Tonight, it was easy, and soon I was asleep.

In the morning, I peeked outside to see if anyone was on the street and then hurriedly threw my camera and overnight bag in the trunk. I hated having people see me pack and know I was going to be away for the weekend. My apartment had bars on the windows and a barred gate on the door, but it also had two wooden shutters over French doors in the bedroom.

They were only held shut by a metal bar in a slot like a latch on a screen door. The bar was heavier than a latch but also looser. And the shutters were so old that there was plenty of space to slip in a wire hanger. It would be easy to pull the latch away even from the outside. I put a bookcase in front of the doors, but it wasn't so heavy that it couldn't be pushed away by a burglar because I didn't want it so heavy that I couldn't move it in case of a fire.

I was eleven when I'd seen the photographs of the burned men hanging out the barred windows of the UpStairs Lounge in the French Quarter, where an arsonist had killed thirty-two people by setting fire to the stairwell leading to the entrance of the second story gay bar. I'd vowed then never to live anyplace with bars blocking the exits, but when David and I had broken up in December, this converted corner storefront had been the only available place I could afford.

It was only a foot off the ground and would be one of the first places to flood the next time we had a 15-inch rainfall. I remembered the last flood while David and I were living near Bayou St. John. By the light of Shabbat candles, after the electricity had gone out, we tried desperately to lift everything off the floor as the water came in under the doors and up through the tiles. That had been three years now, so it wouldn't be long before the next flood.

I'd already experienced four "once in a hundred years" floods in my lifetime. I hoped I could find a better place before the next one, though that would mean moving yet again. David and I had lived in four different apartments together because he could never get along with our landlords, and now with this last move, I was tired of changing addresses and wanted to stay put.

Not wanting to leave for Mississippi right away this morning, just in case someone had in fact seen me pack the car, I read the paper and skipped my morning cereal, more to save the calories than to keep a kosher Passover. I really didn't see how Frosted Flakes could be considered leavened bread. In fact, cereal seemed like such a fast meal that it represented exactly the kind of meal that should be eaten this week, food that could be prepared and eaten in a hurry.

But then, sandwiches could be prepared quickly, too, so that alone wasn't a good criterion. I did want to eat differently this week, to remind myself of the occasion, but I wasn't sure it mattered exactly what it was that I did eat. I'd finished a loaf of bread yesterday, though, and was going at least to avoid that for the next several days.

I exchanged my bar mitzvah tape for my Reclaiming Shabbat and started off to Brookhaven. It had been hard for me to study for my bar mitzvah the year before. I rarely felt like studying anyway, so when I could force myself, I studied Organic Chemistry or Microbiology. I found that the only way I could make myself study the prayers, basic songs like "Mi Chamocha" or "Yedid Nefesh," and my Torah and Haftarah portions, was to listen to a practice tape in the car.

It took twenty minutes to drive out to the University of New Orleans at the Lakefront for classes, twenty minutes to get back home, twenty more minutes to drive out to Southern University to teach, and twenty minutes to get back home. I went through a serious Celine Dion withdrawal, but my chanting was flawless.

Now I was trying to find a tape of all the other prayers I still didn't know. And I'd looked for a tape of Passover songs but couldn't find one in time to be prepared for last night. No one expected me to know those songs, but it was embarrassing not to be able to chant either the Kiddush or the kaddish on Shabbat. It was like going to a birthday party and not knowing the words to "Happy Birthday."

I felt we should have been required to learn these prayers as well for the bar mitzvah, since they were important and part of the weekly service, but we were Reform. I guess the rabbi was scared of chasing away the adult b'nei mitzvah class. I'd been scared myself, but I knew if I didn't do it before medical school, it would be years before I had another chance.

The Reclaiming Shabbat tape had two local cantors, plus a male rabbi and a woman who was the Director of Youth Education, calling themselves Beignet Israel, making a pun using the name of a French Quarter doughnut in place of the nearly identical sounding Hebrew word for "children." On the tape, they performed "Shalom Aleichem," "Mi Sheibeirach," "Adon Olam," and other songs we sang in shul regularly. I wished "Shalom Rav" were on it.

When our cantor sang, "tassim tassim l'olam," I felt such an incredible sense of peace that it alone made the unpleasant trek past the projects in Central City to the synagogue in my old car worthwhile. It had taken me a while to get used to the idea that in Hebrew, the apostrophe was pronounced. "L'olam" was not pronounced "lolam" but "luh olam."

And of course, real Hebrew didn't even have vowels, so the writing was quite compact, even when tiny vowel marks were placed underneath or beside the main letters for those who couldn't manage the language without cheating a little. Listening to the songs over and over on the tape helped me follow along in the prayer book with at least passing competency.

I drove west on I-10 through the cypress swamps to LaPlace and then took I-55 north further on through more swamps. I wished David were with me. He had to take extra morphine to handle the ride, so it was always a sacrifice for him to come. One summer, we'd picked blackberries together. We'd also picked and canned pears a couple of times. He was always a wreck for days after the exertion of a trip, but it was about the only time we ever got to do anything together.

Of course, no one in such pain for so many years could stay nice forever. David had started criticizing my relatives and his own relatives and everyone at synagogue and had become meaner and meaner to everyone. I was the last, but he finally just grew too mean to live with. I felt terrible leaving a sick man I had loved, but I just wasn't strong enough to take it.

Before long, I drove past Hammond, solid ground finally, where my aunt and gay uncle lived with their four children. I should have sympathized with Mark but was instead angry at him for marrying Brenda twenty years ago. Mark was much more homophobic than Brenda, who'd only two years ago found out about Mark, though I'd come out to her years before.

I couldn't pity him, though, because I was too irritated with his praise for Rush Limbaugh or Newt Gingrich or Trent Lott or whoever the currently popular Republican bigot was. I was just glad I'd broken up with my fianceé in Belgium before I totally ruined her life. We still wrote, but at thirty-eight, she still hadn't married. I knew I wouldn't have fulfilled her life any more than Mark had fulfilled Brenda's. Brenda tried to take satisfaction in her children, but her oldest girl, Cathy, was a senior in high school, had gotten drunk this past New Year's, and I'd seen her partying heavily in the French Quarter on Mardi Gras. Brenda's only son, Samuel, however, was serving a mission now in Guatemala.

I had for years felt guilty about hurting Claire when I broke up with her after a three-year engagement. She was truly a wonderful woman. We'd met when she was serving as a missionary in Brussels. We'd become good friends because so many of the other American missionaries spoke English and ignored the few Belgian missionaries, but I enjoyed speaking French once I knew it.

And I genuinely liked this woman. I never once heard her criticize another missionary, raise her voice, or even use bland expletives which all the rest of us used. We began writing after we finished our missions, and I eventually decided that if I had to marry a woman, there wasn't a better one out there. "Had to" sounded so terribly unromantic and unfair to her, so I kept trying year after year to become heterosexual.

I wanted to finish my degree in English before going back to Belgium to teach, so that gave us a few years to get to know each other better through weekly letters and bi-monthly phone calls, and time for me to keep fasting and praying for a miraculous transformation.

I'd had major culture shock when I arrived in Belgium, taking a year to adjust, and then I'd had culture shock again upon returning to America, requiring another six months to adjust to my own country. I'd gone back to Belgium for a summer to study more French and be with Claire, and I felt torn between the two countries and cultures. When I saw *Greystoke*, I was amazed at how the preposterous story of Tarzan described my life. Because I'd experienced two worlds, I'd never really fit in again in either.

We decided to live in Belgium, though, and raise our children bilingual. But I kept postponing the time for my final return to Belgium, not wanting to marry until I knew I could stay married to a woman. When I finally realized it wasn't going to happen, I felt I'd wasted the best years of Claire's life. And perhaps I did.

But at least I didn't waste twenty years of her life. My uncle had been more concerned about his own welfare than my aunt's and so had married her to save himself. He called my coming out a selfish act, but I think there was plenty selfishness to go around. Still, I thought about Claire every time I went up to Mississippi, every time I didn't go up with a wife.

The speed limit on the interstate was 70, but New Orleans roads kept my wheels out of alignment, so I rarely reached it. Still, after a couple of hours, I pulled off on the Bogue Chitto exit, and after another twenty minutes past farms and forests, I pulled up in front of my grandma's house. I sang one last "v'taheir libeinu" and stepped out of the car into the calf-high Easter grass ready for egg-hiding.

The paint had peeled off the porch, and the dog had scratched off the slats and screen on the bottom of the screen door, so the front door was closed to keep out the bugs. My grandma opened the door before I knocked, and I hugged her when I went in. She allowed the hug but could never initiate it. "How've you been?" I asked.

"Fine. And you?" She had lost weight and looked old for the first time at eighty-four.

"Did the acidophilus help any?" She'd taken antibiotics in January and then had diarrhea for two months.

"I never did get any. Annie Ruth had a headache when we went to town, and I hated to make her wait."

"Well, good grief, Grandma," I said, laughing. "After all the headaches she's given you over the years, you can make her wait one minute. What's she going to do, disown you?" I smiled, but I sensed that the real reason she hadn't pursued the acidophilus was because she didn't trust me enough to suggest something helpful. I wasn't in medical school yet, and her doctor hadn't said anything about "good bacteria."

"Well, you know how Annie Ruth can be." Grandma and Annie Ruth had endured a tense relationship for the twenty-five years since she married into the family and converted, though Annie Ruth had mellowed a bit after adopting one baby, Albert, through the Church and another, Wayne, from her drug-using brother after he was put in prison for stealing. Andy and Annie Ruth hadn't arrived with their two kids yet, but they lived only a mile or so away, on the next farm over.

We went to the kitchen, where Grandma checked the vegetables on the stove and the turkey breast and ham in the oven. Then she left the kitchen while I started washing the dishes in the sink. She came back a minute later with a $20 bill. "For gas," she said, looking around nervously as if to check if any of the rest of the family had shown up and might see.

She'd been giving me "gas money" for years, and I was still so poor that I took it, feeling stupid when I did, feeling it meant that at thirty-six I still hadn't made the transition to adulthood. I tried to repay her by paying attention to her. I'd planted a crepe myrtle for her one year, some day lilies another, and had polyurethaned her wooden floors another time, but I never felt I did enough for her, since she always kept doing more for me.

"How's school?" she asked.

"Okay. Immunology's turned out to be a lot harder than I thought. But I have a great lecturer for Cell Physiology. That always makes it easier."

"Have you heard from the medical school yet?"

"I'm on the waiting list."

"You think you'll get in?"

"Eventually." I smiled. "I didn't do too well in the interview. Too grim. It was only a week after I broke up with David."

"Oh."

My being an English instructor for ten years had never impressed anyone in the family, probably because I only earned between $6000 and $13,000 a year, depending on how many classes I taught, only about $5000 a year since I went back to school myself. My sister Lisa had dropped out of high school and married a welder with a Special Olympics medal.

My sister finally earned her GED, divorced, and eventually became an LPN, but she never worked more than part-time and was eager to quit work when she married her second husband, though he barely made enough to support her and her two youngest children.

My sister's oldest son had dropped out of school after ninth grade as well. He was a mechanic and liked to talk about motors, with a smirk that suggested he was superior to "book learning" college folks. I never made an issue of the lack of interest in education most of my family shared, but I was certainly aware of it every time we tried to find common interests, and especially when they tried to make me feel stupid because I didn't know what kind of oil was best.

I'd always gotten along well with my mother, my grandma's oldest child, but she'd died fifteen years ago, right after I came home from my two years as a missionary. Forty-three had seemed middle-aged to me then, but that was younger than either of my partners had been when we met. My dad, still a high priest in the Church, was the only real success in the family, as a contractor who owned his own house in New Orleans, plus a farm up here in the country. I could tell my grandma hoped I'd finally make it, too, that there'd be one less person she needed to worry about.

The dog out front started barking, so Grandma went to see. It was Brenda and her family. They came in carrying clothes and went to claim the rooms they'd be staying in. Then everyone gathered in the kitchen, the two younger girls, Susan and Emma, ten and fourteen, nibbling on homemade cookies from a Tupperware container, bought when Brenda used to sell the plastic dishes at parties.

"Mark's first counselor in the bishopric now," Brenda announced.

"Oh my God," I said. That meant he was second only to the bishop, who was the leader over the congregation. I guess it meant Mark was no longer calling numbers he found on bathroom walls at the rest area. He'd told me several years ago about meeting someone at a hotel after calling such a number, and being surprised to find the stake patriarch, the man ordained to lay hands on any member from seven or eight congregations in the area and pronounce their lineage through the Twelve Tribes and then state God's plan for that person's life.

Mark hadn't talked to me for a few years now about his sexual struggles, but I could hardly believe he'd put them all behind. "Do you *want* to be first counselor?" I asked. "It's a big job."

"Well, the other guy wasn't doing much with it, and I will."

"Besides," Brenda said, "it means I get released from being Relief Society president." She'd been the leader of the women's group in the congregation for two and a half years.

"Congratulations," I told her.

"Thank you. I've been ready to pass that torch for a year."

Soon Grandma had food on the table, and after Emma said a blessing, "in the name of Jesus Christ," we began eating. The good thing about holidays was that so many people were there that I never had to say the blessing. I couldn't say the hamotzi, and I didn't want to pray in the name of Jesus Christ, so I was glad when someone else prayed instead.

We always passed food around to the right. I took some of the peas, green beans, corn, sweet potato casserole, and turkey, but passed the ham on by, hoping that with all the activity, no one would notice.

"Don't you want any ham?" Grandma asked a second later. She always looked so innocent, but her mind worked at full capacity. It was hard not to be thankful for that.

"I've got plenty," I said. She looked worried, but while I was certainly not keeping kosher at home, I just couldn't bear to eat ham during a holiday. It was hypocritical, of course, since I knew damn well I was going to eat cake for dessert. So when I took seconds, I slipped a piece of ham on my plate. Grandma pretended she didn't notice, but I could see her relax. I felt bad either with or without the ham, but at least she felt better this way.

As we finished, my sister Lisa came with her husband and two youngest children, and Annie Ruth and Andy came with their two children. Wayne immediately started running through the kitchen and living room with a toy gun, pointing it at everyone and screaming with delight. It looked so much like the BB gun he'd received for Christmas that I kept expecting to be shot at any moment.

"I want to hunt some eggs!" Wayne shouted.

"Wait till after dinner," Annie Ruth said. "Sit down and eat your corn. You like corn."

"No!" He pointed and shot at his mother and ran back to the living room.

I vacated the table for the second shift. Grandma came from the back porch pantry with a carrot cake. "Don't you want some dessert?" she asked me.

I shook my head. "I know I'm going to eat too much later. I'm going to pass for now."

"There's chocolate cake, too. And lemon pound cake."

"Not just now, thank you."

"And condensed milk cake with coconut cream."

"I'm gaining weight just listening to you."

"There's strawberries and whipped cream in the refrigerator."

"Were you trained by the CIA?" I said, laughing. "Stop it!"

"Speaking of the CIA," Brenda said, "we just got a letter from Samuel."

"Why is that speaking of the CIA?" asked Annie Ruth.

"Because so many people think Mormon missionaries are CIA agents," said Mark, who'd served a mission in Japan.

"We had a kidnap threat in my mission," I said. "Some group called and said they were going to kidnap two missionaries and torture them until they confessed to being CIA agents."

"Did you hear about the two missionaries kidnapped in Russia last week?" Mark asked.

I nodded. "They were released?"

"Uh-huh," said Brenda. "Anyway, Samuel said he still hasn't gotten the peanut butter we sent him. It cost $32 to mail it. He *better* get it."

I started washing the dishes as the others continued talking and eating. I always felt bad I didn't help with the cooking, but at home I ate cereal for breakfast, sandwiches for lunch, and opened a can of vegetables for dinner. I did know how to wash dishes, however, and even though we used Styrofoam plates and plastic cups here, there were still a lot of utensils and pots and bowls to wash, more dishes than could fit on the drainboard.

Brenda's daughter, Cathy, talked about her boyfriend whose father piloted boats on the Mississippi River. Brenda talked about the boy in the next class over from the one she taught who was suspended for pushing another boy against a locker, Annie Ruth talked about the sale at the Cash N' Carry, and I looked out the window over the kitchen sink and watched Wayne chase the dog with his toy gun.

When I was a kid, I loved staying in the kitchen to hear the women talk. It was always about people and so much more interesting than the men in the living room talking about tractors and sports. My brother-in-law now talked about deer hunting. Lisa's oldest boy, who hadn't come today, was twenty. He and my dad talked about tractor pulls every time they were together. And Mark usually wanted to talk Republican politics. But while I found the men's discussion these days as boring as ever, I also now found the women boring as well. That was surely more a comment on me than it was on them.

I hoped it simply meant I was depressed, that it didn't reflect a total disinterest in my own family. I felt bad I didn't like them more than I did, since they were basically decent people. I'd had friends over the years from all walks of life and never felt particularly superior. Before I'd married, I had a wide circle of friends I saw regularly, a couple of doctors, a lawyer, a bookstore owner, a bartender, a landscaper, a cashier, and even an escort.

There was only one thing I absolutely demanded out of a friend, that he be a nice person. Nice. Not smart, not creative, not beautiful, though all those things were great. But I absolutely needed to be around people who were nice.

My family wasn't *un*nice. They just didn't seem overly nice, either. They were just kind of there.

But then, I wasn't overly nice around my family myself, or even away from my family. I was just kind of there, too.

One of the most shocking things I'd discovered at the synagogue was that there were a great many Jews who were not particularly nice, who didn't even feel that niceness was anything worth aspiring to, and yet they were still dedicated to doing good things. I'd never seen arrogant creeps being good before.

I wasn't sure I liked the attitude that it was okay to be a jerk as long as you supported good causes, but at the same time, there was such a serious, legitimate commitment to those good causes that I couldn't discount it. Jerks volunteered to help build houses for Habitat for Humanity. Creeps gave thousands of dollars to buy food for the poor or support a battered women's shelter.

It was comforting to realize I didn't have to be a great person to still be a good person, but at the same time, it seemed a shame people couldn't be both good *and* nice. There were several members of my congregation, of course, who were in fact regularly nice: Emily, who volunteered with PWA's despite suffering from lupus; Alan, who gave me copies of pictures of me in my talis chanting my Torah portion, who took pictures of every adult b'nei mitzvah service for those participating; and Oscar, who always made a point of greeting me when I first started attending, even though he held tightly onto his wife as he did so, clearly afraid of my gayness.

I always tried to speak a few minutes each week with the nice people I knew, hoping some of it would eventually rub off. As far as my family went, Brenda and I could only talk if no one else was around, but someone else was always around, so while I liked her, I still felt I could only rarely communicate authentically with her. My dad was nice financially. I knew he helped my sister out often and knew he'd be there for me if I asked, but he was never there emotionally, so I still had an ambivalent feeling toward him.

But my grandma, her I liked for real. She was a doormat in a lot of ways, but then so was I. Despite everything, though, despite the total ordinariness of our family, she managed to love all of us equally. I had a respect for her that made me pay attention even when I tuned out the others.

I only visited my grandma four times a year, for Easter, Thanksgiving, Christmas, and once in the summer. It was only during the summer visit I was able to talk to her. She knew I wrote down every story she told me, and she'd write notes between visits so she could remember anything new.

She'd told me about her baby brother dying of diphtheria when she was a little girl, about an oldest sister being her first grade teacher, about another sister who bled to death during a tonsillectomy, about her mother keeping the quilt she was working on strung up on slats she could lower down from the ceiling when she had a few minutes to work on it, about the time her mother shot a neighbor trying to steal her corn, about the time Grandma saw a rabid dog and lifted her cousins onto the hood of a car to get them out of the way, and about the time she tried to get a job in town and my grandfather had a fit.

She'd tried to join the Church twenty-five years earlier when the rest of the family did, but my grandfather brought home a six-pack of beer and said, "The day you join that church is the day I start drinking." So she'd waited until he died of lung cancer from smoking before she looked into it again. She also told me about the time she and her next youngest sister came in the house one day after visiting a neighbor, and when she went in the bedroom and looked in the mirror to start changing back into work clothes, she saw the reflection of a man underneath her bed.

Still wearing her good dress, she grabbed her sister and said, "Roberta Lee, we forgot to milk the cows." She pulled her puzzled sister out of the room and ran to get help. Every bit of that I found fascinating, and I dreaded holidays because

I knew it meant the only thing she'd say was, "Don't you want another piece of lemon meringue pie?" And that this would still be the most interesting conversation of the weekend.

I often thought that if given the opportunity, my grandmother could have really been somebody. Then I felt bad for not already considering her "somebody." She would have done something with opportunities if she'd had them, though, and most of the rest of us had done nothing, except perhaps my dad, who was on the other side of the family. The rest of us had so deliberately chosen our mediocrity that it was suffocating at times to be around the whole family and realize that maybe I did fit in more than I'd like.

Even now, I'd never actually done anything with my life. I was always just about to. In one more year I'd be going to my 20th high school reunion, and if I was lucky, I'd be just about to *start* medical school, while everyone else would be only a few years from retiring. Being around my family felt like a high school reunion, too, and always made me see how little I'd done.

It might have been different if I could at least have talked to my family, felt that we had at least accomplished friendship. But I used to feel trapped with my family, feeling I couldn't talk about anything gay, but even when I finally did, no one was any more interested in that than I was in hearing about that new paint job my nephew had done on his pickup truck.

At the synagogue, no one particularly wanted to hear about my Mormon past, and though Brenda and Mark knew I'd converted to Judaism, they weren't particularly interested in hearing about that. No one wanted to hear about Biochemistry, not even other biochemistry students. Even when I felt I really understood a complicated molecular pathway and its regulation and could even draw every molecule in the pathway, I never felt smart enough to do research. I felt too intimidated to talk to my professors, who I was sure would see me as a peasant.

And no matter how much science I learned, I wasn't at all sure how I'd do in medical school, especially with those awful thirty-six-hour shifts at the hospital. I needed nine hours of sleep now. How could I ever survive and become a doctor? I spent twenty-seven hours a week teaching or tutoring, twelve more working in a bookstore, and God only knew how many more in class, lab, or studying. And yet during none of that did I feel very connected to anything.

No one at school or the synagogue or even in the family wanted to hear about the patchwork quilts I made. Brenda and I had been very close growing up since she was only a few years older than I was, and we could sometimes talk about teaching, but that story was so old now that I didn't even want to talk about my own miserable experiences teaching college students who had a 4th grade reading level, much less hear of her 5th graders with a 1st grade reading level.

But I had enjoyed the seder the other evening. I hadn't completely connected there, but I'd come close a couple of times. And when I could chant during services and sing along with songs that didn't even have a printed transliteration, I felt close.

I'd asked the chair of the foreign languages department at UNO last year if Hebrew could be offered as an independent study, and he said no. I went back a few weeks ago to beg. With all the other things I had to do, I knew I wouldn't learn Hebrew unless my GPA was dependent on it. It turned out that Hebrew had been offered as part of the "Critical Languages" program for two semesters now, so I could take it as an independent study after all.

Only the teacher was moving and they didn't have another one yet and didn't want to look for one until they had at least two students signed up. So I'd made fliers and put them on bulletin boards across campus. And one prissy, arrogant girl in several of my classes the past few semesters came to class one day wearing a shirt advertising the Henry S. Jacobs camp, a Jewish summer camp not far from Brookhaven, so I asked her as she was inserting a thread through a beating frog heart if she'd like to learn some Hebrew. She didn't seem particularly enthused, though my timing was perhaps a bit off in the asking.

Last Friday, I'd mentioned the class to Tom, another gay member of Touro. He'd been studying Hebrew for years with his partner and when I mentioned the class said he thought he might apply to teach the independent study. I hoped it would all somehow work out. My learning Hebrew wouldn't make anyone's life better, which was my criterion for deciding if an act was religious or not, but it would make *me* feel better, and I needed something right now to give me a little comfort.

I doubted I'd ever want to make aliyah to Israel, but I wanted to know the option was there. And I wanted to be able to follow the services completely. I needed a lot more practice even just to read the letters, much less understand what I was reading.

"Why don't you fill up that pan with water?" Annie Ruth asked, standing next to me at the sink. "Are you sure that's a good way to wash dishes?"

I was too surprised to answer, but I couldn't help but raise one eyebrow, and she walked off.

Soon everyone had finished dinner, and the adults and older kids hid eggs for the younger kids. Grandma had boiled three dozen eggs the day before, and Wayne had come over yesterday to color them, breaking only four this year. It didn't take long today before several eggs turned up missing, and the dog ran off with a couple.

I hid eggs in easy places, on tree branches or on car hoods in plain sight at eye level, but no one looked at eye level when hunting, so mine were still the last to be found. My sister's eleven-year-old pouted when she couldn't find enough, and then my aunt's ten-year-old became mad that everyone was helping my sister's girl find eggs.

Claire had written a few months ago saying how sad she was she might not ever have children. I told her I had felt the same for years but now saw childlessness as a blessing. That probably wasn't terribly comforting, but I felt more and more glad all the time I didn't have children, though in a sense this fact separated me from most of humanity, made it impossible for me to connect in a fundamental way that almost everyone else shared. I wondered if this was why I felt so distant from my relatives.

My sister Lisa and her family left before supper, loading an old hutch they found in the feed room of the barn onto the back of their pickup truck. They also took large portions of each cake and half a ham. If I was lucky, there wouldn't be much food left to take when I started for home the next day.

Not only did I always gain a couple of pounds each time I visited, but Grandma also sent enough home with me to put yet another pound on me there. Battling my weight had been a constant struggle since I was eleven and spent two weeks in the country with my aunt and grandparents. We'd had hot dogs and homemade ice cream every day.

When my mom returned to pick me up, she gasped that I'd gained so much in so short a time. I was "husky" throughout junior high and pudgy throughout high school. I had lost weight in Belgium, about the only missionary in my mission to do so. I gained it back when I came home. Then at twenty-four, after I graduated with a degree in English, I went on a major diet.

I fasted for thirty days over three months, praying for God to change me into a heterosexual. But I figured that while fasting, I ought to walk a few miles a day as well, since that was how I'd lost weight in Belgium. It was a commandment to keep our bodies healthy, and since I obeyed just about every other commandment, I figured my failure in this area must be why God hadn't "healed" me yet. So I went from 190 pounds to 140 in four months.

The world changed for me almost overnight. People were nicer to me, wanted to talk to me, wanted to be my friend. I recognized instantly the superficiality, that they liked me because I was attractive, though I was the same person as always. But at the same time, it felt good to be liked for any reason. For perhaps the first time, I felt as if I'd crossed into another dimension. In this parallel universe, I was now a part of the world, part of the mainstream. Then I came out and left the mainstream, but the appreciation for my body only became stronger.

That was such a good feeling that I'd worked hard to maintain my weight in the succeeding twelve years. I went up to 150 a few times and had to work back down to 140 again. I hated seeing even one pound added to my weight but absolutely freaked whenever I reached 150. I didn't dislike overweight people and found many heavy men attractive and likeable.

I also argued in defense of overweight people every time I heard a thin person make some ridiculous comment on a subject they couldn't possibly know anything about. But the idea of *me* being heavy again was terrifying. I was already on the edge of society in so many ways. I couldn't face the idea of being pushed totally aside again.

But it was a constant battle. A constant, every day, continual, never-ending battle. So much energy for such a stupid issue. So many hours that could have been used for something useful devoted instead to superficial self-esteem.

And I still ate two pieces of cake after supper tonight. The coconut cake with condensed milk poured into fork holes, with whipped cream on top, was impossible to resist two meals in a row.

Andy and his family finally left for the evening, but even just Mark and Brenda's three girls were getting to be too much. I'd given up the idea of children when I came out at twenty-five, but I'd thought about it again after a gay couple and a lesbian at the synagogue shared custody of a child. To raise my child as a Jew might make the journey worthwhile. But when I spent even a few hours with children, I was glad I hadn't yet met a Jewish lesbian I liked enough to do it.

Around 7:30, I'd listened to as much bickering as I wanted to hear. "I guess I'm going to head on to Dad's," I said.

"You're not going to stay here?" Grandma asked. There were three bedrooms and six people, but I knew she felt slighted that I preferred my father's cabin to her house. I didn't dislike her place, but there was, after all, only one bathroom, and even it didn't have a shower. Grandma always acted surprised, though I'd been staying at Dad's place for the last couple of years when I visited. That made me feel bad, but not bad enough to stay.

"I'm going to study for an Animal Physiology exam I have this week."

"Aren't you going to be scared all by yourself over there?"

"I like it. Shivering burns calories."

"Doesn't it get dark out there in the woods? You're not afraid to be alone?"

"Dad leaves a gun for me."

"Ooooh." She shook her head slightly, worried.

"We haven't seen the place since it was a barn," Mark said. "Mind if we come along to look?"

"Sure." Emma was in the bathtub and the other two girls were in the kitchen, so they didn't ask to come along.

"You want to bring some cake to eat later?" Grandma asked as I walked onto the porch.

"I already ate that piece. But thanks." I smiled, thinking that maybe the reason I'd always liked her was because she was so much a Jewish mother without realizing it.

I drove first, Brenda and Mark following me in their minivan. In just five minutes, we pulled through the open gate on my father's land, drove down a pine needle-covered gravel driveway and up to a small wooden home. I'd been to Dad's place so rarely that I didn't even remember the structure as a barn. There was an old feeding shelter just off the driveway in the woods that David and I joked about using for a sukkah, though technically sukkot couldn't be permanent structures.

"How long's he had this cabin?" Brenda asked as we walked up to the front door, using the light from my headlights to show the way.

"He finished it with Karen." I remembered his third wife, from New Orleans, whom I'd liked quite a bit. After her father died, though, she'd suddenly become very Catholic, and Dad finally couldn't take it. His second wife had been Mormon but a major bitch, a Relief Society president who gossiped about all the secrets she knew, so Dad had gone after sweetness the next time.

This last time, he went for a country girl, deciding that a common background was the safest bet, and it seemed to have worked out well enough these past few years. Libby was Baptist, as my dad had been raised, so while neither of them went to church often, they didn't seem to have any conflicts there.

I gave Mark and Brenda a tour of the two tiny bedrooms, tiny kitchen, closet laundry room, and living room with a free-standing iron fireplace with a pipe leading through the roof. The wood was unfinished all throughout the house, giving it a rustic look I liked. Though I'd grown up in the city, I sometimes felt more at home up here, even though every time I met anyone here, I was glad I lived in the city.

"He's got central air and heat?" Brenda asked, pointing to a thermostat.

I nodded. "This place is a lot nicer than my apartment," I said. Dad always did quality work. I'd planned to have him build a house for me one day, but it would be several years yet before I could afford that. Dad would be retiring in two more years and then moving up here permanently. I smiled, remembering the rough house plans I'd drawn when I was sixteen, shortly after I'd been ordained a priest by my father, and shortly after I'd read Anne Frank's diary.

The plans included a secret room large enough to hide a family of Jews. If Jews never needed it, I could just hide valuables, or the year's supply of food the Church told us to keep, an idea I still thought useful. Now even if I could hire my dad to build a house for me, the hidden room would be pointless, unless people came to take Mormons away, or some other group.

"Would you hide me if people came to round up Jews again?" I asked, perhaps a little too abruptly.

Brenda and Mark both stared at me a moment. "Of course," Brenda said.

"Would you hide me if people came to round up gays?" I continued.

Brenda started to speak but stopped. Then Mark said, "I doubt it would be safe at our house."

"Would your friends hide Mark?"

"I believe so."

I wondered if those days would ever really come. It seemed impossible, and yet the Holocaust had happened so recently that I personally knew two women who'd survived Auschwitz-Birkenau. Thinking about the future in any context was difficult. I could rarely see more than a year or two down the road. As a Mormon, I would never have imagined myself a Jew. As an English instructor, I would never have imagined myself in Biology.

I'd started back in college four years ago to begin work on my prerequisites for medical school, just after David and I became partners. I'd thought about it for a couple of years before that but was too afraid of the change it would demand. I hadn't had math since 10th grade and never had any physics or chemistry. I'd hated dissecting frogs in high school. I didn't know if I could handle medicine.

Unfortunately, David had no insurance and wasn't happy with the care he was getting at Charity hospital. I didn't think he would still be alive by the time I was finally a physician, but it seemed the only way to ensure we'd have the money to take care of him, or at least be able to understand the medical literature enough to decide what the best treatments were.

And yet, that was only part of the reason I signed up for remedial math and started my life over again. A bigger reason, one I didn't tell anyone, was simply that I was so tired of being poor. I wanted to build a custom home with a hidden room. I wanted to have a career that paid enough that I could escape the country if the fundamentalists took over. I wanted a job that would be in demand so I could make a living wherever I ended up after fleeing.

When the rabbi interviewed me before my conversion, he asked if I was willing to face another Shoah if it came to that. As a Mormon, I'd been led to believe we might face that ourselves. Our history wasn't as awful as Jewish history, of course, but Mormons had their pogroms, too, kicked out of state after state, their crops and homes burned, their temple destroyed, their prophet tarred, feathered, and shot.

It was legal in Missouri to kill a Mormon up until I was in high school. I'd long believed I might have to face real persecution for being Mormon. I personally had never suffered more than being spit on a few times. Of course, there was the man in Brussels who'd come after me with a knife, but he'd been easy to outrun, so I'd never felt truly scared by him. Still, I was always aware it was possible Mormons might face real trouble again one day. I'd often read books about the Holocaust just so I might perhaps be better able to deal with it if it ever did happen.

Then when I came out as gay, I read about Nazis killing gays, too, and I knew most religious people in America hated us. I'd once seen the bumper sticker, "Kill a Queer for Christ."

So when I came out, I told *everyone*. I wrote letters to the paper about gay rights. I wanted to make sure my name was on someone's list, so I wouldn't have the option of "passing." I'd know I had to fight.

But as a Jew who'd watched *Schindler's List*, I knew the rabbi's question was more than just theoretical. Still, what I told him was, "I had a friend who was stabbed to death two years ago by a gay basher. Anyone coming for you would be coming for me, too. But yes, I'm prepared to face another Holocaust."

"You won't have to," he replied. "Not in America."

Even if he was right, I needed to become a physician so I'd have enough money to help rescue other Jews elsewhere if it ever came to that. I was still terrified of the responsibility of other people's health, but I'd met so many mediocre doctors over the years that I honestly thought I could do as well as most and hoped I could do better.

I'd also seen so many injustices in the system that I hoped to have some power to help reform health care. I'd read several books about interns and residents and dreaded those impossibly miserable years that had to come before I'd become a physician. The one good thing about being an older student, though, was the realization that four years would fly by, even miserable years. The downside to that realization was the feeling that life was passing me by before I'd managed to do anything.

Even though I now recognized how many Jewish names were listed as donors to various charities, the charities rarely included environmental concerns, issues which I very much wanted to support. I dreamed of being able to buy a huge chunk of land and planting it with trees. I wanted to give more than $10 a year to Israel to plant a single tree. There was so much I wanted to do but would never be able to do as an English instructor.

"One good thing about Mormon families," said Mark, "is that among all the returned missionaries, we know enough languages to be able to run somewhere if we have to."

"But America is Zion," Brenda said. "We won't have to leave here."

"Spoken like someone who fits in," I said. "The rest of us need to at least consider the possibility. Apparently even first counselors think about it sometimes."

Brenda looked at Mark. "Is that why you keep telling me to learn a language?"

He laughed. "No. I just think it's fun to feel more connected to the world as a whole."

"I don't want to connect to the world. I have a hard enough time connecting to myself."

"I have trouble just switching to dialect when I come to Mississippi," I said, laughing. "Which reminds me. I better 'cut off' my headlights before my battery runs 'plum' empty."

Brenda and Mark followed me outside. "I'm not sure you got the dialect right," Brenda said.

"I told you it was hard."

They left for Grandma's house, and I went inside and luxuriated in the total silence of the place. There was no phone and no T.V. I really had brought my notebook to study for class, but I knew that once I was here I wouldn't study. I sat on the sofa and looked around the room just enjoying the atmosphere. A 150-year-old Bible lay on the coffee table, next to a ceramic pitcher in a basin. A calendar of John Deere tractors hung on the wall.

I'd made a quilt of a tractor plowing a field and given it to my dad for Christmas the year before. It was the first present I'd ever given him that I could tell he liked. He kept it at his wife's house. My Mom's old quilts were here.

I looked around a few more minutes and then went out to the car to unpack. It was a bit eerie, hearing footsteps passing in the dark and assuming they were the calves Dad had bought a few weeks earlier.

Back in the cabin, I took out *In the Beginning* by Chaim Potok and read for a couple of hours before going to bed. It was pitch black even after I let my eyes adjust, so I had to leave a light on in the other bedroom as a night light. I loved being out here in the country, but every time I was here, I thought of how far away the police were, even if I had a phone to call 911.

There had to be rumors about my dad's queer boy, and even though my father was well-liked, I couldn't help but worry. If a couple of drunk good ole boys ever decided to come fuck the fag, I hoped I could keep my wits about me. The gun was in the corner by the door leading to the bathroom. I tried to forget about that and instead think about yesterday's seder for a while as I lay in bed. I eventually fell asleep.

The next morning, I went back to Grandma's for breakfast—sausage and homemade biscuits. She offered some pear preserves David and I had given her.

Brenda and her family went to church in town, as did Andy and his family. Grandma hardly ever went, attending only long enough after her baptism ten years ago to qualify for going through the temple to be "sealed" to the family. She was still basically Methodist, however, always asking why Mormons didn't believe in the Rapture.

When I finally told her I'd been excommunicated, she said, "Oh, dear. I don't even know if the Mormons are right, but I figured if I joined like the rest of you, we'd all at least end up in the same place."

I helped Grandma make some potato salad, took a picture of her at work in the kitchen, and then washed dishes before everyone arrived for dinner. I had only turkey today, but I again ate pieces of two different cakes for dessert. Then around 2:00, I gave Grandma a hug and told everyone goodbye. "You're leaving so early?" Grandma asked.

"Yeah, I've got to finish filling out an application for Charity hospital. I keep putting it off. I'm going to volunteer one afternoon a week in the emergency room."

"Oh, my. What will you be doing?"

"Probably not much. But it's a pretty unhappy place. David was there for almost two days straight once. I figure I need to show the medical schools I know what I'm getting into."

"Oh, dear."

I hardly ever did volunteer work, and even then it was usually one-shot deals, like cleaning up after the AIDS walk, or planting trees on neutral grounds. But I had a couple of free afternoons each week despite my bizarre work schedule, and I wasn't studying like I should. I figured I might as well volunteer. So far this semester, the only volunteer work I could claim was helping the curve in Immunology class. My overall GPA after four years was 3.8, but I had a B- average in Immunology and might get a C if I wasn't careful.

"You can't fill out the application tonight?" Grandma rarely begged, and I again felt bad for disappointing her, but I felt I couldn't really connect with her while everyone else was there anyway.

When we were alone, she might ask if I was still HIV negative, or ask which of us in the relationship was "the man," looking confused when I explained we both were. She might ask what I thought of Wayne, or of Annie Ruth. When everyone was together, she was a completely different person, existing only to serve. If we were alone, she'd easily let me help her in the kitchen, and we'd talk as we worked. When everyone was there, she'd say, "Don't you want to let me do those dishes?"

When we were alone, we could talk about God, and about life, and about death. "I don't want to go like my mother," she'd told me. Her mother had a stroke and was bedridden for a year before she finally died. My own mother had gone quickly in comparison, suffering a mere six weeks of absolute misery with leukemia before she too had a stroke and died.

"I hope you die in your sleep, Grandma."

"I do, too."

We might say little more than that, but we had this conversation about death almost every time I came up by myself. She said I was the only one in the family who would talk to her about it. It seemed ridiculous to pretend she wasn't going to die, and if talking about her hopes for an easy death comforted her in the meantime, it seemed cruel not to allow her the release.

She wanted to know what I expected in the afterlife, if I thought I could still be with them when I died, considering I was gay. "I honestly have no idea what to expect," I told her once. "All I know is that it had better be worth all this trouble, or I'm going to be mad."

I'd said it jokingly, but she replied in all seriousness, "I hope so, too."

As a Mormon, I'd believed the traditional story, that we were here on Earth to be tested, and if we passed, we'd have the opportunity for eternal progression and eventual godhood, after which we'd create worlds and allow others the same opportunity. For the past ten years, I no longer had any clue what to expect.

I had read Harold Kushner's *When Bad Things Happen to Good People* long before I met David and converted, and it had seemed like the first halfway acceptable approach to

God, eliminating most of the stupid things people said about Him. But there had to be some *point* to believing in God, and I didn't know what that point was. Just believing was meaningless.

My rabbi had told me lots of Jews didn't believe in an afterlife at all. If this life were all we got out of being created, though, I didn't see how creation was doing any of us much of a favor. There *had* to be something more. The rabbi's explanation was to ask what a goldfish would say it wanted of heaven—clean water, plenty of fish food, and no mean fish to eat him. The fish, he said, was incapable of comprehending it could ask for more. It couldn't comprehend Beethoven or Mozart or anything beyond its own highest experience.

Likewise, we humans could have no concept of how truly wonderful the afterlife would be. And a merciful and loving God would see to it that all except perhaps the most rotten of us would receive it.

But that answer was every bit as unsatisfying. If we received such an incredible afterlife almost universally, what was so bad about murder? All we really did then was help people leave a mediocre and often horrible life for a beautiful one. If the afterlife was really so incredible, why not help everyone cross over to a spectacular existence?

It didn't make sense that we ever needed to be here in this life, now, unless this life itself mattered in some way. Why make us come here at all if the plan was to give us eternal bliss? Did we need eighty years of misery to appreciate it? Then why did some people only live for a few months or even just hours?

It just didn't make sense. Life had to have some meaning. There had to be a point. And it absolutely had to be important that we *do* something while we were here, though that still wouldn't explain infant mortality. This life might only be a fleeting part of our overall existence, a mere apostrophe in a long word. But the apostrophe was there for a reason. Ignoring it changed the word entirely. There had to be more to life than just passing through.

But *what* were we supposed to do? "Make the world a better place." It sounded so trite, and that answer raised a dozen more questions, but it was the best thing I could come up with so far. Somehow, before I died and passed on to whatever lay ahead, I had to do something to make life better for others.

I looked at my grandma. I wanted to make the world a better place, so I was leaving early and disappointing her. Good grief.

"I need to take a long walk to work off this cake," I said. It was a lame excuse, and she knew it, but I'd write her a long letter this week, and maybe I'd paint her living room when I came up this summer.

"You want me to pack you some before you go? There's a whole German chocolate cake out back no one's even touched yet."

"No. I can't afford the calories. It's too hard to resist if I have it with me." I hugged her again and went out to my car.

Grandma stood on the porch to watch me leave. I backed up by the old dairy barn, waiting for Wayne to run past, chasing a one-eyed cat with his gun, and then started down the driveway, waving to Grandma as I went around the bend. As awkward and unpleasant as I often found these family holidays, I always felt a certain pain as I left that I felt at no other time.

I hoped Grandma would stay healthy for however much longer she'd be here. I hoped I could find a way someday so that despite disappointing her regularly, I could still make her feel special.

I pulled onto the road, drove past the neighbor's twin silos, and let out a long sigh. Then I turned my tape louder and tried to sing the words whose meaning I didn't even know.

Two hours later, I was in New Orleans, and after unpacking the car, I took a walk through the Marigny and the Quarter, hoping to walk a good ninety minutes or so to burn off at least one piece of cake. Walking past Good Friends, I saw lots of men wearing outrageous hats for the Easter bonnet contest.

I waved at a couple of guys I knew and walked on, starting to feel comfortable again in my old neighborhood. After I'd walked long enough to work off the guilt of that fourth piece of cake, even if not all of its calories, I headed back for the Marigny. I always walked against traffic, as it gave me an opportunity to cruise drivers heading toward me.

David and I hadn't had sex the last couple of years we were together since he always hurt so much, and I hadn't wanted to even consider dating again after a second failed relationship. But I did want to have sex again sometimes now that I could. Though street contacts were rarely satisfying, I did occasionally pick someone up.

I wasn't particularly in the mood this afternoon, but as I crossed Elysian Fields, a cute Hispanic man drove past and smiled. I smiled back, and a block later, he drove by again and again smiled. He kept circling me until I reached my apartment a few blocks later, and when he paused as I reached my door, I nodded, and he found a parking place.

When he came up to the door, however, I realized that he wasn't Hispanic after all. He looked Middle Eastern. He smiled, and he didn't seem to notice the mezuzah on the doorpost, the one David had bought for me the day I went into the mikvah, so I let him in. He instantly began fondling me, and I fondled back, but we were in my living room, with my menorah only a few feet away. Surely, he saw it.

He grabbed my behind. "I'd really like to fuck you," he said, squeezing my cheeks.

I sighed. This was not going to work. "I'm sorry," I said. "I shouldn't have led you on. I'm really not much in the mood today."

He instantly grew cold. "Okay."

I led him back to the door, and he left without looking back. He might have been a perfectly decent man, I realized, but what if he had in fact noticed I was a Jew? I didn't buy into the sexism that even lots of gays demonstrated, that being a "bottom" was somehow inferior to being a "top." I liked both and had been mostly a bottom with my first lover and mostly a top with David. I could adapt when I needed to. But I didn't want to take the chance that this guy was a

Muslim, and that he felt superior while fucking a Jew. Some Israelis didn't like that. I couldn't have enjoyed the experience wondering the whole time what he was really thinking.

Of course, maybe I'd just missed a good chance to connect with a Muslim, or simply a good chance to connect with another human being. I shook my head. Life had last been simple when I was ten years old. I'd had a quarter of a century since then to get over that fact, and yet every day it still seemed an amazing discovery.

I'd probably never fit in with the gay community since I never went to bars, hating the smoke and the loud music. I'd never fully fit in with Jews even if I ended up knowing more Jewish history or Hebrew than many of them. And I was sure I'd never be a typical medical student or doctor. Of course, I never really had fit in anywhere during my life. I had always simply hoped I would.

But I was just going to have to accept that other people would always see me as peculiar. Maybe that wasn't so bad. Regardless, it was simply going to be so. At least as a Jew, it was okay to think for myself. I didn't really have to fit in to still fit in.

I filled out my application to Charity and stamped the envelope, setting it on top of my bookbag so I'd remember to mail it on my way to school tomorrow. Then I watered my potted trees in front of the living room window: two pecan trees, two pear trees, a walnut tree, an oak, and a cypress, all grown from seeds I'd gathered.

Someday, I'd have land to plant them on. I wished I at least had a porch or balcony so they could get full sunlight. I took one of them with me now and placed it on the sidewalk to catch the late afternoon sun and then sat on my front steps with my Animal Physiology notebook.

Renal function. Okay. I turned on the switch to that part of my brain, took a deep breath, and started studying what I needed to know.

Sue a Jew

"What's your name?" the woman demanded, taking out a pen and grabbing a piece of note paper.

"Ryan Silver."

"If you don't find my checks by Friday, I'm going to sue you."

"You do realize I have no control over the postal service?"

"You ordered the checks. You're responsible for them. And if I don't have them by Friday, I'm switching banks."

"All right, Mrs. Nix. I'll keep looking for them."

"Don't look for them. Find them."

The woman stalked off, and Ryan forced a smile as the next customer came to his window. He'd just been promoted to Teller 2 a few weeks earlier after only six months at the bank and was hoping to make a career in finance. After graduating from the University of Southern Mississippi in Hattiesburg with a degree in art history, he'd quickly realized he needed to do something less esoteric with his life. He'd moved back to Brookhaven, applied at the bank, and gotten the job within two weeks of leaving school.

He wondered, though, if it had been wise to rack up $42,000 in student loan debt for a degree he'd never use. Was it possible to enrich your life and make yourself miserable at the same time? He'd felt so up when he reached for his diploma, only to feel quite down the very next day.

He'd finished his six-month amnesty from Sallie Mae, and from his last paycheck he'd had to write a $276 check. He'd just received a raise for his promotion, and immediately he was losing money. Up one day and down the next. He wanted the direction to always be up, up, and up. Did life really mean very much if the direction was down just as often?

"Hey, Ryan, how you doing today?"

"Great, Mrs. Stevens. That's a lovely blouse you have on."

"Thank you. You're such a dear. I just got one of those service surveys from the bank in the mail, and I'm going to give you a good rating."

"That's very sweet of you, Mrs. Stevens. What can I do for you today? You have Kimberly's surprise party all planned?"

She set two jars of coins down on the counter. "Could you run these tomorrow and deposit the money right into Kimberly's account? I don't want it to go in today because her birthday's not till tomorrow. I simply won't have time to get to the bank tomorrow, so I had to bring it in today."

"That'll be no problem. I'll put a note on this and put the jars in the vault to be run first thing in the morning."

"That would be heaven."

The rest of the day went much the same way, some good customers and some bad customers, some easy transactions and some hard ones, some customers complaining that loan rates were going up, and some complaining that money market rates were going down. Though Ryan enjoyed his job for the most part, he was still happy when he balanced, ran his checks, and left for the day.

"Stay out of trouble," said Jim, the manager, as Ryan headed for the door.

"Oh, I don't know. There's an old lady in my building I was planning to beat up."

"Procrastination is sometimes a virtue."

"Yep."

"And Jews need whatever virtues they can muster."

Ryan smiled, though the joke irritated him. When he'd first started working at the bank, Jim had gone down a list of things Ryan would need to be on the lookout for. One was a type of fraud called "kiting" checks, but Ryan had misunderstood.

"I don't appreciate you slurring my people," he'd said a little testily. Jim had looked at him in confusion, and Ryan went on. "'Kiking' is an offensive term."

Jim stared a second longer and then laughed. Ever since, he'd gone out of his way to make "playful" slurs against Jews. Ryan liked Jim well enough, but he kept a list of all the jabs, just in case he ever needed ammunition in a discrimination lawsuit. Since he'd just been promoted, he hoped that would never be necessary, but when he got to his car, he still wrote down the latest remark.

Driving home, Ryan was still thinking about what Mrs. Nix had said, and what Jim had said, and he didn't see the cat run out in front of his car. He felt the thump, though, and in his rear view mirror, he could see the cat lying dead in the street.

"Damn." He shook his head. Other cars were right behind him now, so he couldn't stop. "Sorry, Grandma."

Ryan himself didn't believe in reincarnation, and if he were ever to consider the idea, he felt people would come back as people, but his grandmother who'd died a year ago had always said she hoped to come back as a cat. Would she now come back as mouse after a brief stint as a predator? Just what did the afterlife really offer anyway, if life itself didn't offer very much? Was there even a God running the world to begin with?

And if there was, did things like career choice and losing checks and anything else matter much, if Earth life were just one-billionth of your existence? In that case, simply being "good" was the only job truly worth pursuing. But that was only if there was something beyond all this mess now. Everything in his experience seemed to tell him there was no God up there to believe in, yet Ryan still held out just the slightest hope, which was dimming a tiny bit more every day.

If there was a God, though, Ryan didn't want to see a burning bush, or a finger coming out of a cloud, or parting waters. He could be convinced much more easily. All he needed was a 1916-D Mercury dime as proof.

Ryan collected coins, but only the "Mercury" or Winged Liberty dimes and the Walking Liberty half dollars. He preferred silver to gold, and these were hands-down the prettiest two silver coins ever minted in the United States. Ryan wanted the 1916-D not only because it was rare but also because he'd had one years before, when he was a child, found in a little coin purse in his great-grandmother's attic.

He'd traded it with a boy in the neighborhood who also collected. The other boy was a few years older and knew exactly what he was getting. Ryan had felt thrilled to get ten whole Mercury dimes in place of the one. Then when he found out he'd been swindled, he felt a tremendous weight of injustice which remained with him to this day.

Life obviously always had its ups and downs, but for Ryan, it seemed to have more downs. His books were stolen out of the university library cubicle where he'd been studying. His laptop was stolen from his dorm room. A middle-aged professor had come on to him and then "lost" his final paper and given him a lower grade for turning it in "late," all because he'd refused to sleep with her. His father had been killed by a drunk driver. His mother had died of breast cancer.

Ryan wasn't sure he even wanted to do something as simple as marry and have children, until God could prove to him in some way that life was somehow more than just bearable. It wasn't enough that *maybe* there was a heaven where there *might* be some reward. Life itself needed to be worth living if he was going to bring any more life to it himself.

Ryan pulled up to his apartment complex and climbed up the stairs to his place. The first thing he saw when he walked inside was his Botticelli print. Primavera always struck him as one of the loveliest paintings of all time. Ryan had learned Italian so he could study art more easily, and he'd managed to get to Florence just once and see the painting in person.

He now celebrated the spring equinox, May Day, Passover, and Easter, anything related to springtime. A time of renewal and life after a dreary winter seemed a promise of something celestial and eternal, despite its transience. Looking at the painting every evening helped Ryan keep hoping just a little longer.

"Hey, Charles," Ryan said over the phone a moment after he'd kicked off his shoes and ripped off his tie. "Up for some fun this evening?"

"I don't know. I'm feeling kind of down."

"What's up?"

"My girlfriend's pushing me to get married. How do you say 'married' in Italian?"

"Sposato."

"It's funny how someone can say they love you one day and then the next day they want to break up."

"What happened?"

"Betty got down on one knee and proposed, and I said I'd have to think about it. She wasn't impressed."

"Why don't you just move in together?"

"She thinks that's a sin."

"But you're already having sex, aren't you?"

"Yes, but moving in means it's all premeditated."

"And bringing the condoms doesn't?"

"It's complicated, Ryan. You wouldn't understand these things."

Ryan immediately felt his temper flare. "Jews don't understand sin? We have 613 commandments."

"Yes, but…"

"But?"

"Well, you know."

"We're damned no matter what we do so it's all moot?"

"Well…"

Sometimes, Ryan wanted to knock Charles down a peg. Still, it was impossible not to live among all these Christians and not wonder at least once in a while if you were on the wrong side of the fence. The Brookhaven synagogue was housed in an old Baptist church near the public library, and they only met for high holidays and a couple of other times a year, when the congregation could save up for a visiting student rabbi. There wasn't much of a righteous momentum behind it all.

Ryan sighed. "So come on over and I'll cheer you up."

"Thanks, Ryan. You never let me down."

"I'm a rock. Oh, wait, that was Peter and the Catholics."

"They're going to hell, too."

"At least I can drag some Christians down with me."

"I'm still trying to think of a way to pull you up. How do you say 'heaven'?"

"Paradiso."

"You like classical music. Heaven's full of it."

"Whatever. Bring some condoms. Maybe I can find a nice girl this evening to not sin with."

"Me, too, now that I have my freedom back."

It was only Thursday night, but Ryan took Charles to a country/western bar. There was a line dancing lesson from 8:00 to 9:00, and Ryan flirted with one girl while Charles flirted with another.

After Charles left with his girl for some unpremeditated sex, Ryan decided he ought to try it as well. "You up to coming back to my place for a while?"

The girl looked down shyly but held out her hand for Ryan to take and lead her to their cars. They weren't in his bedroom two minutes before she was naked and kneeling on the bed. Ryan was up in an instant, and soon the girl was going down on him. Then she was flat on her back and Ryan was inside her. She smiled and giggled playfully while they had sex, and it ended up a rather pleasant experience.

"That was heavenly," the girl said, sighing.

They lay on their backs for a few minutes afterward, holding hands, with Ryan contemplating asking the girl for her number. And her name, which he'd forgotten already.

Then the girl got up on her knees and tugged at Ryan's hand. Was she up for a second round?

"Come on, let's pray."

"Huh?"

"I always pray for forgiveness after I have sex. That way I don't have to go home feeling guilty."

"I already don't feel guilty."

"Are you saved?"

"No."

"Then pray with me. It would be so great if our having sex could bring you to Jesus."

"I'm a Jew."

"You could be a 'Jew for Jesus.'"

"Those are called 'Christians.' I'm happy as a Jew."

"Are you really happy?"

Ryan was silent a moment. "You need to leave now, uh—"

"Rebecca. Accepting Christ will make you free."

"You need to leave, Rebecca."

"It's my duty to tell you you're going to hell."

"I'm already there."

Ryan listened to the door close behind Rebecca, and he lay in bed awake for a long while. He heard a cat howling down in the parking lot behind his building. Was that his Grandma? Or someone else's grandma? Should he put out some food?

Coming back as a homeless cat didn't strike Ryan as what he wanted of an afterlife. Or coming back as a slum kid in Mumbai. Nothing short of an actual paradise would do. That must be why Ryan preferred Dante's *Paradiso* to his *Inferno*, which was far more popular a work among most readers. Ryan read it in the original and marveled at the beauty of the language. He also preferred Milton's *Paradise Regained* to his more successful *Paradise Lost*.

Neither work described the Paradise Ryan wanted, though he wasn't sure just what he did want. He remembered the student rabbi on one Yom Kippur talking about what was in store after death. He posed it this way: "If you asked a goldfish what it wanted in the afterlife, it would ask for a bigger bowl, clean water, enough food to eat, and no mean fish to eat him. It wouldn't be able to ask to hear Mozart or see Michelangelo's sculptures or read Flaubert. Those things are too far beyond his earthly experience to imagine.

"It's the same with us. What lies ahead is so far above what we've experienced that we aren't in a position to imagine it."

It was mildly comforting, Ryan supposed, but it still circled the simple fact there was no certainty *anything* waited for them at all on the other side, even fish food.

While Karl Marx wasn't a Jew many people wanted to quote, Ryan had to wonder if the man had been right when he said that religion was the opiate of the masses. It would be nice to believe in heaven, to feel comforted, but would that really change his life in any tangible way?

Would believing make him more or less likely to try to right the multitude of wrongs he saw in the world? Ryan gave $25 out of each paycheck to a different charity, but it seemed such a petty way of making the world a better place, and every time he saw how little he was doing to bring others up, he felt more and more down.

He continued musing wearily about life and death and everything else for a while longer and then eventually drifted off to sleep.

The next morning, Ryan was at the bank fifteen minutes early, pulling his cash drawer out of the vault and setting up his work station. He studied a little from his New Accounts manual to get a head start on his next promotion. He'd be able to move up another notch after he passed the New Accounts test.

At 8:45, once he was officially on duty, Ryan ran Mrs. Stevens's coins. There was a machine with five cloth bags attached underneath. The employee could pour coin into a tray on top, feed it slowly in, and the machine would sort everything by size, tallying it up as it went along. Ryan always carried a pocketful of change and once a week or so when he had to run coin, he spread it out slowly in the pan, searching quickly for old coins. If he saw something, he'd pick it up and replace it with a new coin from his pocket. He really wasn't supposed to do it, even though he wasn't shorting the customer as much as a penny, but as a coin collector, he couldn't help it. He'd found three wheat pennies, a buffalo nickel, and two silver Roosevelt dimes in the six months he'd been at the bank. No Mercury dimes, but it was fun to look.

There was nothing in the two jars today of any interest.

Most of the day went along smoothly. Ryan cashed some checks, made some deposits, printed out some money orders, transferred some funds from one account to another, most of the normal everyday transactions. Then, just before lunch, Rosalyn came in. Ryan tried to delay letting his customer go, so that Rosalyn would end up at someone else's window, but the other tellers were doing the same thing, and she ended up in front of him.

"Hi, Rosalyn," Ryan said cheerily, hoping she'd have something easy instead of her usual pain-in-the-butt transaction.

"I had four copays at the doctor's office, and they say I haven't paid, but I'm sure I have. I saw three copays on my checking statement, but I didn't see any on my Visa statement."

"Maybe you did miss paying one."

"Well, I need to know for sure. I don't want to waste fifteen dollars. We aren't all rich Jews."

"If it isn't on your checking statement or your Visa statement, is there any other way you would have paid?"

"Maybe I missed it on my Visa statement. Could you look it up?"

Ryan went through the first five screens of the difficult Visa program before getting stuck and having to call the Card Services department. They told him the statement he was looking for was too old to be on that program, but they promised to email him instructions for this other program which he'd never used.

They did, and it was amazingly simple, easier than the usual program. But on the last step, Ryan was only able to open one month at a time, and when he did, *every* statement for that month appeared, and there was no way to request a specific account number. He had to scroll through hundreds and hundreds of numbers to look for the one he wanted.

The transaction had already taken thirty minutes, and there was no end in sight. Rosalyn stood in front of him, sighing heavily and shifting from foot to foot, looking at her watch every few seconds. "Waiting for the Rapture?" she asked. "Oh. No, you wouldn't be, I suppose."

"Rosalyn. This is going to take a while. Why don't I call you when I find it?"

"You are so incompetent. Do they even train you guys? If you don't find my copay and I have to pay again, I'm going to sue you. I'll take you to small claims court. Don't think I won't."

She stomped away, and Ryan closed his window. He clicked open his email so he could ask Card Services how to narrow the search, and he found a second email from them telling him just that. The instructions had come in two parts. Goddammit.

Ryan hadn't brought his lunch and so walked a couple of blocks to the supermarket. He needed some fresh fruit to calm him down. Apples were on sale, so he grabbed two Granny Smiths and headed for the check out.

"That'll be $2.19."

"Uh, these are on sale."

"It's $2.19. You don't have $2.19?"

"They're on sale."

The cashier sighed and walked slowly, slowly over to the produce section and then slowly, slowly back. She rerung the sale without looking at Ryan. "That'll be $1.09."

Normally, Ryan would have paid such a small amount with cash, but he was irritated, so he handed the girl his credit card.

"Silver, huh? No wonder you had to Jew me down."

Ryan pulled his card back. "Forget it. I'm not hungry. Keep the damn apples. They look wormy anyway."

As he started walking off, the girl called after him, "There's no money in heaven, you know."

Ryan turned around but kept walking backward. "There's Mercury dimes," he said. "And Walking Liberty half dollars. Everything beautiful is in heaven. Sorry you won't be there." Then he turned and was out the door.

He sat on the curb in the parking lot to get some sun.

It's Friday, he reminded himself. When he got home from work, he'd light some candles, have a glass of wine, and read some Potok. That always lifted him up.

He breathed deeply and tried to meditate and was feeling better by the time he clocked back in after lunch.

But it didn't last long. Mrs. Stevens came marching up to his window only a moment after he'd opened up. "Oh, hey there," he said. "How's Kimberly's birthday going?"

"Not good," she said curtly. "I told you I didn't have time to come in today. But when I looked online at my statement, I saw you only deposited $80.84 in my account from all those coins I brought yesterday. I *know* there was at least a hundred dollars in there. I want to know what happened to my money."

"I ran everything in the two jars. I took care of it myself."

"If you don't find the rest of that money by the end of the day and deposit it before the bank closes, I'll press charges. I'll sue."

She turned and stormed off. Ryan shook his head. The woman was usually so nice, and now without any provocation, she'd turned into a bitch. Could anything God had in store after death make putting up with all this crap every day worth it? He'd watched *Schindler's List* last Sunday, and when he came to work the next day and casually mentioned the movie to Jim, his boss had put on an exaggerated frown and said, "Did you cry?" Maybe Ryan wasn't living in Nazi Germany, but lots of everyday Americans were pretty shitty, too.

How could there be a God when even in the "best" country people were awful? In the rest of the world, Israelis oppressed Palestinians, Shiites oppressed Sunnis, Tutsis oppressed Hutus, and it all worked exactly the other way, too.

Ryan picked up the phone at his station and called up Charles. He had to see him tonight, spend time with someone who was at least at times reasonably decent to him. He wasn't supposed to make personal calls at work, but he held up a check and looked at it, pretending he was talking to someone about it.

"Hey, buddy, how are you?"

"Want to meet after work for dinner?" Ryan asked. "My treat."

"I can't. My girlfriend wants to talk."

"You gonna get married?"

"Maybe I'll agree to a two-year engagement or something. That way I have time to weigh the pros and cons."

"Well, I'm glad things are looking up."

"Up and down. Hey, how do you say that in Italian?"

"Su e giú."

"Well, Betty and I are going to do a lot of su e giú tonight."

"You guys have fun."

Ryan hung up, feeling down. Maybe he'd watch *Wheel of Fortune* tonight over dinner and then put in a DVD. He'd been meaning to watch *Far from Heaven* for a while now.

Things quieted down for a bit in the bank, and Ryan overheard two of his fellow tellers talking. One was going up to Jackson the next day to see family, while the other was going down to McComb to see friends.

Ryan felt very alone.

Maybe he should move to a larger city once he had more bank experience under his belt. Up to New York where there were plenty of Jews. Or down to Miami, where there were almost as many.

Perhaps he could start doing volunteer work on Saturdays. There *had* to be some value in making the world a better place, even if this was all there was to existence.

"Are you Ryan?" asked a man about forty, standing challengingly in front of his window. Ryan's name was on the nameplate, he wanted to say, so it should be clear who he was.

What now, he thought.

"Did you take my Rebecca home last night?"

"Excuse me?" Had he even mentioned to Rebecca where he worked?

"I don't want you having sex with my daughter!" The man spoke loudly, and a few people nearby turned to look.

"There's no danger of that, sir," Ryan said calmly.

"If my daughter gets pregnant with any Yids, I'll sue your ass. Stay away from her."

The man walked off, leaving Ryan standing there with his mouth open.

A moment later, Ryan felt a touch on his sleeve. He turned to see Jim at his side. "Ryan, I can't have you causing trouble and embarrassing the bank. I'm going to have to give you a written warning. And I'll have to think about whether to demote you back down to Teller 1."

Ryan nodded. After Jim left, he looked at his watch. 4:15. Just forty-five minutes left of this awful day.

He processed a couple of easy transactions and then his heart sank when he saw Mrs. Stevens coming back in. She came straight to his window and plopped a jar on the counter.

"Ryan, I found this at home. I must have forgotten to bring it. Sorry I went off on you earlier. Here, I brought you a slice of Kimberly's birthday cake."

"Oh, that wasn't necessary. I'll run this coin before we close today."

"Thanks so much, Ryan. You have a good weekend."

After she left, Ryan carried the jar to the vault. He knew he should have felt better after the apology, but somehow all he could think was that she could still be mean again the next time he saw her. You could never really depend on anybody, no matter how nice they might seem at any given point.

Even if there were a God, one day He could give you manna in the wilderness, and the next he could allow the Holocaust to occur.

Ryan wanted to believe in absolute goodness. He wanted to believe in something as good and liberating as Botticelli's creation. If a mere human could create something that good, surely a God could produce something better than what Ryan saw around him every day.

But Ryan wanted to do more than just believe. He wanted to be a part of that absolute goodness.

He decided he'd sign up the next day to deliver food to shut-ins on Saturdays. If no one else was going to be good, he'd just have to do it himself.

Ryan stopped. If there were a food delivery program for shut-ins already established, then he wouldn't have to be good all by himself. There really was goodness already out there. It was just a matter of tapping into it, helping it flourish and sprout new growth.

He poured the jar of coins into the tray, absentmindedly spread them out, and started feeding them into the funnel. There was a Canadian penny he had to take out and put in a bin that went to charity. Any time an employee found unaccounted-for loose coins, or foreign coins, they went in that bin.

Ryan looked at his watch. 4:24. Hang in there. Hang in there.

Out of the corner of his eye, Ryan saw something white in the tray. It was that special color of dirty white that signaled silver. Even though he didn't actively collect the pre-1965 Roosevelt dimes and Washington quarters, it still gave him a little thrill simply to find silver.

Ryan reached into the tray before the silver went down the funnel and picked up the coin. It was a Mercury dime. Excellent.

He squinted to see the date.

1916.

Ryan's heart skipped a beat.

He turned over the coin, hoping, hoping.

There was the D. It was the right size D, too. It was probably real.

Oh my god.

He looked at the beautiful coin a moment longer and then slipped it into his pocket, quickly throwing a dime from his other pocket into the tray.

After the coin finished running, he bundled all the bags up and wrote out a cash ticket to sell them to the vault, and then walked back to his station to deposit the money into Kimberly's account.

Ryan was punching keys in a daze.

So did this really mean there was a God? Or was it just coincidence? Luck? Chance? Was he being bad for doubting, when he'd told himself before this would be proof?

"Hey, Ryan," said Cheryl, a regular who'd just come up to his window. "I need $20 for the weekend. You gonna have a good one?" She always flirted, and Ryan was never sure if he should pursue it.

"Yes," Ryan told her. "Yes, I am. Want to help me deliver food to old people?"

Cheryl laughed. "I don't think so. Sounds awful."

"I'm going to enjoy it."

He handed Cheryl twenty dollars and thought about putting his Mercury dime into a cardboard holder with its cellophane window, stapling it shut, and slipping the coin into that one empty space in his plastic coin page.

Finally, finally, after all these years.

He thought for a long moment and then picked up the phone.

"Hello?"

"Mrs. Stevens. It's Ryan from the bank."

"Yes?"

"You need to come back and pick something up. I found a rare coin in your jar. It's worth about $300. You might want to bring it to a dealer."

He understood now why that kid had swindled him all those years ago. Didn't make it right, of course, but he finally understood.

He hadn't thought it possible. Who would even *want* to understand sin?

He wished he hadn't called Mrs. Stevens.

"Oh, heavens!" she said. "I'll be right over."

She stopped in five minutes before closing, and Ryan explained to her that if the coin wasn't a fake, it was very valuable, and to be very careful with it. She thanked him and headed off with a big smile.

Ryan balanced and was out by 5:10. As he reached his car, he saw a scratch along the door. Someone had hit the car and hadn't left a note.

"Bummer," said Jim, walking by a moment later. "I guess what goes around comes around."

Ryan wasn't quite sure how to take that but decided to let it slide. He saw a crumpled paper bag on the asphalt and picked it up and dropped it in the trash can a few feet away.

"You can't work your way to heaven, you know," Jim said, opening his car door. "It's a gift."

"You *can* work your way there," Ryan corrected. "You can work to *make* heaven, or work to make hell."

Jim smiled condescendingly and shook his head as he climbed into his car. But Ryan walked around the parking lot a few more minutes, picking up more trash. A young man passing by saw him, stooped to pick up a piece of paper, and then tossed it in the can with a backward grin as he moved on.

Ryan smiled and climbed into his car. If he could just nurture that little bit of God in himself, perhaps he could make God real. There was a certain freedom in believing, and a certain freedom in *not* believing. But Ryan needed the freedom of creation.

He pulled out of the parking lot to head home, and at the first stoplight, the car behind him tapped his rear bumper. Ryan got out to make sure there was no damage, in the mood to shrug it off, but the man in the car behind him jumped out shouting. "What kind of an idiot stops short like that? It was *your* fault! I can prove it! I have witnesses! I'm gonna sue!"

Ryan smiled at the man, nodded politely, gave him the finger, and then sat back down in his car and drove away.

The Tarot Reader

The day started off poorly when I dropped my cell phone in the toilet. I had a phone sex buddy in New York, a Lubavitcher rabbi I'd met online, and we'd both been about to climax when the phone slipped from my hands. It was ruined, so I had to order a new one, and I'd be without a cell for a couple of days. I hoped Shmuel wouldn't think I'd abandoned him at a crucial moment. It was important for me to be dependable in my relationships, even if I'd never actually met the person I was having an affair with.

I left my apartment on St. Roch and walked over five blocks to Elysian Fields, where I caught the 55 to the University of New Orleans on the Lakefront. Living in the Marigny, just outside of the French Quarter, made getting to work easy. Just one bus, from one end of Elysian Fields at the river to the other end by the lake.

I was an English instructor, my schedule virtually the same every semester—composition courses at 8:00 and 9:00 on Monday-Wednesday-Friday and again at 8:00 and 9:30 on Tuesday-Thursday, the hours nobody else wanted. I was a morning person, however, so it didn't bother me. Though I was Reform, I never taught classes on Saturday. I held office hours immediately after my weekday classes and graded papers if no one came to see me.

By 1:00, I was finished for the day, though often I still had to grade at home. But I could grade at 1:00, or at 3:00, or at 5:00, or at 8:00. Flexibility was one of the things I liked about my job.

And it didn't hurt that I could sit on my stoop at 1:30 in the afternoon and catch the eye of someone taking a late lunch, who was driving slowly by, hoping to find someone just like me waiting for him. It was like a mini-vacation every day, but I also liked all the real vacation time that came with the job.

On my last trip between semesters, I'd gone to New York and attended a gay synagogue. I was thirty-two and still single, but I very much wanted to marry another Jew. I wasn't a fanatic, but I liked Judaism and wanted it to remain a vital part of my life. I even went to the mikvah at Beth Israel once a month. I was usually alone while I was naked, and it wasn't a sexual experience with another man I was looking for. It was a way to be sexual and intimate with Judaism itself.

Still, most of the time, I felt very frustrated by my inability to connect Jewishly with anyone. Here in New Orleans, Temple Sinai had a gay havurah that met irregularly. I wasn't a member of Sinai but had given them my name and address so I could be notified about upcoming meetings, but months would go by with no notice.

Then I'd call and the secretary would tell me of the meeting I'd just missed. It was February now. I'd missed the Hanukkah party a couple of months ago, and as far as I knew, the Passover seder was the next scheduled meeting.

I'd met a couple of Jews at French Quarter bars over the years, but they were even more secular than I was, almost anti-Jewish in their condescension, so I hadn't wanted to date them. One of my fellow instructors at the university was a gay Jew, but he was one of those haughty intellectuals who turned me off. I liked intelligence and education, but I believed in being down to earth as well. I had a couple of Jewish pen pals on the internet, but no one I was willing to move across the country for.

Today in my first class, I had my students write an argument paper. I usually gave them a choice of two topics. It was often something like gun control or cloning or using cell phones while driving. I forbid the topic of gay rights because I knew I couldn't be objective, and I forbid the topic of abortion because I'd never seen a good student paper yet either pro or con on the issue.

Today I offered using animals as research subjects and whether a person should marry within their religion. I usually had several fundamentalists of varying faiths, so religion was always a popular subject. I once had a cute Jewish student write a paper entitled, "Deadly Swine Flesh in America," but he'd been too fanatical and strait-laced for me to consider, even once he was no longer my student.

I stayed at school till 3:00 to finish grading papers and then caught the bus home. It was too late for lunch and too early for dinner, so I decided to take a walk through the Quarter. February was a good month, before the blazing heat started that would last half the year. I'd hated Israel the one time I'd gone, as it was like an oven, too.

On my walk today, I kept my eyes open for anyone cruising. I passed a Laundromat on Barracks, and the Verti-Mart deli, and a few art galleries. Even when the sexual pickings were slim, the Quarter could always be relied on to offer something interesting. I passed a schizophrenic homeless man who always haunted the corner of Ursulines and Burgundy. I walked by a used book store, and a voodoo shop with a man inside wearing a boa constrictor around his shoulders. I stopped by my mailbox on Bourbon Street to pick up my mail, in a private shop run by two evangelical lesbians, and then I decided to walk through Jackson Square.

A black woman there sang *a cappella* in one corner, and a guy with a scruffy beard played a guitar in another. There were a few painters with their work displayed, one a nun I talked to regularly, and as usual, there were a few tarot readers. I usually paid them the least attention since I considered them charlatans, but today I noticed a cute guy maybe just a few years younger than I. He was reading a book, and I was about to walk on when the title caught my eye. *How to Pray as a Jew.*

He looked up as I walked over. "Want me to read your fortune?" he asked.

"No. I was just wondering about the book."

"It's not *How to Pay as Jew,*" he said wearily. "I've heard that one before."

I laughed. "No, I have a copy of your book myself, but I haven't gotten around to it yet."

"You a Jew?"

"Yes."

"Have a seat." The man motioned to a plastic chair beside his small table. "I'm Albert." He offered his hand.

"I'm Isaac. After Singer, not the one in Genesis." I shook Albert's hand.

"I'm affiliated with Tikvat Shalom," said Albert. "You?"

"Touro. What do you do? You make a living at this?"

He shrugged. "I do pretty well. Started about a year ago. I'm also a student at Southern. I'm working on a degree in Social Work."

I nodded. "You'll obviously be poor like me, but it's a useful career. A helpful one."

"And what do you do?"

"I'm an English instructor at UNO."

"You sure you don't want me to read your fortune? See what good you're going to do in the world?"

"I don't believe in Tarot."

"Some people think it originated with Kabbalah. No one knows for sure. But it helps pay the bills. And I've got an extra bill today. This morning I was out back mowing the lawn for the first time in three months, and I dropped my cell phone and ran over it with the mower."

"No kidding?" I laughed and told him what had happened to my cell phone.

"Looks like we were meant to be out of contact with the world for a few days." Albert grinned as if he'd said something clever.

"What part of the world do you want to avoid contact with?"

"Houston mostly. I moved here a few years ago to attend the seminary on Carrollton."

"The seminary?"

"I used to be Catholic. My family's Portuguese descent." He tried to catch the eye of a tourist passing by but failed. "So one day I was doing a paper on marranos and learned about some of the rituals they kept after being forced to convert. It turned out that my family did some of those things, too, like lighting candles on Friday evening. So I figured my ancestors used to be Jewish. I started studying Judaism, I liked what I learned, and I converted back. Of course, that meant changing careers."

"You could have become a rabbi."

"I'm not sure I could learn Hebrew. I'm not very good with languages. I had a Cuban boyfriend for a while and couldn't even learn the most basic Spanish."

"Was he Jewish?" I asked.

"No. I'd like to try dating a Jew next time. Jose was cute, but he had a bad temper. We broke up after he beat me."

"Yikes."

"I found out he was having sex on the side, and I called him a slut."

"You sure you don't belong in the pulpit?"

"Do you believe in monogamy?" he countered.

I'd only had two relationships, one for six months, and another for just over a year. Both ended when my partner strayed. "Yes," I said. "I do."

"Would you like to go out sometime?"

"Sure," I said.

"Can you come over this Friday evening for Shabbat dinner?"

Albert gave me his address on Spain Street, in the Marigny, not far from my own place. We exchanged cell phone numbers but weren't sure we'd have replacements in time, so I was simply to come over around 6:00. I walked home then, passing a deli with the sign, "Poboys, muffalettas, Jesus is Lord" in the window.

Back home, I read a few stories by my namesake and then watched the news. It was only Tuesday, so there were three days to wait till my date with Albert, and I was horny now. Around 10:00, I went out to the Phoenix to have a quick look around. I ran into Steve, a bar buddy I had sex with occasionally, and invited him home. I fucked him and then sucked him off, and he headed back to the bar, still after more.

I wondered if going to the bars showed a lack of respect for Albert, since I'd chosen actual sex over beating off. Surely, I didn't have to be monogamous even before the first date, but if I was genuinely interested, why wasn't simple masturbation enough?

Wednesday night, I went a couple of doors down to my friend Michael's apartment, and we played Scrabble.

Afterward, I fucked him, too, and then let him fuck me. I suppose I believed in monogamy while in a committed relationship, but I wasn't in a committed relationship *yet*, and I believed in freedom *now*.

Thursday night, I stayed home and graded papers, and then I graded more papers on Friday afternoon, but finally it was time to go over to Albert's place. He lived upstairs in a house converted into two apartments. His was a one-bedroom with a nice-sized living room and a decent kitchen and bathroom. Albert had a menorah on the mantelpiece by his bricked-up chimney. Beside it was a bookcase filled mostly with Jewish books, several by Singer. "Why did you have to mow the lawn if you have an upstairs apartment?" I asked.

"Because the people below won't so much as pull one weed all year," he replied. "Typical renters. No sense of commitment."

It was almost dark by the time Albert had shown me around the apartment, and he wanted to light the candles before the Sabbath began. "I'm not a stickler about lighting fires on the Sabbath, but I do like lighting the candles at sundown."

Albert said the prayers as he lit the candles, and then he brought out the dinner. It was fairly simple—some roasted chicken with green beans and bread. It wasn't challah but still was good. No butter, of course, though neither of us was a stickler on that point, either. We had some wine with the dinner.

"Any serious boyfriends in the past?" Albert asked as he took a bite of chicken.

"A couple," I replied. "One guy I dated in college. He was also an English major. He wasn't ready to settle down. I was tempted by other guys, too, but he was the one who fooled around. Then a couple of years ago I dated Randy for a while. I was sucking him off one day and noticed crabs. It's kind of a giveaway."

"I don't know why guys can't be happy with what they have."

"If penguins can be monogamous," I said, "we should be able to manage it as well."

"Though I suppose a lot of primates aren't sexually committed," Albert said pensively.

"Well, some primates live solely on grass. And some primates swim underwater to eat. We can't base our own species on what other primates do. We're supposed to be God's greatest creation. Is His best work genetically flawed from the start?"

"Maybe humans are evolutionarily programmed to mate with as many different partners as possible to ensure the greatest chance of reproducing," Albert said, "but if God gave us a soul, and the ability to tell right from wrong, He must expect us to rise above our DNA."

"You had anyone else besides the Cuban?"

"A couple. I dated one guy in the seminary on the sly. One of my professors. Even having sex with one guy was more than he was supposed to be doing."

"Maybe some of our rules aren't very realistic."

"You should be able to keep *any* vow you make."

"I hope he at least gave you a good grade."

"Oh, I always got good grades," he said. "Except in Latin."

We talked throughout dinner, and afterward, Albert put in a DVD of *Left Luggage*, a Jewish movie, and we watched that. We talked a little longer, and then Albert said, "Want to move into the bedroom?"

"Sure."

I followed him to the bed, and we took off each other's shirts, kissing as we fumbled with the buttons. We were soon in bed naked, and after fondling each other for a while, I fucked him and then sucked him off. We lay cuddled in one another's arms, Albert lightly caressing my shoulder.

"Want to stay the night?"

"Yep."

"Good." He paused. "If you hear banging on the door in the middle of the night, it'll be Jose. He's kind of stalking me. But I wouldn't worry."

I smiled, trying to be convincing. The offside to commitment was the unstable person who became absolutely fixated with his partner. That didn't sound any better than sneaking sex on the side. And in this case, it seemed Jose was doing both. Was it possible that even someone obsessed with the object of their love *still* couldn't commit?

I wasn't sure I wanted to get into the middle of the physical side of a philosophical debate. Albert certainly seemed nice enough, but I sure didn't want to deal with a violent ex-boyfriend who made headlines.

Albert and I cuddled throughout the night, and there was no banging on the door. The next morning, Albert readied himself for Tikvat Shalom. I'd probably try his congregation soon if we kept seeing each other. It was Conservative, not Reform, but I could probably live with that. It just meant my commitment to Judaism would have to move up a notch. We agreed to meet next Friday for Shabbat dinner again. Then we kissed and I left to get ready for Touro.

We continued to meet on Fridays for the next few weeks, and occasionally during the week I'd see him reading Tarot cards on Jackson Square. I told him about my parents and my sister with two children, who all accepted me. Albert told me of his parents and his brother, all of whom had difficulty accepting both his gayness and his Jewishness.

I told him of my first job, making kosher pizza, and he told me of his first real job, as a counselor in a camp for mentally handicapped youths. I told him how I'd campaigned for the Democrats in the last governor's race, and he told me of his volunteering for the Human Rights Campaign. We took a couple of walks through the Quarter, browsing through antique shops, and he tried to get me to agree to a Tarot reading, which I again declined. We had bagels one afternoon and beignets another. We sat on the levee and watched the ships go by on the river. We enjoyed Shabbat dinners together, and we enjoyed the Jewish movie and circumcised sex that came afterward.

At school one day for my 9:00 class, I had my students write argument papers either for or against monogamy, and for or against marriage. They took to their papers immediately. Everyone had an opinion on the matter. I read a couple of passages from the Talmud on the subject while my students scribbled away.

Soon, I knew Albert and I would move into sharing Saturday nights as well, and then monogamy would kick in. But it hadn't just yet, so this Saturday night, I went to the Phoenix. I watched the regulars play pool, and I cruised some new guys who came in. One guy, about forty, with a goatee, chatted with me for several minutes but then moved on to someone else.

It was probably just as well. Maybe monogamy should kick in now. I supposed if you stayed a virgin until you married, it was obvious when the monogamy started. Perhaps there was a reason for the traditional rules. I should just go home.

Then another cute guy, maybe twenty-five, came over, and I reconsidered the timing of the monogamy yet again. "Hi, I'm Isaac," I said.

"Alberto." He had an accent. A lot of people from Central America came to New Orleans.

"What do you do?"

"I'm studying to be a priest."

"No vows yet?"

"No vows." He smiled.

"Where're you from?"

"Portugal."

"Really? I know another guy named Albert whose ancestors are from Portugal, and he was studying to be a priest, too."

Alberto seemed to grow more interested. "You know this other Albert well?"

"We're dating."

"I see." He paused. "But I can come home with you?"

I nodded, we finished our drinks, and walked a few blocks to my apartment. There were no preliminaries—we just took off our clothes and he started fucking me. But he didn't bother to suck me off or give me a hand job afterward. We lay in bed, and I wondered again if I should have switched to monogamy earlier. It was so hard to know just when the right moment was. After only one date seemed too soon, but there was never any other clear line in the gay world. It would have to be well before moving in together.

Was the line simply whenever a couple had the discussion and committed verbally? Somehow, that seemed too late as well. I felt that by the time I brought it up at dinner, Albert would say, "Well, I thought we were being faithful *ages* ago, and you're just now willing to start?" What did it mean that I was still afraid to "miss out" on a few last sexual adventures?

I wondered if all this uncertainty meant the gay way of life truly was inferior. Perhaps the Orthodox were right. Shmuel said he never had any "real" sex with other men, just phone sex and beating off to online video from friends. Did that count? Was he obeying the letter of the law? That's what we Jews were good at, after all.

"Tell me more about this guy you're dating," Alberto said.

"Well, he's a great guy, very sweet, and socially aware." So why wasn't I with him tonight?

"Does he like to get fucked?"

"Uh, yeah." Talking about Albert made me feel I was betraying him more than being in bed with Alberto was.

"Does he yell for you to fuck him harder?"

"No, but perhaps we shouldn't—"

"I used to date a guy named Jose, from Cuba. He liked me to fuck him hard. I'd never been with a guy before him. I'm not really gay. I just like fucking guys."

I didn't say anything.

"But my last boyfriend liked to fuck around, so when I found out, I hit him. He fucked around just like you fuck around."

I still didn't say anything.

"I think guys who fuck around deserve to be punished."

My heart began beating fast.

"What are you thinking?"

"I'm thinking your name is Jose."

"It is."

Fuck. Was I going to end up in the hospital? Of course, I could hardly blame Albert for getting me into this mess. If I'd just kept my dick in my pants…

"You know, Albert's a liar. He says he's Jewish, but he still has a rosary. I've seen him pray the rosary. And did he say he was monogamous? That whore fucks around all the time. I got syphilis from him."

"So what do you really do?" Maybe I could change the topic and lower the tension.

He smiled darkly. "I work at Macy's. That's where I met Albert."

"How long have you been in America?"

"I'm a U.S. citizen. You can't have me deported."

"Who wants to deport you? I was just making conversation."

"You gonna keep seeing Albert?"

"I'm not sure."

"That means yes."

"What's it to you?"

"I still love him. I want him back."

"I don't think he wants to see you anymore. There's no excuse for hitting."

"Sometimes there is."

"If you still love him, why are you having sex with me?"

"Because you touched him last."

"Revenge is not love."

"Sometimes it is."

I sat up and started putting on my underwear. "I think we're done here. It's time for you to leave."

"You kicking me out?"

"I need to get to sleep."

"Right."

But he got dressed without any more complaints, and I was able to see him to the door without incident. After he left, I sat on the edge of my bed, shaking. Even when a young couple knew they weren't committed yet, they didn't usually want to hear about their partner's other sexual encounters. But now I'd have to tell Albert I'd met Jose, which would be even worse than just a random hook-up.

Jose said he still loved Albert, but what did it say about commitment when a guy so focused on you could still so easily justify fucking a stranger? And what did it say about me that I was judging Jose's sexual choices rather than my own?

Even worse than these concerns was the doubt Jose had placed in my mind about Albert's own ability to commit. But I knew Jose had lied about who he was. He'd been impersonating his ex-boyfriend, even before he knew who I was. That was pretty damning. This couldn't wait till Friday, though. I'd have to call Albert in the morning.

I beat off, thinking about my buddy Michael, wondering why I wasn't thinking of Albert, and then went to sleep. The next morning, I graded some papers and called Albert around 10:00. "Can I come over?" I asked.

"Oh. Sure. Give me a few minutes to clean up. Is 10:30 okay?"

"I'll see you in a bit." Albert had never worried about me seeing his place messy before. Did he have someone over? I wondered if it mattered. If I hadn't been at the pivotal point of monogamy myself last night, there was no reason he needed to be.

But I'd never actually lied about having sex, and I wanted to see if he was lying about the reason he wanted me to wait. So I walked right over and stood on the sidewalk a few doors down to watch. Then I felt dirty. Was I turning into a stalker, too? Was this what commitment led to?

I didn't want to be more of an asshole than I already was, so I turned and took a short walk, returning right at 10:30.

When I knocked on the door, Albert opened it with a smile. I could tell instantly that whatever secrets Albert might have, and we all had some, he was clearly more trustworthy than Jose. Or than I was, for that matter. "To what do I owe this pleasure?"

"I ran into Jose last night." I walked in and Albert shut the door.

"Did he hurt you?"

"He fucked me."

"Oh." We were silent for a moment. Then he shrugged. "I saw it in the cards."

"Yes, I'm a slut, too. Just like him."

"I wasn't going to say that."

"I'll be monogamous from now on. I was on the verge of monogamy anyway."

Albert looked at me. "Do you really want to be monogamous? It needs to come from your heart."

"Well, I want you. And I'll do whatever it takes to have you."

Albert was silent for a moment. "If it doesn't come natural, it's never going to work. You'll always feel suffocated."

I shook my head. "No one *likes* paying taxes, but we enjoy having roads and schools and a postal service. No one *likes* paying their temple dues, but we do it to be a part of a community. No one *likes* fasting on Yom Kippur, yet we get more out of the day if we do. This is where we're different from Christians. Jews don't have to *like* obeying the commandments. We just need to do it."

"But if you're not monogamous because you're only thinking of me, there's always the danger you'll slip up."

I laughed. "Albert, there *will* always be that danger. I can guarantee it."

Albert frowned. "Then—"

"Can you promise you'll always fast on Yom Kippur every year for the rest of your life?"

"Well…"

"Can you swear you're reporting all your Tarot-reading money to the IRS?"

"But—"

"Don't you like roads and schools?"

"What's your point?"

"Even monogamous penguins can't predict the future. All we can do is commit to always do our best at love."

Albert suddenly looked glum. "I think about other guys, too. I went to the bathhouse two weeks ago." His shoulders slumped. "What are we going to do?"

"Maybe we can watch Israeli porn together. Or have sex while reading the Talmud. Maybe have sex while you're reading the Tarot for my future."

"How long can gimmicks last, Isaac?"

"I don't know," I said slowly. "But I like even the regular things we do for sex, so why would I get tired of it? I still like vanilla ice cream after thirty-two years of vanilla."

Still, I knew this meant no more sitting on my stoop, no more friendly sex with fuck buddies I genuinely liked. Could I ever find satisfaction with just one man?

"Maybe gays are emotional 'renters,' not real homeowners," Albert said sadly.

"Having sex with my best friend has to be better than sex with a casual bar buddy I have a limited amount in common with, no matter how nice he may be, even if all I'm after is friendly sex."

"What about hot sex?"

I shrugged. "It's hot for now, but I think if hot sex is a priority, a person will inevitably commit adultery. I don't think it's possible to maintain hotness with a partner you've had sex with a thousand times."

Albert looked glum again.

"We can always fantasize about other guys when we have sex, though, can't we?" I asked softly.

"Isn't that still cheating?"

"We have to make *some* concessions to our DNA."

Albert nodded slowly. "What if we make it ten years, and then…"

"We can only live one day at a time," I said. "No amount of Tarot can change that."

Albert stood up. "I'll be right back," he said.

I sighed, wondering if the whole idea of a relationship was a fantasy in the first place, but still willing to give it a serious try. If "trying" wasn't already admitting to failure.

Then Albert came back with something in his hand. He held it out.

It was a tightly knit blue kipa with a white border. I looked up quizzically.

"I'm studying to become a bar mitzvah. Why don't we beat off into my yarmulke while I recite my Torah portion?"

I laughed. "I guess hot sex for a gay Jew is rather specific." I unzipped my pants and pulled out my penis.

Albert smiled and began stroking himself as well.

I really didn't know what the future held, but I suspected if we could keep thinking outside the box, the box wouldn't be able to confine us entirely. We stood there staring at each other, bringing ourselves closer to orgasm with every stroke. As I reached climax a few moments later, I realized I was fantasizing right now about Albert. I smiled.

And when I came, I shouted his name.

The Convert's Mezuzah

I got four stitches trying to put up my mezuzah. It was the first of April and almost seven months had passed since I'd moved to Seattle after the hurricane devastated my hometown of New Orleans. I was able to save some of my Jewish books and my menorah and tallis, but my kipot and mezuzah were left behind.

I'd been attending the Reform synagogue here on Capitol Hill a couple of times a month, but I'd just never gotten around to buying a new mezuzah or kipa yet. Finally, this morning, I went to the gift shop and picked out a Lenox mezuzah for my bedroom doorpost and one light blue kipa for my head.

But while trying to put up the mezuzah, I discovered that the screws were too small, or rather, my screwdriver was too big. I'd bought a small case of screwdriver heads of different sizes that slipped into the handle and were held by magnets, but now when I retrieved the box, I saw that it was closed with a thin white plastic strip pulled tight. I couldn't get scissors underneath it, so I thought I'd try a steak knife.

The blade wasn't all that sharp, so I had to push hard to cut through the zip tie. When I did, the knife went flying into my left hand, cutting a gash in the fleshy part between the thumb and forefinger.

It didn't really hurt, but when I could see the inside of my hand, I knew I was in trouble, and I felt an intense flash of anger for having been so stupid. I rinsed off the wound quickly, and since blood was now dripping onto the floor, I grabbed a paper towel and applied pressure.

Then I headed out the door to the bus stop. Normally, I took my shoes off when I got to my apartment, but fortunately, I hadn't taken them off yet after coming home with the mezuzah. And while I was in no position to put on a jacket, it was probably 50 degrees outside and bearable.

Just as I got to Broadway a block away, a #60 pulled up.

"Is it okay if I ride without paying?" I asked sheepishly, still applying pressure to my hand. "I'm going to the emergency room at Harborview. I cut myself."

"Sure. Get on."

It wasn't that I didn't have $1.25. I just didn't want to let go of my hand long enough to reach in my pocket for my wallet.

Within five minutes, I was at the hospital and headed for the emergency room. The waiting area was filled with fifteen or so people, and six more were in line just to see the triage nurse. This was going to take a while.

I was a little miffed to see that one of the men in line had a tray of food from the cafeteria. How ill could he be if he had time to get lunch before waiting in line?

But the line moved quickly and within twenty minutes I was talking to the triage nurse. "Can I see the hand?" she asked. When I showed her, she nodded. "Yes, we'll have someone look at that. On a scale of one to ten, how much does it hurt?"

"It doesn't hurt at all."

She gave me kind of a funny look, and then she nodded again. "They'll call you in a few minutes to the registration booth."

It was twenty more minutes before I could register and another fifteen before I was called in back. A nurse practitioner looked at my hand.

"What happened?" she asked.

"I was trying to open a box with a knife," I said. "Apparently, you're supposed to be careful when you do that."

"Well, we're going to put in a few sutures. We'll have to clean it and numb it up first."

The cleaning was easy, just pouring water over it. The numbing was more involved, requiring an injection of anesthetic into the wound. It burned like hell, and I grunted a few times.

"Now we'll put in the sutures."

I looked away as the nurse got out her curved needle. I could feel her touching the skin, but it didn't hurt. However, she was having trouble tying the thread, and it took a full half hour for her to put in four sutures. Finally, though, she was finished, and she wrapped my hand in bandages. It was a bit overdone for such a small injury, but the nurse practitioner smiled and said, "This way, you'll get some sympathy."

I thanked her and walked home, about a twenty-five minute walk. Then I finished putting up my mezuzah. I was afraid at first to finish hanging it, worried I'd associate bad memories with the day, but the stitches were from my own stupidity and not the mezuzah, and I'd waited long enough to put it up already.

Though my menorah was prominently displayed in the living room, I didn't feel like I lived in a Jewish home until my mezuzah was on the doorpost. I suppose I was only nominally Jewish at best, but I wanted to do more, and be better.

I had the day off and needed to do something fun with the rest of the day. It was rare to get a Sunday off, which was partly why it had taken me so long to get to the synagogue gift shop in the first place. It was a lovely day, and though I'd already walked half an hour, I took another walk now, north to Volunteer Park.

There was an old stone water tower about eighty feet high, and an Asian art museum, and a greenhouse full of plants. Also, some of the trees in the park were flowering, cherry trees with their pink blossoms. Soothing to see all the beauty.

But it was impossible after coming this far not to walk along the road where gay guys parked to cruise. I walked past four cars with guys inside lightly fondling the crotch of their pants to let people know they were on the prowl. Two of the guys were heavy and unattractive, one was average, and one was too good looking to approach. But I didn't go up to any of them.

I didn't really have anything against anonymous encounters. I simply didn't have much interest in sex these days. It had been ten months since my partner, David, had died back in New Orleans of liver cancer. We hadn't had sex the last several weeks of his life, and he'd apologized several times for letting me down, but I assured him sex was the least of my worries. Even now, I'd only had sex three times since coming to Seattle. I just couldn't seem to get interested any more.

Walking back along Broadway, I passed an African art shop, a Mexican restaurant, and a Buddhist shop. There were a few other restaurants, a tobacco shop, and a piercing salon, and then I saw two young men in suits waiting at a bus stop. Mormon missionaries.

I stopped at the bus stop as well. One of the guys was dark-haired, good looking. The other was blond and average looking. Both were about twenty years old. It had been a long time since I'd seen a missionary. Even longer since I'd been one. I had been excommunicated from the Mormon Church fifteen years ago and had converted to Judaism five years later.

I'd only been a Mormon for fourteen years, since I was nine, having been nothing before that, so I would soon have been a Jew as long as I'd been a Mormon. I certainly knew more about Judaism than I knew about Mormonism, but there was a lot more to know about Jews. Their history was 4000 years longer.

I wondered, though, how Mormon missionaries would treat a Jew. Or a gay Jew, for that matter. It was purely out of morbid curiosity, and perhaps a sense of nostalgia, but I turned to the dark-haired one. "Are you guys Mormons?"

"Yes." He looked me up and down. "Have you heard of us before?"

"A little here and there over the years."

"What have you heard?" The blond now turned to me and smiled, too.

"Oh, that you believe in families, that sort of thing."

The dark-haired one nodded happily. "Anything else?"

"You had some prophet named John Smith."

"Joseph Smith."

"Oh, that's right."

"Have the missionaries ever talked to you before?"

I'd baptized five people on my mission to Sweden nineteen years earlier. "No," I said. "I'd like to talk to you guys sometimes, but I just want to tell you up front I'm happy as a Jew and probably won't convert. I just want to hear what you have to say. If you don't think I'd be wasting your time, I'd like to invite you over sometime."

"No, we'd like to talk to you."

I gave them my address and phone number, and they gave me a paperback copy of the Book of Mormon and their phone number. We arranged for them to come to my place Tuesday evening. They didn't say anything about my bandaged hand, and just as we were finishing exchanging information, their bus came and they climbed on.

I went back to my apartment, feeling a little guilty over the deception, but also glad to be able to talk to missionaries again. Though I had gone to my bishop and requested excommunication when I no longer believed in the Church, I still had fond memories of my time in Stockholm as a missionary. It might be fun to tap back into that briefly.

Back in my apartment, I decided to read for a while. I'd just finished *Jewish Literacy* by Joseph Telushkin, an enlightening book, but now felt like returning to a novel I'd begun earlier, *Jurassic Park* in Swedish. I was almost halfway through and read thirty more pages now.

The next day I went back to work at Money Grows, a check cashing place here on Capitol Hill. It was the first job I'd found after moving to Seattle, and though it paid $5 an hour less than I made as a bookstore clerk in New Orleans, it was the only job I'd been offered so far, despite continually applying for others. With two English degrees, I wasn't a very marketable guy and had to take what I could get. Switching to a new city and a new career wasn't easy.

"Hey, Robert," said my coworker Henry as I came through the two locked doors into the secure work area in back. "How was your weekend?"

I showed him my hand.

"Wow. What happened?"

"Masturbation injury." Almost all my coworkers were gay, so I could joke with them.

"Well, it's the first of the month, and we've been getting lots of government checks today, so let's get you on a drawer quick."

Monday was a slow loan day, fortunately, but I did get Social Security checks one after another most of the day. We always got at least a couple of homeless people every day, and always a couple of people cashing $1500 or $2000 checks. I wondered why they didn't go to the bank instead of us, but I'd quickly learned these were the people banks didn't want. Many had substance abuse issues or gambling addictions or were mentally ill. Some were just socially awkward. We had one woman come in today wearing a bathrobe and slippers. We got all kinds.

Mike, one of our regulars, came in. He looked homeless, but once when I made a casual comment about the good weather we were having, he'd said quickly, "Oh, I have an apartment." Still, he was usually filthy, and one of my coworkers had written a note in the computer under his name, "Could someone please burn a dead muskrat and improve the smell when he comes in?" But Mike was always pleasant and polite, and I made sure to keep extra protein bars or chewy granola bars at work so I could give him one when he came in. My coworkers disapproved, and I don't suppose it was much of a mitzvah. It was easy, after all, to be nice to nice people.

Not everyone who came in was nice. Just before the end of my shift, I cashed a check for a guy, and his total cash back was $80.01. He only wanted $20 in cash, though, and he wanted the rest put on his Visa debit card. It cost $2 to load the card, so I put $58 on the card. Then I realized I should have put the penny on as well, but it was too late, so I handed the customer $20.01.

"I said I only wanted $20 back," the customer snarled. "Now I have to carry a penny around in my pocket all day. Can't you get anything right? You're so incompetent. I can't believe you're causing me so much inconvenience. I sure hope I don't get you next time I come here."

He continued complaining for another minute or so, and though I rarely envied my customers, this time I couldn't help but think, "If carrying a penny is your biggest problem, I wish I was you."

Soon my shift was over. I counted my drawer, finding it a nickel over, and before long I was home. It was drizzling lightly, but I took a half hour walk down Broadway past where the stores ended at East Roy and where Broadway became 10th Avenue East, and I continued north past a lovely Italian mansion on Howe.

After half an hour, I turned and walked back to East Denny, where I walked over a block to my apartment on Nagle by the new fountain at Cal Anderson Park. So I got in an extra hour of walking today. I'd gained five pounds since moving to Seattle and now weighed 155. I wanted to get back down to 150, or better yet, to 140, where I was happiest.

I got on the internet to a bear site I'd recently joined, since I had a beard and liked other guys with facial hair, and browsed through some profiles. I sent a few messages to guys in Stockholm, wanting to make a few more Swedish friends.

My partner David had been a French professor who also knew Dutch and Swedish, and I missed speaking it every day.

I also wrote to several people in Seattle, hoping to find friends in general. One of my coworkers had mentioned the "Seattle freeze," and I was beginning to understand what he meant.

While on the internet, I checked out the site for the gay Jewish congregation that met once a month in Seattle. I'd emailed them a couple of times when I first moved, but they'd never responded. I asked my own synagogue on 16th if they were having a congregational seder this year, and they weren't, so I decided to check if the gay group was.

And in fact, it was. I'd called to confirm a reservation, leaving a message, and wondered if they'd call back since they never emailed back. Mormons had always been much more enthusiastic about accepting new members than Jews were. I never liked to admit to Jews I was a convert. I figured they'd be even less interested in me. But with a last name like Anderson, it was clear from the start I wasn't a regular Jew.

Signing up for the Passover seder had put me in a Jewish mood, so I looked through my DVDs, found *A Stranger Among Us*, and put it in the DVD player. It wasn't great, but I enjoyed seeing Jews again.

The next day, work went well enough. Government checks started tapering off, but SMHI checks started coming in, from clients of the mental health clinic nearby. Most of the people were functional, though one guy came in with his pants down around his knees. Though his shirt was covering his genitals, it was clear he was behaving inappropriately. It was tiring to have to be a moral authority even at a secular job.

"Sir, you're going to need to pull your pants up," I said as he came to my window.

"Can't," he said, thrusting a check at me. "I shit in my pants."

At this point, I could smell he was telling the truth, and I tried to conduct the transaction as quickly as possible. Other customers looked at him in horror, and one customer walked out. After my customer left, before waiting on the next customer, I washed my hands, went out in the lobby to spray Lysol on the counter in front of my window, and then I washed my hands again.

The rest of the day went okay.

I got off work at 6:00, ate a fat-free bologna sandwich, and tidied up the living room. At 7:05, the elders rang the buzzer to my building, and I let them in. Elder Stuart, the dark-haired one, said a prayer, and then Elder Osgood, the blond, asked if I'd read any of the Book of Mormon they'd given me.

I hadn't, but I wanted to sound more interested than I was, so I thought back to the ten or so times I'd read the book to a story I'd liked. "I read about a guy trying to preach to another, and they both fell down unconscious," I said, "and a woman went to gather everyone in to look."

"Oh, that would be King Lamoni and Ammon in the book of Alma," Stuart said. They seemed pleased with me.

Thank God I'd remembered the story correctly. I listened then as the elders told me about Joseph Smith praying and seeing God the Father and Jesus Christ, and how they'd restored the true church through Joseph. At the end of the lesson, they asked if I had any questions. I felt it was too soon to ask about their position on gays. I wanted them first to see me as a good "investigator."

"No," I said, "but I'd like to hear more. Can you come back next week?"

They wrote down some verses for me to read, prayed, and then left. I decided this time to read a little, so I looked up the verses they'd left. Every one was about Jesus Christ. I'd told them I was Jewish, and they apparently felt they needed to emphasize Christ. That had certainly not been the focus back when I was a missionary.

I put the book down and picked up *To Life!* by Harold Kushner. Much more to my liking. Then I put in a DVD of *I Love Lucy* season four and watched a couple of episodes.

Work over the next few days was more of the same. The only real incident was a guy trying to exchange a million dollar bill for smaller denominations, and the continual war among my coworkers over what temperature to set the thermostat at. Also, there was my regular frustration at finding loan files out of order, Thompson coming after Tucker, for example. I made a joking comment about it every time I found a misfiled folder, but it truly irritated me.

What was so difficult about filing? I'd mastered the alphabet back in the first grade. On the same note, I often found names of check makers misspelled in the computer. Not only was there an entry for U.S. Treasury, for instance, but also one for U.S. Treassury, one for U.S. Treasure, and one for Untied States Treasury. Good grief. I always felt it was a matter of honesty to do a good job at work, to do what I was paid to do. It was a contract, and I felt sinful if I didn't keep up my end of it.

To hone up our obviously weak writing skills at work, and for a little diversion, our boss had posted a sheet on which we were supposed to write down good drag queen names. I'd written down Katrina D'Bris, and the other gay workers contributed Melody D'Amour, Crystal Kleer, Sofanda Peters, and Polly Propylene. Today I added Helena Handbasket. The one straight guy at our store offered X-Ray Ted and Poor Nomad. I told him, "It is *so* obvious you aren't gay. Those may be good band names, but they're awful drag queen names."

On Friday, I got off work at 6:00 and walked two blocks from the store to the synagogue for services. I'd lost my tape of prayers in my hasty move from New Orleans, so I couldn't listen to it as I fell asleep at night like I used to, but I knew my prayers well enough after becoming a bar mitzvah that I could say them without any trouble during services.

Still, that tape had a couple of my favorite Hebrew songs on it, too, like "Adon Olam" by David Yakobian, and I missed being able to sing along at home. This congregation had different tunes than the ones I knew. It was going to take a while to get used to them. At the oneg after services, I had a cookie and stood around while everyone else talked to each other. No one approached me, and I was too nervous to approach any of them, feeling like an impostor.

On my way home, I stopped at QFC to buy a gallon of milk. I decided to also check out the cereal aisle. I only bought it if it was on sale. Both Honey Smacks and Apple

Jacks were half price today, so I wanted a box of each, but there was a cute guy nearby also looking at the cereals, and I was too embarrassed to pick out such juvenile boxes while he was looking. I just pretended to be taking a while to make my decision, but he was taking a long while, too.

I wanted to flirt and tried to catch his eye, but he never glanced at me. He would certainly look if I picked out a kid's cereal, though. But why was he taking so long? Was he working up the nerve to say something? I finally got tired of waiting for him to do anything and decided I might just have to embarrass myself anyway.

Before I could reach for the Honey Smacks, though, the cute guy picked up a box of Trix and walked away quickly. A man after my own heart. Too bad he wasn't interested in me. Perhaps he was embarrassed, too. We missed so many opportunities for such stupid reasons.

Ooh, Life cereal was on sale, too.

Monday morning before work, I went back to the emergency room to have my stitches removed. I thought about taking them out myself but was too chicken. The cut still looked open after the sutures were removed, so I kept a Band Aid on it.

Then Tuesday night the elders came back. Elder Osgood gave a prayer, and then Elder Stuart asked, "Did you read any of the passages we marked for you?"

"Yes," I said, "but they were all about Jesus. I have to say, as a Jew, that has to be the least interesting part of your message."

"Well, we *are* Christians. It's an important part of our message."

"I can get Christianity anywhere," I said. "What makes you different? Why should I come to you and not another Christian church?"

"Well, we have the Plan of Salvation," Osgood replied. "It's the purpose of life. We have a lesson about that we can teach tonight. Does that sound good?"

I nodded, and they began taking turns as they talked about how we lived with God before coming to the Earth, came to Earth to get a body and be tested, and would join God again after death. It was essentially the same lesson I used to teach as the second lesson. If nothing else, Mormons were consistent.

After the lesson, Elder Stuart asked, "Do you have any questions?"

It still seemed a little early to ask about gays, but I could let them know I was a liberal. "What is your position on blacks?" I asked.

"Oh, they're treated equally in the Church. They can hold the priesthood."

"What about interracial marriage?"

"We have no problem with that."

Interesting. That certainly had changed. While black men were given the priesthood back in the late 1970's, there had still been for a long time a reaction against interracial marriage. Hopefully, that was changing now. It was a good sign.

"What's your position on women?" I went on.

"Oh, they're completely equal, too."

I raised an eyebrow. "So they can hold the priesthood now?"

"Oh, no," said Osgood. "There are still appropriate roles. Women are mothers. Men hold the priesthood. But really, women are better because they don't need the priesthood."

Oh, please, I thought, but I nodded as if considering. "What about women working outside the home?"

"We believe someone should be home to raise the children."

"So it would be okay if the woman got a job and the man stayed home?"

The two elders looked at each other. "Well, uh, sure, but it's probably best if the woman stays home. Women are usually better caregivers."

Well, that position certainly hadn't changed since I'd left the Church fifteen years ago. But I'd asked as many questions as I dared today. The gay issue could wait till next time. "Okay," I said. "Do you think you guys could come back next week?"

"Sure," said Elder Stuart. "But do you think you could come out to church this Sunday?"

Ugh. Even though I wanted some contact with Mormons again, church was a little too much. "No, I have to work this Sunday," I lied. "Maybe next week." A good Jew wouldn't lie, I thought. But then, a good Jew probably wouldn't have Mormon missionaries over.

"Okay. But will you read more of the Book of Mormon?"

"Of course."

After the elders left, feeling guilty for allowing the Mormon influence, I watched another Jewish DVD, the movie *Ushpizin*. But that was way more Jewish than I was, about an Orthodox couple in Jerusalem during Sukkot. I felt as alienated from that experience as I did from Mormonism. Feeling a little down, I read more of *Jurassic Park* in Swedish before bed.

At work the next day, I had a man try to get a loan by giving me a Social Security awards letter as proof of income. It showed he received $3000 a month. That was the first clue something was wrong. I took the letter in back and compared it to the other award letters we received. The fonts were different. It was counterfeit.

I went through the motions of processing the loan but clicked on "Invalid proof of income," and the loan was denied by the computer. The customer walked away unhappy. I felt conflicted enough working for a company that took advantage of desperate people.

Even on good days, I was taking 6% and 10% out of the checks people gave me. And we charged several hundred percent interest on the loans. When we took in a loan repayment, we were told not to alert the customer that their paperwork might not be in order to reloan, because then they might not pay us back, given that almost all of the loan customers took out loan after loan every two weeks, caught in the trap.

Once, I took in a payment of $795 and then had to tell the customer she wasn't eligible to take out another loan. She said she'd be evicted, and she sat down in our lobby and cried for ten minutes. I needed to find a more righteous job.

Though I usually worked with my gay colleagues, today I was working with two straight women. One was supposedly Native American, but she looked as white as I was. The other was a nineteen-year-old Cambodian girl named Sally, always bubbly. She'd taken out a loan at a competitor's store last week so she could buy an expensive pair of shoes she wanted. When she told me, I just smiled and nodded. I wasted money on books and DVDs, so who was I to judge?

Today, Sally talked about having kids. "I want to name my daughter Naisa," she said. "Don't you think that's pretty? It's Asian spelled backwards. I want to name my daughter after where she's from, and I think spelling it backwards is clever."

"That's harder to do if you're from England," I said with a straight face, and she frowned.

"Speaking of England," said Marilyn, my other coworker, talking to us while processing a man's check, "my parents are going on a cruise of Europe." Her parents were two lesbians. "They're making stops in Spain, France, Italy, and Greece." She handed the customer his money and then turned to me with a sincerely puzzled look. "Is there some large body of water in Europe that you can get to all those places by boat?"

I found that Christians often didn't have as strong a commitment to education as Jews had. That was at least one thing about Judaism I felt I could identify with.

The rest of the day went well, and after balancing my drawer to the penny, I went home. I ate a fat-free bologna sandwich again and then took a shower. At 8:00, I was supposed to meet a guy from the internet at the coffee shop around the corner. I'd said I was only interested in friendship, but with gay guys, sex was always a possibility, and I was nervous.

I went to the coffee shop ten minutes early and ordered a warm milk with almond flavoring. Since I was no longer Mormon, I was allowed to drink coffee but found I simply didn't like the taste, so when I went to coffee shops, I either drank hot chocolate or warm milk. But I wanted to buy it early. It seemed too awkward to meet someone while still standing in line.

I found a table with a clear view of the line, and I sipped my milk while waiting for Tom to show up. We'd been chatting for a couple of weeks. He was in his mid-forties, several years older than I was, but his photo still looked good. Even though I was primarily interested in friendship, it was impossible not to consider dating again. I missed David, and no one could replace him, but eventually I'd want another partner, so I had to be open to the possibilities. I'd rather marry a Jew again, but you had to take what was available.

At 8:05, Tom walked into the coffee shop. He looked around and finally caught my eye. He didn't wait in line to buy anything but came straight to my table. "Hi, Robert," he said, sitting down.

"Hi. Good to meet you."

"It's a relief to see you look like your picture."

"Was it hard to find the place?" I asked.

"Oh, no. I'm pretty familiar with Capitol Hill even though I live up in Greenwood."

"You don't mind living so far from downtown?"

"No. It's peaceful out there. You like it here, with all the street kids and panhandlers?"

"It's vibrant here. Alive. I'm only seven blocks from the nearest skyscraper. I can walk to the grocery or drug store. I'm a block from the bus stop. I like it."

"So what do you do again?"

"Check cashing."

"Oh."

"I used to work for Barnes and Noble in New Orleans. But my store got eight feet of water in it, so I was out of a job. You think a job like that will last forever, but not if the city is destroyed."

"Well, I have a federal job, so I'm more secure. I work for the post office."

"Now that's something I hadn't considered yet."

"They're signing up for the exam now. You ought to go for it."

"I generally test okay. Maybe I will."

We chatted for forty-five minutes, and it seemed to go well. Perhaps we'd meet again. Tom gave me his phone number before he left, which seemed a good sign. I put my cup in the bus tray and walked a block back to my apartment. Then, while I was thinking about it, I went online and applied to take the postal exam. It was worth a shot. At least it would be a more ethical job.

It was late, so after emailing some guys in Sweden, I got in bed. I masturbated while thinking of David, and then I went to sleep.

The next day I worked the 7:30 to 3:30 shift, my favorite. It included two things I didn't like, ordering money from the bank to be delivered the following day, and having safe control, which meant having to count all the money in the safe, usually around $20,000, and being responsible for it. But the hours were good. You got work out of the way and still had a little of the day left.

Other shifts I worked regularly were the 10:00 a.m. to 6:00 p.m. shift, the noon to 8:00 p.m. shift, and the 2:00 p.m. to 10:00 p.m. shift, when I had to help do the closing paperwork for the store, which had to be done daily even though we stayed open twenty-four hours. That consisted of running a money order report, a Western Union report from each terminal, a utility pay report, and running a loan report and depositing to the bank electronically any loans due that day which hadn't been paid back.

Then, in addition to these shifts, one week every five weeks, I had to do the graveyard shift, from 10:00 p.m. to 8:00 a.m. But graveyard shifts had the benefit of giving me the opportunity to listen to my European music and my Jewish music, which I couldn't do when my coworkers were there, and I also had time to read more Chaim Potok and Isaac Bashevis Singer. I was hungry to feel authentically Jewish, yet somehow always felt instead like I was playing dress-up.

The only real incident today was that the guy who had shit in his pants the other week came in to cash a check, and he urinated on himself while I waited on him. When another customer complained about the puddle, my boss, Cliff, went in the lobby to mop it up. "I swear," he said, pushing the mop back and forth, "it's worse than having a puppy in the house."

After work today, I took a shower and prepared a large salad to take to the seder tonight. I put in Romaine lettuce, yellow peppers, orange peppers, red tomatoes, black olives, green pickles, and mushrooms. I also bought some Italian dressing, no Ranch or anything like that because I'd been told the potluck was meat, no milk. I didn't keep kosher myself and had no problem with eating cheeseburgers, but I didn't want to upset anyone by breaking the rules, so I brought Italian.

Just before 5:00, I caught the 43 downtown and then switched to the 17. We drove out to Ballard, went past the locks, and kept going north another twenty blocks. I got off at 85th and Loyal as the computer had told me, but it also said that I then needed to walk west half a mile.

The only thing west was a staircase going down a heavily wooded hill. I decided to try it and walked down the steep stairs. After a while, I came upon a small road and a parking lot. I crossed it and went down more stairs. Now I was at a little road that led under a railroad track. There were no cars anywhere.

I walked under the tracks and ended up on a desolate beach. There was an abandoned beach house and nothing else. It was dusk now, getting cold, and starting to rain. I hadn't brought an umbrella.

I'd clearly gone the wrong way and now would be late. I saw some buildings way off in the distance to the south and started walking, figuring I could call a taxi from there, but a few hundred feet down, I saw a police car parked off to the side of the road.

I approached the officer and asked, "Do you know where the Golden Gardens bathhouse is?" I hated to say the word bathhouse. It sounded so decadent.

"It's right there." The officer pointed to the deserted beach house I'd passed. I saw no lights, but there were a couple of cars out front. I thanked the officer and headed back.

I peered in one of the windows, and there were several people busily setting plates at about twenty tables. This must be the place, after all. I looked back up the dark trail I'd just come down. There was no way I was walking back up that hill in the dark and rain after the seder. I'd have to get a ride from someone.

I walked in, paid my $20, and brought the salad to the kitchen. Money was another difference between Mormons and Jews. Mormons had lots of free activities, but with Jews, everything cost something. If there was a special speaker on Tuesday night, it cost $35 to hear him.

Even attending services at high holidays required the purchase of a ticket. It would have been like charging Mormons to attend General Conference, which was instead free to everyone. Mormons would never have done anything to discourage attendance. This was a major cultural difference, and I hated that I was still feeling Mormon on this point. If Jews did it this way, it was a perfectly valid way of operating, and I wanted to like it.

But perhaps these were just annoying "bank fees," rather than the 10% tithing cut the Mormons had forced me to pay in order to feel communion.

I wandered about the large room and was surprised when three separate people came over to talk to me. In the little over seven months I'd been going to the synagogue on Capitol Hill, only one person had ever said hi. One of the people tonight who approached was a lesbian who was the president of the gay congregation. Another was a man who was a librarian at an engineering library, and the other was an attractive man in his forties who happened to also live on Capitol Hill. He said he and his partner could give me a ride home tonight after the seder. His name was Marty, and his partner's name was Steven.

Before too long, fifty or sixty people had shown up, with just a few more men than women present. When it was time to sit, I decided to be one of the first. I didn't want to place myself next to one of the people who had spoken to me and make them feel I was being a leech. If I sat first, no one would feel either slighted or conversely put out.

I was happy, though, to see that Marty and Steven chose to sit next to me. Across the table sat a straight family with two boys about nine and eleven. The mother told me, "We always come to this synagogue because we want our boys to grow up liberal." Tonight, the boys took turns reading the four questions. Everyone had haggadahs, or haggadot, to be correct, and we all took turns reading. We sang "Dayeinu," of course, and after all the ritual foods were finished, we got up to serve ourselves in the kitchen for the real meal.

I chatted with Marty and Steven throughout the dinner. Marty was an insurance adjustor, which had to be even more boring than working in the bookstore had been. Steven was a medical equipment salesman. I wouldn't have liked that, either. But they made lots more money than I did, and they seemed happy with their jobs. I was even more surprised to learn that Steven had been Mormon and had served a mission to New York. He was now as much Buddhist as Jewish. I decided not to mention my own Mormon past just yet, and I was irritated that I felt a slight disappointment that he wasn't a "real" Jew.

"Do you guys ever like to go on walks?" I asked, hoping they'd want to develop a friendship with me. "Or watch movies? I have lots of gay and Jewish DVDs."

"Sure. We'd love to get together sometime." Marty gave me his email address and phone number. There was no way to tell if anything would develop, of course. After the meal was over, everyone helped clean up and put the tables away, and then Marty and Steven drove me home.

The next day at work was Friday, always a busy day. I did about ten loan transactions in addition to cashing thirty-five checks and processing several Western Union sends. There was a long line of customers almost the entire day. One time, an Asian guy who'd waited patiently for his turn finally got up to the window. "Cheeseburger, please," he said with a thick accent.

I thought I'd misunderstood and asked him to repeat himself. "Cheeseburger, please," he said again. I tried to explain that we were not a fast food place, and he walked off, looking confused. Other than that, the only odd customer I had was a man who wanted his change all in five dollar bills, and he sniffed each one at the window before leaving, asking me to exchange one of them for another five because it apparently didn't have the right smell.

On Tuesday, the elders came over again. I was growing a little tired of our meetings, still feeling uncomfortable about deceiving them, so I figured this would be the day I came out. "Did you read any more of the Book of Mormon?" Elder Stuart asked.

"I read a story about two guys fighting, and one cut off the other guy's head, and the headless guy kept trying to fight." It was one of the other stories I remembered after all those years, and since I hadn't read any of the book this week, I had to pull up what I could.

"Oh, yes," said Stuart. "That was Mormon after all the Nephites turned bad, and there was a big war between the Nephites and Lamanites."

I nodded, trying not to look surprised. 95% of the Book of Mormon was the history of the Lamanites and Nephites in America, but one book was the story of the Jaredites, a completely separate people, and even after fifteen years away from the Church, I remembered that the story I'd mentioned came from the Jaredite account.

After the lesson, Elder Osgood asked, "Do you have any other questions for us tonight?"

"Well, I was wondering about your position on a couple of other issues."

"Like what?"

"What do you think of abortion?"

"Oh, it's a terrible sin. Next to murder."

"Next to? But not actually murder?"

"No, but next to is bad enough."

"You know, in the Torah, there's a passage that says if a pregnant woman is attacked and loses her baby, the attacker should be fined, but if the woman dies, the attacker should be put to death. So it's pretty clear that the fetus doesn't have the same value as a human life."

"Well, we go by the Bible, not the Torah."

"Do you even know what the Torah is?"

"It's the Jewish scriptures."

"It's Christian scripture, too. It's the first five books of the Bible."

"Oh."

"This passage was from Exodus, and it seems fairly clear."

"So you're pro-abortion?"

"No, I'm pro-choice. But as I'm a man and not dating a woman right now, I don't suppose it's really an issue."

"Well, you'd have to be pro-life if you were baptized."

I raised an eyebrow. "You can't have a difference of opinion in your church? There are plenty of Jews who are pro-choice, and plenty who are pro-life."

"No, truth is truth. You have to believe the truth to be a Mormon."

"I see. Well, what about gays?" I asked. "My rabbi is gay. Do you ordain gay priests?"

"Gay people are excommunicated from the Church," Elder Stuart said. "The most important commandment is 'Be fruitful and replenish the Earth,' and gays don't do that."

I laughed, unable to stop myself. "Even cats and dogs multiply. And rabbits and rats. I would have thought God expected more out of us than to be like the lowest of animals. Besides, the Talmud says that whoever brings up an orphan is seen as if the child was born to him. Don't Mormons believe in adoption? I thought you guys sealed your families to you in the temple. Don't adopted kids get sealed to their parents? Don't they count? And believe me, adoption isn't the only way gays can have children."

"Homosexuality is wrong. People can try to rationalize, but God forbids it, and that's all that matters."

I decided to back off for now, though I would certainly come back to the topic another day. "What about divorce? Do you permit that?"

"We discourage it, but there are times it's necessary," said Stuart.

"Any other questions?" asked Osgood, in a tone which clearly implied he was tired of the discussion.

"You don't like telling me what you believe?" I wasn't normally confrontational, but it irritated me that they were trying to shrug me off.

"The important thing is Joseph Smith and the Book of Mormon. You need to pray about that. We don't need to get distracted by all these other things."

"I'm sorry," I said. "I didn't realize Mormons were so simplistic. Jews are anything but that. I didn't mean to make you think." I was being a snot and knew it, but these guys reminded me so clearly why I'd left. The nostalgia was quickly fading.

"Do you think you'll be able to come to church this Sunday?" Elder Osgood asked tersely.

"No, I have to work again." This time, it wasn't a lie.

Instantly, the expressions on the missionaries' faces changed. "Well," said Stuart, "we can see you're not progressing. If you're not truly serious about this, we need to spend our time with other people who are really searching for the truth." They stood up. "If you ever do decide to come to church, maybe we can come over again."

I held back a laugh and escorted them to the door. They'd rejected me even before I had a chance to tell them I was gay. I wasn't good enough for them even as a straight person. I probably should have felt offended, but I was too amused.

After all, I'd told them up front I wasn't going to convert. I only felt mildly guilty now for wasting their time, since I knew on the other hand that I'd helped their statistics reports to the mission president, and I knew stats were important to missionaries. It was a business, after all.

"You'll find that things never go quite right for you from now on," said Osgood at the door. "You've had your chance. The Lord won't forgive you for rejecting the gospel."

"Oh, well."

"I can see from your attitude you really love wickedness more than truth. But actions have consequences, and you'll have to live with yours for eternity."

"It's nice to see that all your friendliness these past few weeks was so genuine."

I closed the door behind them, and despite knowing I was okay with God, a little of the Mormon guilt came rushing back. It was foolish really to have let them in. It was like an alcoholic thinking he could take just one drink. Once I let myself be influenced, it was hard to break away again. I was lucky I ever made it out the first time.

They baited you with the good stuff, and then forced you to feel bad about yourself the rest of your life. I supposed Jews had their guilt, too, though. Guilt probably had its purpose, but I thought it also likely did more harm than good in people's lives.

I took a short walk after they left and discovered I was more irritated than I'd originally believed. Perhaps I'd tricked the elders into coming over because I was lonely, but they had pretended interest in me, too, simply to fill a baptism goal. I remembered that as a missionary, I'd been told specifically to look for people who had recently moved or who had new jobs, anyone in emotional turmoil who might feel vulnerable.

Of course, my mission president hadn't said "vulnerable." He'd said "prepared to hear the gospel." But there had been an element of predation involved in missionary work that I had never liked, and now I'd experienced it from the other end. I went around the block an extra time and then decided to watch a movie before bed.

I considered the Mormon missionary movie *The Best Two Years* to get a last dose of missionary life, still morbidly drawn to it for some reason, but I finally decided on *Parting Glances* instead, an early gay film. It took me a very long time to get to sleep after the movie was over.

Work the next day went about as usual. A black woman in her fifties named Esther came to cash a check. She wore a scarf across her face, but I didn't think she was Muslim because she also wore a cross around her neck, and a Star of David as well. And she usually wore a heavy bike helmet, too. I think she was just trying to cover all the bases. I understood.

A couple of days later, there was an incident when I was cashing a check for an attractive guy in his early fifties. We had kind of a bantering conversation back and forth as I processed the transaction, and then he said, "Why don't you write your phone number down on the receipt?" He smiled, and I thought, "He's cute enough. Maybe it's time to try a little more dating. Or at least some sex."

It might get me out of my funk. So I was just about to write down my number when he added, "You know, because sometimes I need to call the store, and I don't have your number here." I flushed but casually wrote down the store's phone number, grateful I hadn't yet written my own down. Such an idiot.

Perhaps I needed to take some advice from Alcoholics Anonymous. "Easy does it" was a key ingredient in having the right attitude. I needed to stop trying so hard. Maybe it was like childless couples who try and try to get pregnant, and it's only when they give up trying that they finally conceive.

The phone number incident wasn't the end of the idiocy for the day, however. The worst part came about an hour before I was supposed to finish my shift. We had the key to our cash drawers hanging from plastic bands around our arms, and as I finished a transaction, I pushed my drawer closed with my hip, but my key was dangling from my arm and got caught up and locked in the drawer.

There was no way to get it out, and no way to open the drawer without it. We had to break the drawer to open it, and I felt like a complete fool. Had the missionaries dusted their feet off on my doorstep? Maybe God really was starting to punish me.

If that was the case, though, then so be it. I may have been prone to guilt, but I was also prone to stubbornness. I was gay, and I was a Jew, and that's just the way it was going to be.

"Well, I hated that drawer, anyway," Cliff said. "I had already ordered a replacement for it, so I'll just go get it out of my office."

I then processed a very difficult loan flawlessly, and at the end of my shift balanced again to the penny, so I felt a little better. Guilt could bring about self-fulfilling prophecies, and if I was going to let others influence me, I needed to think more about Norman Vincent Peale. Positive thinking was something worth trying.

I got off at 5:00 that afternoon. Synagogue services started at 6:00, and though the synagogue was only a couple of blocks from work, I decided to go home first rather than sit and wait. Besides, I hadn't brought a tie or kipa to work, and I wanted to dress up for shul. I realized I didn't really "believe" in religion now as I used to as a Mormon. I saw too easily how it could be corrupted.

But I still wanted to believe at least a little. Be a part of a religious community.

When I got home, I saw a message flashing on my answering machine. I pushed the play button. "Hey, Robert," said a male voice. "This is Marty and Steven. I know this is last minute, but we were wondering if you wanted to come over and have Shabbat dinner with us tonight, say around 7:00. Give us a call if you get this message."

I smiled and then sighed. I really, really wanted Jewish friends, but I realized nothing might even come of this at all, if I acted too clingy with them. I needed to keep things in perspective. Be careful.

I called back to accept the invitation and then walked five blocks over to their house at 7:00. They had a small, two-bedroom home a couple of blocks east of Broadway up by Harrison. There were blooming purple rhododendron bushes out front and prints of a Panini painting and a Piranesi etching in their living room, plus other pieces I didn't recognize. One looked like a medieval Madonna, which seemed an odd thing for Jews to have in their home.

"I'm glad you could come," Marty said, giving me a kiss.

"Hi, sweetie," said Steven, also giving me a kiss. "I'm going to finish up here in the kitchen while Marty gives you the tour."

The house was spotlessly clean, something I could never manage, and the furniture was modern but with hints of the traditional, so it probably wouldn't be out of style in just a few years. I saw a Renoir print in one bedroom and those of a couple of other French impressionists. What looked to be an original painting of the Duomo in Florence hung in the other bedroom. In the hall was another Madonna.

"You can see we like French and Italian art," Marty said. "Jewish art is usually abstract, and we like representational. But we only have one original, a painting we bought in Florence a couple of years ago. It isn't a masterpiece, but it reminds us of good times there. We like van Gogh, too, but we find that prints don't convey enough of the beauty of the original to be worth the effort, and we obviously can't afford the real thing."

"I have three framed prints on my walls," I said. "One is a Michalopoulos print of a New Orleans scene. One is a photo of Paris, and the other is a photo of Stockholm. My three favorite cities. I may eventually have to look for a Seattle scene, and certainly New York, and maybe Tel Aviv if I ever get a chance to go there."

"Well, we're going to Israel for a week in the fall. If you want to come along, we could share a hotel room. It would make it more affordable for all of us. Think about it."

"I will."

"We better get downstairs for dinner."

Marty lit the Shabbat candles and said a prayer in Hebrew, and then Steven served us a salad, green beans, carrots, and rigatoni with a cream sauce. They had wine but I drank water. Even though I had "permission" to drink alcohol after leaving the Church, I chose not to drink, not wanting to take the chance of becoming an alcoholic.

Addiction to Mormon guilt was enough. I didn't need any more obsessions. It made me feel less authentic, but it was a decision I wanted to keep. I wondered if it was really because I still believed it was a sin. Perhaps there was no way to ever cure oneself of guilt, or of a particular cultural background, any more than of alcoholism.

"No meat, I see," I commented. "Y'all keep kosher?"

Marty shrugged. "An Orthodox Jew wouldn't think so. We don't have separate dishes for milk and meat. But we don't mix the foods at one meal. And we don't eat pork or shellfish."

"The separate dishes didn't evolve for hundreds of years after the Torah was written," Steven pointed out, "so we don't feel it's necessarily a part of truly keeping kosher. Lots of things that have been around for hundreds of years haven't been around for thousands, and even those which have been around for thousands still haven't been there right from the beginning, so we kind of make our own rules."

"A lot of people would think we're bad Jews," Marty went on. "We like being Jews, but we also like to have minds of our own. I suppose we're 'cafeteria' Jews, picking and choosing what we want to believe, but I think God wants us to pick and choose, to truly evaluate things and not just follow blindly. Any child can follow blindly. God wants mature followers who can think."

I nodded. "Well, you're way more Jewish than I am," I said, while still feeling immeasurably more comfortable with this message than that of Osgood and Stuart.

"Don't say that." Marty shook his head. "You have to determine for yourself what makes a good Jew. Don't let others tell you what to believe about yourself." I nodded, thinking that this was exactly what I'd done as a Mormon. It was like continually taking out payday loans, always investing more and more into a company that only functioned if I forced myself deeper and deeper into debt. I didn't need to do the same thing as a Jew.

We talked of other things then, about two more drowned, decayed bodies being found in an attic in New Orleans this week, about the 2001 earthquake in Seattle, about the ongoing mess in Iraq, and about the upcoming trip to Israel. It would be so extravagant to go along given my present income, but I had a little saved up, and sometimes, you just had to do things even if it wasn't practical. I'd have to put in a vacation request as soon as they settled on a date.

After dinner, we retired to the living room to chat some more. Steven said they had another single Jewish friend named Gary who hadn't come to the seder, but they might try to get us to meet sometime. Marty told me how he and Steven met seven years earlier at a used book store looking through the mysteries.

Then Steven pulled out a DVD of *Walk on Water*, an Israeli movie I hadn't seen, and we watched that. Finally, around 10:30, I hugged and kissed them both and walked home, feeling better than I had in a long time. Eight months wasn't long, but it sure felt long without a solid circle of friends.

Back home tonight, I emailed Tom again, and my friends in New Orleans, and my Swedish friends, but then I decided to look on the gay site for guys in Israel. It might make the trip there more interesting if I did decide to go, and even if I didn't, I wanted a stronger connection to Israel. Just donating to plant trees there every year wasn't enough. Perhaps having friends might help. I wrote to a Dubi, an Ari, and a Chayim and I figured that was a good start.

Then I went on Craigslist and started looking through the job ads. I submitted four resumes and made a commitment to myself to send out four more each day until I had a job where I didn't have to be a predator.

I went in my bedroom, lightly touching my mezuzah as I walked in, and then undressed and climbed in bed. I read a little more of *Jurassic Park* in Swedish before putting on my one good Jewish CD, of the Effi Netzer singers. I turned out the light and listened to music as I slowly fell asleep.

Vampires of the Blood Atonement

It was nearing the end of Tisha B'Av and Chayim hadn't spoken to me all day. I was fasting along with him, as I did for Yom Kippur every year, too. He never recognized the sacrifice, or empathy, or emotional support, or whatever else one might call my participation. It was only natural I'd follow the commandment to fast, he told me, even if I wasn't a real Jew, simply because it was the right thing to do. So there was nothing for him to acknowledge, other than the fact that I wasn't observing each of the remaining 613 commandments as well.

Still, we'd made it through almost eighteen years together despite our religious differences. But Chayim had kept his distance all day today, wouldn't talk about the destruction of the temple, wouldn't even spend time reading the Talmud with me as we usually did on Sundays. We'd missed most of the weekend already, but I hoped we could still salvage the evening once the sun went down.

I opened the door of my mother-in-law cottage and looked toward the main house. No visible sign of life. I hesitantly approached the bedroom window, feeling like Count Yorga, but decided to be a man and head for the back entrance instead. When I tried the knob, of course, I discovered the door was locked. I took a deep breath and knocked.

After waiting almost two minutes, I knocked again, more loudly. Thirty seconds later, the door opened with a jerk.

"You know I don't like you coming to my house, Nathan." He tugged nervously on his long, bushy beard.

"There are no Hasidim spying on us right now."

"You don't know that."

I thought about the campus police at Brigham Young writing down license plate numbers at gay bars. I remembered a friend in my student ward who was brought to the Honor Code office for helping carry an overstuffed chair into his girlfriend's apartment. He'd apparently been alone with her for over ten minutes, and his roommate reported him. But Mormons had nothing on the ultra-Orthodox.

"Chayim, what's wrong? Something's wrong."

Chayim quickly surveyed the back yard and then ushered me into the house. Normally, I wasn't allowed past the kitchen. I'd only seen the living room half a dozen times since we'd pulled down all the blinds and stood under our own chuppah all those years ago. Most of the walls were covered with bookshelves containing thousands of books, most in Hebrew but many in English, plus a handful in Yiddish.

The only artwork was a copy of his framed ketubah from his first marriage. Rivka had died twenty years ago while giving birth to their second child, who also died. His firstborn then died six months later of pneumonia. Chayim and I had met another six months after that tragedy in a support group. I was mourning the loss of my entire family as well.

They'd cut off all contact when I came out as gay and was excommunicated from the Mormon Church. I supposed to them I was the one who was "dead," or perhaps "undead," since I was still walking about, but they weren't the ones in mourning—I was. Chayim was one of the few members of the group who understood my need to come to the meetings.

A year later, after I moved into the mother-in-law, Chayim painted our own ketubah and hung it over my sofa. None of his friends were allowed into my apartment, and I was never allowed to speak to any other Hasidim when they came to visit Chayim in his home. If anyone asked, I was "the lodger" who also turned on any lights or appliances for him on the Sabbath.

Standing in the sanctuary of the living room, I wanted to give him a kiss, but I could sense something in the air, something heavier than leftover incense from yesterday's Havdalah. I felt like Christopher Lee in one of the Hammer films we liked to watch late on Saturday night after the Sabbath was over.

Dracula about to be destroyed by holy water or sunlight...or maybe this time by a Magen David. We'd huddle under a tallit, feeling a little thrill at the irreverence, and watched the scary movie. I always felt safe in his arms.

Chayim touched the top of his kipa now as if to adjust it and then motioned for me to sit on the sofa. I sat on one end and he sat on the other, with a space between us. On the coffee table, open, was the Tractate Sanhedrin Part IV, the eighteenth volume of the Steinsaltz edition. We'd gone through one volume each year we'd been together.

He was studying Talmud today without me.

"Have you met someone else?" I asked softly. He spent so much of his time with other Chabadniks.

Chayim closed his eyes and lowered his head. "You know I would never do that."

"Then what?" I asked and, after an awkward pause, added, "Is it the sex?" I'd had myself circumcised for him back at the beginning. I'd become a Reform Jew before he would agree to marry me, and I'd immersed myself in the Orthodox mikvah before Shabbat every week since then so I'd be ready for Sabbath sex. The mikvah was really about purifying women, but gay Jews had to adapt as best they could. Hasidim lived by rules, and when there weren't any, Chayim just made something up.

"Yes," he said. "Yes, it's the sex."

Even though I'd suspected it, I still felt as if I'd been slapped. I always did everything Chayim wanted in bed. And out of bed, too. I'd legally changed my name from Henry to Nathan. I'd left my job as a bus driver and started cooking at a kosher deli just to make sure I knew the rules. I'd studied both spoken and written Hebrew, though I still used the dots when I read alone in my room. I sang songs it took me years to understand, learned a dozen prayers, even paid for a handwritten scroll to put in the mezuzah on my front doorpost.

Of course, I just pretended to insert scrolls in all my other mezuzot. I had to draw the line somewhere.

I thought of all the hoops I'd jumped through to appease my parents and the Church. Seminary, a mission to Singapore, a religion degree from BYU so I could start teaching for the Church Educational System. In the end, one could never jump through enough hoops. I'd thought things would be different if I moved to Atlanta.

"Nathan," he said, "it's not you. It's the book."

"You can't be serious." He'd sold fewer than two thousand copies.

He shook his head. "It's being reviewed in Jewish papers everywhere."

I tried not to feel dismissive. Chayim had always been a bit self-important—"There will be no minyan if I don't show up!"—but whatever extra attention he was getting now was screwing up my life, so I had to take it seriously. "It'll pass," I said. "I'll just lie low for a while."

He moved toward me and grabbed my hand. "The book's been nominated for the National Jewish Book Award."

My mouth fell open. Chayim's *Anne Frank after Fifteen* detailed what Anne's life might have been like had she survived the Shoah, and by extension, what the millions of others killed might have done with their own lives. I personally found the writing a bit pedestrian but certainly never said so to Chayim. The only truly remarkable scene in the entire novel was one where as an adult living in Israel, Anne hid some Palestinians in her home during a tense two-week period in the 1970's.

I doubted the real Anne Frank would have ever moved to Israel.

"Okay," I said slowly, "then we just need to be careful until the winner is announced. If it's not you, things will get back to normal. I…I can move out for a few months."

"We can't be together any more at all," Chayim said, "whether anyone else ever reads that book or not."

"But why?" I looked at the velvet tefillin bag on the end table, filled with leather boxes and leather straps. I thought of my garments, which I still wore on days I knew Chayim wouldn't be asking for sex. "I'll become Conservative," I said. "Orthodox."

Chayim brushed back the hair from my forehead and gently kissed me.

"Ani ohev otkha," I said.

He nodded. "I love you, too." He sighed. "But I also love Judaism. Even more." I watched him close his eyes in response to the look on my face. "Ahava hi pashut ahava. Hi af pa'am lo musberet."

The same thing we'd always told ourselves to justify our relationship.

"Like Anne says in my book, 'We don't get a pass because of what we've suffered. We're held to a higher standard instead.'"

It was what I'd always heard at church, too. Every religion had *some* truth, we were taught, but Latter-day Saints had it all, and therefore the Lord expected more of us. "I'll start looking for a new apartment right away."

"Todah."

I leaned to give him one last kiss, but he shook his head. I nodded, exited out the back door, and walked across the yard to my apartment. Standing in my tiny living room, I stared at our ketubah, wondering if I should take it with me or leave it behind. If I didn't pack it, Chayim would need to destroy it. I took it off the wall and set it on the kitchen table.

I spent the next hour or so pacing back and forth from the living room to the bedroom to the bathroom to the kitchen and back over and over again. Chayim had forbidden me from hanging any representational artwork, just as he refused to display any in his own home. I had two framed prints featuring quotes I liked hanging on either side of the ketubah.

One of them said, "To be kind is more important than to be right," and the other reminded me that, "If you are not a better person tomorrow than you are today, what need have you for a tomorrow?"

Thoughts could be as beautiful as images.

There was no point delaying the inevitable, so I sat at my computer and started looking for an apartment. I found one closer to the deli and sent an email asking the landlord for an appointment at his earliest convenience. He called not fifteen minutes later, and even though it was almost 6:30 already, he asked if I could come see the apartment right then.

A desperate landlord could be a good thing. I drove over, took a look at the place, and signed the lease on the spot. I was even able to negotiate free basic cable. I handed over a check for the deposit and another for the first month's rent, but the landlord promised not to put them in his account until he'd finished his credit check on me.

The place was tiny, and right next door to a convenience store with bars on its windows, but the interior was clean and sufficient for my needs. I went back to my mother-in-law and plopped down on the sofa. That couldn't have gone better if directed by HaShem himself.

I guessed I could start calling God Heavenly Father again.

I turned on the television and began flipping through channels. I wasn't in the mood for *Little House on the Prairie* or *Mr. Selfridge* or an infomercial on how to make my skin look younger. *Ice Road Truckers* was on The Weather Channel. The truckers this week were having problems with the melting permafrost. I wanted to watch my DVD of *The Vampire Lovers* again with Chayim. We rarely enjoyed any vampire movies made after the early 1970's and certainly didn't like the Mormon-inspired vampires of the Twilight series.

But we'd loved *The Brides of Dracula* and watched it over and over. Chayim and I had even once made a dubbed version of the movie, which we renamed *The Husbands of Dracula*. He'd felt so guilt-ridden over the emotional slip into polyandry that he insisted I go to the mikvah two weeks in a row untouched before he considered me pure enough again that he could allow himself to come over and fuck me.

I wanted a copy of our recording, but I expected Chayim had already destroyed it. Just like I'd destroyed my Annie Lennox CD back in the 1990's when trying to rededicate myself to the Church as a teenager. I remembered the album had been released on April 6, so I'd felt the Lord must have approved of it.

Until my Young Men's teacher told me the music was unacceptable for the singer's hairstyle alone, much less for her mannish personality. It wouldn't do to sell the CD, as it would then just corrupt someone else. It had to be destroyed altogether. I understood fully what Chayim was doing with our marriage.

In all the years since, I'd never bought another copy of that CD, with its great "Why" and "Walking on Broken Glass." When I heard the song on the radio these days, all I could think of was Kristallnacht.

I vaguely remembered there also being a track on that album about vampires. Maybe I'd mail a copy to Chayim anonymously on his next birthday so he'd know he was still loved.

Or maybe it was finally time to look ahead. I needed to make arrangements for the move. Perhaps Tuesday or Wednesday after work. I'd just about depleted my bank account with the checks to the new landlord, and I didn't have many friends who could help me. I wasn't close to anyone at Temple Sinai or at the deli. It was too hard to avoid mentioning Chayim, so it was best not to talk to anyone at all.

I wondered…

Back in the day, the Elders Quorum had always helped members of the congregation move. Did Mormons still do that? If Chayim was rededicating himself to God, perhaps I should do so as well. It might be a way of keeping us on the same page, even if in different books. Perhaps I could even find a single mother, someone who'd had children before joining the Church, so her ex wouldn't still be sealed to them. I could have a wife and kids sealed to me for all eternity.

The possibilities excited me. Until I realized there was no way any sane person would rely on a sandwich maker to support them. And no sane person would still believe everything the Mormon Church commanded in the first place.

If I'd learned anything at all over the years, it was that people were not inanimate objects to fill holes in one's life. Though to be honest, I'd met my fair share of dildos at church in my Single Adult days.

So I was probably facing a lifetime of celibacy, but I'd spent the last eighteen years without friends. Perhaps now I could have friends in place of sex.

One thing or another was always going to suck some of the joy out of life, no matter which path I chose. Might as well be Mormon again. At least I understood the rules there. I wanted community in my life, even if the community wasn't fully accepting. Despite reading three hundred books on Judaism and attending Torah Study and services both Friday evening and Saturday morning, I still felt like a stranger even in the least strict version of the faith.

I could simply never learn enough. I was always getting things wrong. But Mormons believed in "milk before meat." Nothing was ever very complicated to master there.

I looked up the phone number for the nearest ward and left a message. Then I took one of the knitted kipot Chayim had given me one year for our anniversary and beat off into it before climbing into bed.

The next morning around 10:30, just after concluding a sale, I received a call from the missionaries. I sneaked into the back of the deli and answered. "I used to be a member and now I'm returning to the fold," I explained. "So I want you to baptize me, but I also need to see if the bishop can get anyone to help me move to get away from a sinful situation." I paused to see if there'd be a reaction. There wasn't.

"I only have a bed," I continued, "a sofa, a table and chairs, and a dresser. Oh, and an end table." Books were among the most miserable things to move, but almost all the books I'd read in the last several years were those I "checked out" of Chayim's personal library. Really just whatever he brought over and assigned me to read.

"No one can help tonight because of Family Home Evening," said Elder Carter, apparently the senior companion, "but Elder Casterlin and I need to get in our service hours this week, so we can call a couple of members and help you tomorrow night. Will that do?"

"Sure, thanks!"

"And afterward, we'll teach you the first lesson."

I laughed. "I expect I can still recite all eight myself."

"See you tomorrow at 6:00?"

I gave them my address and hurried back to my sandwiches. Just after noon, Bishop Littleton called. "I'd like to talk with you in my office," he said. "How's Wednesday at 7:30? I expect we have some serious issues to discuss."

"Yes, Bishop." Another interview about sex and masturbation. Did I have a lifetime of that ahead of me again? To whom did I confess that I was tired of confessing?

"You should know I'm a professional therapist trained in counseling," he went on, and for the first time, I wondered if God was behind all this unexpected tumult in my life. Perhaps everything had led me to this point right now so I could finally get the direction I needed. I felt a sudden sense of relief and comfort that I'd only ever known back when I was a Mormon.

"Wonderful," I said. "I think I need some real counseling." I laughed.

"Fantastic, fantastic. I'll give you my card when you come in Wednesday, and we'll make an appointment for you to come down to the clinic. If you're struggling financially, we can always work out a payment plan." He laughed, too. "We'll have your blessings restored quicker than you can say 'flip.'"

Or before I could run back to Sinai. At this rate, I'd be rebaptized within a week or two. I'd had to take a year-long Intro to Judaism class before my rabbi would even consider letting me become a Jew by Choice.

The rest of the day, Sandra, the woman who worked with me behind the counter, kept nudging me to get moving again. I would stop what I was doing and start staring at the pastrami on rye and the corned beef. I would linger over the chopped liver and stuffed cabbage, the blintzes and kreplach, the knishes and kugel. But it wasn't as if I were quitting my job,

I reminded myself, just Chayim. I'd still make the knoblewurst every day, have a herring for lunch.

At least I could finally stop worrying about trying to like gefilte fish, though, the nastiest dish known to man. And there was no reason, I supposed, that I couldn't start looking for a Gentile job when I had a chance.

Plus, I could look forward to ward socials serving scalloped potatoes and lime jello. Comfort food. It was comforting to think about.

After work, I parked down the block from Chayim's house as usual and walked past it directly to my cottage. Once inside, I went straight to my closet, untaped a box hidden in the farthest corner, and removed the lid. I pulled out my highlighted triple combination, fingering my name in gold lettering on the leather cover. I dug out my copies of *No Man Knows My History* and *Blood Atonement and the Origin of Plural Marriage*. Books which had led me to forego a career of teaching Church history.

A career, I realized in retrospect, that probably paid about the same as making matzoh ball soup did now.

I called up the missionaries and asked if they were available tonight despite all other Mormons being asked to turn off their televisions and cell phones and computers. "I never had Family Home Evening with the members while I was on my mission," I said, "but things may have changed in the last couple of decades."

"No, we're free," Elder Carter said excitedly. "Would you like us to come teach you this evening?"

"Have you eaten yet?"

"No."

"You guys up for a free meal?"

"Are you kidding! What time?"

The elders looked so young when they arrived that my first thought was they'd sent the deacons to collect fast offerings instead. I expected Chayim had seen the young men walk past his house in their white shirts and ties and wasn't pleased, but their presence could only strengthen his alibi that there was nothing between us, so I didn't let it bother me. Elder Carter and Elder Casterlin shook my hand, and then I invited them to the kitchen table. They sat, looking at their plates filled with kasha and tzimmes.

"It's all good. Really."

They glanced at their six-inch long dill pickles on the side. I never was very good at balanced meals. I ate what I wanted to eat, as much as I could while still trying to feel like a Jew. Since I was inviting the missionaries over, though, I had no idea why I didn't just prepare macaroni and cheese. Or hot dogs and fries.

"Well, uh, since this is your home, Brother Hamer, why don't you offer the blessing?" Elder Carter gave me an encouraging nod.

I suddenly remembered the overwhelming condescension of the Church. At least when Jews looked down on me for not being knowledgeable about religious etiquette, they were usually right.

I started right into the Mezonot and followed immediately with the Ha-adamah. I realized we were supposed to eat some of the kasha before moving on to the second blessing for the vegetables, but there was no way these guys were going to call me on it. In fact, the elders looked at me as if I'd just forced them to partake in a Satanic ritual.

Soon, I'd be wearing a green apron and a baker's hat as I stood in a prayer circle making secret handshakes with the people on either side of me.

"Dig in," I said. "We can talk about the Church while we eat."

Elder Carter picked at the onions in his kasha, and Elder Casterlin looked suspiciously at his carrots and yams.

"Look, guys, I made the least offensive dishes I could. Just taste it."

They did so and seemed to resign themselves to their fate. This apparently took so much concentration, however, that they remained silent for the next few minutes.

"You need to know I'm gay," I said. "I've had sex with three different men and been in a monogamous relationship with the last one for eighteen years."

Elder Carter, who was taking a break from his kasha for a moment by switching to his pickle, paused halfway into a bite.

"Did…did you repent?" Elder Casterlin managed.

"I know I'm not allowed to have sex anymore," I replied, "but I can't honestly say I understand why. If Joseph Smith can have thirty-three wives, I'm not sure why I can't have just the one husband."

"But Joseph only married those other women to make sure they were provided for," said Elder Carter. "He didn't have sex with them."

There was no need to get into a debate, I told myself. With a degree in Church history, my pointing out the truth would be like forcing Jews to dig their own graves. That steadfast milk before meat mentality kept members from asking the most basic of follow-up questions. "If he married the women and young girls just to provide for them," I said, "wasn't that rather cruel?"

"Huh?"

"He's condemning them to a lifetime without sexual or emotional intimacy, condemning them to a lifetime with no children of their own, all just to make sure they have food and a place to stay."

The elders looked at each other.

"Why not just give them food and a place to stay because it's the kind thing to do," I pressed, "without the accompanying chains?" So much for not arguing. But I supposed it was impossible to study Talmud for so many years without enjoying a little argument now and then. I tried to divert the conversation from Mormon doctrine to Jewish history, explaining a little about Sukkot, Pesach, and Purim. Plus my favorite holiday, Tu B'Shevat.

The elders allowed the conversation while they concentrated on their food, but as soon as Elder Carter finished his last bite, he said, "We aren't here to learn. We're called to teach."

"Okay. Teach me something about Jews."

"We're here to talk about Jesus."

"Jesus was a Jew. So were the Nephites and Lamanites."

Elder Carter and Elder Casterlin exchanged glances again. Perhaps I was being a jerk, I thought, taking a long sip of water to shut myself up. People often said Jews were obnoxious. I realized uneasily I was being just as domineering over them as Chayim had been with me. I was just going to be quiet now and listen to whatever they wanted to say.

"Yes, the Jews and the Nephites and the Mormons have all faced persecution for our commitment to the Lord. Jews may have the Holocaust, but we have Haun's Mill. We all understand what it is to be committed to our faith." He continued on as I bit my tongue. It was true, I suppose, that Mormons had sometimes been accused of human sacrifice in their temples, but they never faced anything like the Blood Libel.

I remembered Anne Frank writing in her diary that while many various groups had been oppressed throughout the ages, there was something different about the suffering of the Jews. That diary passage made her insistence on establishing a Palestinian state many years later a provocative ending to Chayim's novel, despite the scene being handled too quickly and superficially.

Chayim thought he was being so mature and daring, and he'd refused even to address the likelihood that Anne was at the very least bisexual.

When the elders finally finished the lesson by bearing their testimonies, I asked if Elder Casterlin could say the closing prayer. The familiar, bland words left me feeling a bit melancholy, and I watched them walk out to the street. I lingered at my door, looking at the soft light emanating from Chayim's bedroom window.

The next morning, I almost ruined a batch of bagels, but Sandra stepped in and saved them in time. By mid-afternoon, she was looking concerned. "You go on home," she said. "I'll cover for you. It's a slow day anyway."

I grabbed all the empty boxes I could find from the back of the deli, just as I'd done the day before, and went home to finish packing. Most of my clothes were already in the dresser and could be transported in the drawers, and the remaining clothes from my closet fit in just a handful of boxes. I'd bought some packing paper on the way home last night and now put my dishes in a few more boxes.

I didn't have two sets like Chayim did, and last night was the first time I'd invited anyone over to eat in years, so there had never been any need to house very many. Another two boxes for food, and I was ready for the elders to show up with whatever members they were able to guilt into helping.

It seemed as if every religion relied heavily on guilt.

Was that the best God could do?

The missionaries knocked on my door first. Soon after, two men from the Elders Quorum arrived with their pick-up trucks, a Brother Petrie and a Brother Carlson. With me carrying a few things in the back seat of my own car, we only had to make one trip to the new apartment. I handed each of the four helpers a two-liter bottle of 7-Up as a thank you.

The married men headed back to their families, and the missionaries moved a box off the sofa and immediately began to teach me another lesson. I of course knew the correct way to answer their loaded questions, and the evening advanced smoothly. After I gave the closing prayer "in the name of Jesus Christ," the elders visibly relaxed.

Their vulnerable faces reminded me how lonely mission life could be, and I thought maybe we should spend a few minutes just chatting. Missionaries lived to recount exciting anecdotes in their emails home to prove their missions were worthwhile.

My biggest thrill had usually been trying to smuggle copies of the Book of Mormon across the border without being arrested.

"Are you enjoying your mission?" I asked.

The elders looked at each other quickly. "The numbers aren't great. But it's the quality that counts, not the quantity."

"Happy to be of service," I said. I couldn't help but feel a little saddened that I was the best they could do. "Living up to expectations can be hard." I didn't expect it would be helpful to share my own experience and bring up the dishonest way the elders all used to travel back and forth between Singapore, Malaysia, and Brunei in our search for investigators.

Or the missionaries who were jailed for a few days or kicked out of the country permanently for lying at the airport. One border guard called me a "blood-sucking leech" when he realized I wasn't really there to "visit friends," but he didn't want to be bothered with the paperwork and let me through. At the time, I'd honestly thought I was being brave going undercover for the Lord.

"I had my name put on the prayer roll at the temple," said Elder Carter, "and the very next day you called."

"The Lord works in mysterious ways," I said and they both smiled.

I didn't like being a service project, so I kept asking the missionaries questions about their lives back home. Elder Carter talked about one of the Boy Scout leaders being excommunicated, though no one knew why. This led Elder Casterlin to mention how the Teachers Quorum instructor in his ward had just stopped coming to church one day and would never explain his reason.

"The Boy Scouts and Teachers Quorum?" I said, trying not to sound like a middle-aged man. "I keep forgetting you guys weren't even old enough to be part of the Single Adults group before you left home."

"Well, we've been through the temple," Elder Carter said a little defensively. "Taking the same oaths they did in Solomon's temple. That makes us real men."

I stopped and took a long look into their adolescent faces. I wasn't at all sure I was going to be able to do this. The vacuum in their personalities was sucking the life right out of me. But where else was I to go? I couldn't stay with Jews because of our vastly different levels of knowledge and belief, but if I couldn't be with Mormons for the same reasons, what was left? Perhaps I should I try spending time with Episcopalians. Or Catholics. Or Buddhists. Without converting to anything else this time. They could know what they knew and I could know what I knew.

Or maybe it was best just keeping to myself. After all, I was pretty used to that already.

But a solitary dog chained in the back yard wasn't the same as a dog running free, with or without a pack.

I stood up. "I'm going to be busy the next couple of nights, so why don't I call you when it's time to set up our next appointment?"

"You aren't bailing on us, are you?" Elder Carter asked, his eyes narrowing. "Getting us to help you move by saying you'd be rebaptized and now going back on your word?" He looked at his companion.

I gave him a tight smile in return. "I thought you needed to get in your service hours anyway."

He didn't answer as he and his companion picked up their soda bottles and left. I leaned against the closed door for a long moment, wondering what to do. They were damned irritating, but I *had* promised, hadn't I? May as well give them their stats, even if I stopped going to church the following week. Who was hurt by that?

Somehow, though, I couldn't help wondering when I was finally going to start doing things for myself and not just to please others. What did *I* want? It was way too pathetic that I didn't know the answer. A moment later, there was a knock at the door. The missionaries were apparently back for a last, withering word. I'd let them deliver it. What did I have to lose? I opened the door.

"Brother Petrie," I said, surprised. "Did you forget something?"

He nodded, and I motioned him inside with a frown. As soon as the door was closed, he immediately pulled me toward him and thrust his tongue into my mouth. He must have been waiting outside all this time for the elders to leave. Brother Petrie grabbed my hand and placed it on the crotch of his jeans. I luxuriated in the passion of his kiss and the hardness beneath the denim, but after a moment, I pulled back.

"I don't have much time," he said. "I need to get home." He reached forward to unzip my pants.

Oh saya Astaga. Another lifetime of closets.

"Brother Petrie," I said, "when the divorce is final, feel free to stop by again."

He gave me a puzzled expression at first, an expression which quickly changed into one of anger. "Faggot!" he said. He yanked open the door and walked out.

Faggots were the kindling used to burn Jews at the stake in the Middle Ages. Homosexuals were usually just hanged.

Mormon apostates, however, were either shot, stabbed, or had their throats slit back in Brigham Young's day. Death alone wouldn't suffice. Heretics could only atone for their sins through the spilling of their blood.

I hung up some of my clothes, put a stack of dishes away, and lined up a few of my DVDs on a built-in shelf in the living room. I carried some toiletries into the bathroom and set my alarm clock on top of my bedside table. The rest could wait until tomorrow after I returned from the deli. Just as I was stripping to get ready for bed, my cell phone rang. I looked at the number. Chayim. I felt my heart skip a beat and picked up.

"Hi, neshama," he said. "I miss you already."

I didn't say anything.

"Maybe…" he went on, "maybe in a few months, you can move back in. I won't rent out the cottage. Maybe…maybe we could still get together once in a while."

I still didn't say anything. I didn't know what to say.

"Are you busy right now?" he asked, sounding a little more confident. "I could come over and fuck you." He giggled in embarrassment. "I cut a hole in the middle of an old tallit. I can—"

"I love you, Chayim," I said softly, "but I love myself, too." I took a breath and said what I had to say. "Shalom."

I hit "End Call," set the phone next to my alarm clock, and took off the rest of my clothes. I filled the tub as deep as I dared and then dunked myself, holding my breath as long as possible.

Then I stood up and let the water slowly drip off my body. After toweling myself dry, I put on a pair of clean garments, lay on the freshly made bed, and looked about. This was my home now. I'd hang up my two framed quotes, add a few photographs of stately trees, and send my old framed ketubah to the gay archive in Los Angeles.

I closed my eyes and concentrated until I could see my favorite mission companion clearly in my mind, the day he showed me how he learned to suck dick while in jail. Then I beat myself off vigorously, shouting "I'm coming!" in three completely unrelated languages.

The Golem of Rabbi Loew

Rabbi Judah Loew was a lonely man. This was partly because he was the chief rabbi of Prague, and great men are always kept at a distance by those who admire them. People are a little afraid of these men. Part of it, too, was because he was very intelligent, and while also humble, he often found it difficult to commune with the masses. And part of it was because his wife, Pearl, while a diligent homemaker and mother, was simply not the love of his life.

Rabbi Loew had five children and loved them all. But Pearl spent more of her time with them than he did. He spent much of his time in classes with his students instead. His oldest daughter, Miriam, had married the best student, a dedicated young man named Isaac, and Rabbi Loew loved Isaac as well.

But this was where the trouble began. Rabbi Loew felt such a deep kinship with his son-in-law and spent such a great deal of time with him that he began feeling lonelier than ever.

What Rabbi Loew wanted was to spend his nights as well as his days with a man like Isaac.

Rabbi Loew knew that what he wanted was a terrible sin. The Torah said so. Thus, the rabbi prayed fervently for many months to be delivered of his evil passion.

But one day, in the early part of 1560, something else terrible happened that would change the rabbi's life forever, and the lives of those in his community.

"Rabbi, have you heard?" It was Yudl, the blacksmith.

"What is it, Yudl?"

"They say that a small gentile boy is missing. They say the Jews have killed him to put his blood in the matzoh for Pesach tomorrow. They say they are going to search the ghetto until they find the boy. What are we to do?"

Rabbi Loew frowned. This was not the first time the Blood Libel had afflicted his people. On many occasions, dozens of Jews were killed in revenge for these supposed murders. How was he to protect his people this time?

"I will pray to heaven, and our Maker will deliver us."

"Rabbi, Pesach begins tomorrow. The raids could commence at any moment."

"We will be delivered."

Rabbi Loew closed the door to his study and prayed. He had prayed this passionately before, for God to send him a golem. The rabbi had asked for a soulless man to be brought to life, just for him, someone he could be with but whose soul would have already departed, so that the rabbi could not corrupt him as he might a living man. Rabbi Loew felt that in this manner, he could have the company he so desired, without sinning quite so much, and without causing another Jew to sin as well.

The rabbi's studies told him that a man taking part in a sexual relationship with another man was not forbidden so much because it was a sinful act in itself, but because God wanted to distinguish the Jews from other peoples. But for whatever reason, if it was forbidden, Rabbi Loew would not do it, unless God could send him a man without a soul, and he prayed for a miracle every day.

But now Rabbi Loew doubled his efforts. He prayed even more fervently for his people to be protected from their current threat.

When Pearl climbed up later to announce that the evening meal was ready, Rabbi Loew sent her away and continued his prayers. He must receive an answer before morning.

He prayed hour after hour, sending his pleas to heaven. Finally, though, he fell asleep on the rough floor of his study.

But there, he had a dream. He would find a lifeless man on the bank of the Moldau River, and he would write the letters EMET on the man's forehead with clay from the ground, and spelling "Truth" in such a manner would bring the man to life. This golem would help protect the Jews.

It wasn't the exact golem the rabbi wanted, but he knew it was more important to save the community than to appease his personal desires.

Because the Jews were not allowed outside the ghetto during the nighttime hours, Rabbi Loew waited anxiously until morning before taking Isaac with him to the river's edge. They did indeed find a large dead body on the bank, just as the rabbi knew they would.

Isaac put his hand on Rabbi Loew's arm. "Father, we should leave quickly. If we are found beside this dead man…"

"Do not fear. It is the will of heaven. I have dreamed it. Look at the yellow circle on his sleeve. He is one of us. This man will help deliver the Jews of Prague."

Isaac looked at his father-in-law worriedly but did not dare contradict the man. Rabbi Loew knelt beside the corpse and dug his finger into the mud next to him. He carefully wrote upon the man's forehead and then leaned down over the man.

He'd hoped for such a long time for a golem to be his companion that he desired terribly to kiss the still figure, even with Isaac looking on. He touched his lips to those of the dead man, and then an inspiration came upon him. He forced his breath into the mouth of the man. He did it again and again as Isaac gasped beside him.

But then the golem coughed and opened his eyes.

"May the heavens save me!" Isaac said fearfully. "You've brought a man to life. You've breathed life into him, just as God did with Adam."

Rabbi Loew looked up at Isaac, who was staring at him in awe.

"It was God's breath coming through me. I'm no Creator. But this man will be a Savior to us."

"A Savior? Is this the Messiah?"

"No, Isaac. Just a man to help us in these difficult times."

The man on the embankment was looking up wonderingly at Rabbi Loew. The rabbi felt a sudden wave of compassion for the soulless creature who was sent to serve him and the other Jews of Prague. He brushed his hand across the man's forehead and nodded kindly at him.

"Come, Isaac, let us help this man to rise."

The two men put a hand under each of the hulking man's shoulders and helped him to an upright position. The man sat looking around in confusion.

"What is your name?" the rabbi asked gently. He expected the man no longer had a name, but he wanted to be sure.

The man stared at him.

"From whence do you come?" asked Isaac. "Can we help you to your home?"

The man stared but said nothing.

"Can you speak?" asked Rabbi Loew uncertainly. He hadn't expected that, but perhaps without a soul, the body was incapable of speech.

The man looked at him a moment and then slowly shook his head.

"But you can hear me?" the rabbi asked.

The man looked at him another moment and then nodded slowly.

"May God preserve us!" breathed Isaac.

"That is exactly what shall happen," said Rabbi Loew. He turned back to the man. "Your name is Joseph. You will live with me. But we need you to assist us."

The man looked at the rabbi and again nodded.

Rabbi Loew explained the danger the Jews were facing and told Joseph he must inspect every cart and bundle that came into the ghetto that day. The rabbi suddenly suspected that one golem would not be enough, but then he repented of his doubts. God had sent this creature, and God would help the man do what must be done.

Rabbi Loew stayed with Joseph all day. There was more than one road into the ghetto, and the rabbi was not secure in his knowledge of which entry to monitor. He prayed and felt that it was the main entrance which carried the danger, and he posted Joseph there and then stood off to the side and watched.

Joseph moved as if he had inspected carts all his life. Since his life had begun only that morning, perhaps it was true. Without a word, Joseph stopped every cart that approached the ghetto, and every person carrying a bundle. Every merchant instinctively feared his huge presence, and each meekly allowed Joseph to search his belongings.

Joseph searched cart after cart throughout the day, and bundle after bundle, but he let everyone pass into the ghetto. The afternoon sun was sinking low in the sky, and Pesach would soon begin. Would Joseph be able to prevent a disaster?

Just then, Joseph turned to look at Rabbi Loew and gave him the slightest hint of a smile. Rabbi Loew's heart began beating a little faster, and he suddenly knew that all would be well.

Late in the afternoon, two Gentiles entered the ghetto with a cart on which lay the carcass of a pig. What were those men doing bringing something so unclean into the Jewish neighborhood? Most Gentiles traveled around the ghetto rather than through it, even if entering the ghetto would shorten their journey. It irritated Rabbi Loew that these men were bringing swine among his people, even if their final destination lay elsewhere. It was a deliberate offense, one the rabbi had not witnessed before. He wanted to be charitable yet felt his muscles tense.

He wanted to hurry the scowling men along, but Joseph stopped their cart as he had everyone else's. Rabbi Loew felt the tiniest flash of irritation. It was possible to be too dedicated. People had said it of the rabbi as well. And anyone could see at a glance there was no place to hide a dead child in this cart.

At least the golem was thorough, however. Rabbi Loew supposed it would not hurt to slow these goyim in their journey, annoy them just enough that they would choose a different route the next time.

But what was Joseph doing now? He seemed to be prying into the carcass itself. He would need to go into the mikvah to purify himself before he could partake of the seder this evening.

Rabbi Loew watched as Joseph reached his hand into the belly of the pig and slowly pulled out a child's arm. He continued tugging, and the arm was followed by the body of a young child.

"Stop! Cease what you are doing!" shouted one of the goyim.

The other man began running, but there were several onlookers, and Rabbi Loew quickly ordered them to grab hold of the two men. Then he sent Shmuel, the fishmonger, to run and bring back a watchman. The rabbi was fearful that any officers of the law would believe whatever story the men concocted, but when two men arrived a few minutes later, they saw the evidence clearly and took the two criminals away, with their heads hanging down in despair.

The rabbi, however, was experiencing great joy. "Joseph! Joseph! You have saved us! Let us hurry now to the mikvah and then let us enjoy the wonderful seder Pearl has prepared for us!"

Rabbi Loew grasped Joseph by the hand and led him through the streets until they arrived at the mikvah. He told Joseph to undress and did the same, and they both stepped into the pool of water and immersed themselves.

Rabbi Loew looked over at Joseph, who seemed a near perfect example of God's supreme creation. The rabbi remembered his sinful desire for a golem to grant him the company he craved, but he had to admit that the Master of the Universe had seen the truer need that existed for a golem, to serve all the people and not merely the rabbi.

Rabbi Loew looked again at Joseph sitting beside him in the water. Perhaps simply being able to cleanse themselves in the mikvah together regularly would be all the company the rabbi would need. He already sensed a deep kinship with this man. Purifying themselves together was a closeness he'd never felt before with anyone. God had answered his prayers, after all, as well as the prayers of his people. He felt happier than he had felt in many, many years.

"You have brought a guest home for the seder," Pearl noticed as the two men walked into the house. "What a blessing for us." She smiled warmly at the golem.

Pearl had prepared a lovely meal, and though she seemed initially disturbed by Joseph's dumbness, and had to scold the two youngest children who giggled at his lack of speech, the meal went well and lasted into the late hours as they recited the Haggadah. The deliverance of the Egyptian Hebrews had never held as much meaning for Rabbi Loew as it did tonight after the ghetto's narrow escape and with his own liberation from the bondage of loneliness.

"Where will our guest sleep?" Pearl whispered after the children were in bed. "We have so little room now with Isaac and Miriam's little baby."

"I will prepare a blanket in my study."

"But Judah—"

"Tomorrow I will buy a small cot and place it in my study for him. Joseph will stay there for the time being."

"How long—"

"Dear Pearl, Joseph has been sent to us by our Eternal Father." He leaned over and whispered into Pearl's ear. "He is a golem. God has brought him to life to protect the Jews of Prague."

Pearl gasped but nodded. "I will treat him as I would Isaac or anyone else who joins our family."

"That is good, Pearl. You are a kind woman."

"And you are a great man."

"It is God who is great."

Rabbi Loew brought a pillow and two blankets to his study and motioned for Joseph to follow. As he prepared a place for Joseph to sleep, the silent man began undressing. Rabbi Loew realized he would need to find some new clothing for the large creature. He would need more than the clothes he wore today. The rabbi would see to it in the morning.

"You will sleep in my study, Joseph," Rabbi Loew said, "among the Torah and Talmud and every other sacred book I own. You have been created especial by the Almighty, and it is appropriate that you rest among His writings."

Joseph lay on one blanket and pulled the other up to his chin. It barely covered him. Then he moved his lips as if to speak. But Rabbi Loew could hear nothing. Joseph moved his lips again and then beckoned for the rabbi to lean down. Rabbi Loew knelt on the floor and put his ear next to Joseph's mouth. Would the creature be able to speak only to him, only in private?

Rabbi Loew could feel a soft wind against his ear but could still hear nothing. Disturbed, he turned his face toward Joseph's, and as he did so, his nose brushed against that of the golem. He should have pulled back but was too captivated by the young, strong face so near. He looked into Joseph's eyes.

They wrinkled a little at the corners, and Rabbi Loew realized that Joseph was smiling. Suddenly, the rabbi felt a hand on the back of his head, felt Joseph pulling him even closer.

They kissed. It was a long, sultry embrace of lips. Rabbi Loew could not pull away with Joseph's hand behind his head. But he did not wish to pull away.

After a few, lingering moments, Joseph released him, and Rabbi Loew stood back up, resting one hand on his desk to steady himself.

"Joseph, you have been sent by God. He has created you to comfort me. And I will ask God's help so that I may comfort you as well." He bowed his head slightly and left the room.

The rabbi joined Pearl in their bed, his mind in a fog. God had not only performed one great miracle today, he had performed two. Rabbi Loew wasn't certain how much of the story he could reveal to his students, but he wanted the Jews of every generation to know at least part of the magnificent mercy God had shown his followers.

As the days passed, Rabbi Loew told his best students that he and Isaac had formed the golem out of clay and performed secret rituals and offered special prayers to bring him to life. Only Isaac knew what really happened, and he agreed that Rabbi Loew's story was better for the people.

Otherwise, they might believe Joseph was simply a waylaid traveler they'd rescued, or an imbecile who'd wandered in from another town, or some terrible sinner cast out from another community who had then lost his speech as a punishment from God.

Rabbi Loew worked diligently to see that Joseph continued to be a blessing to the Jews of Prague. He assigned Joseph to carry water every day for the sick and the elderly. Joseph stood guard at weddings. He roamed the streets and was seen continually by the city's inhabitants, which both comforted them and reminded them to behave justly.

Joseph caught young boys trying to steal apples from the fruit vendor. He captured a gonif trying to run off with some of the cobbler's tools. He assisted Yudl, the blacksmith, in his shop after the man was beaten one evening by goyim.

Joseph was loved by many, respected by others, feared by some, and tolerated by the remainder of the population. But Rabbi Loew was greatly admired, and no one spoke against Joseph in public, whatever they might say in private.

Every week, Rabbi Loew took Joseph to the mikvah, and every evening after they'd purified themselves, Rabbi Loew would remain a long while in his study with the creature, and he would always leave with a serene, thoughtful smile on his lips.

One day as another Pesach approached, Joseph became agitated. He took Rabbi Loew by the hand and led him to the kitchen, where Pearl was preparing matzoh. He pointed to the bowl, pointed to his mouth, and then held his stomach with an agonized expression on his face. He repeated these actions three times.

"Dear husband, what can be the matter? Has poor Joseph lost his senses?"

"No, Pearl," Rabbi Loew said. "He knows of trouble afoot." The rabbi put his hand on Joseph's arm. "Joseph, have you seen something? Have you overheard something?"

Joseph nodded vigorously.

"Is there a danger to the people?"

Joseph nodded vigorously again.

"Can you prevent something bad from happening? Can you show me where I must go to warn others?"

Joseph grasped Rabbi Loew's hand firmly and pulled him forcefully out of the house. He led the rabbi quickly down the street and around the corner to the bakery Abraham owned. Joseph pushed the door open with one hand and pulled the rabbi in after him with the other.

He pointed to the matzoh baking and held his stomach with a pained grimace on his face. Then he pointed to two new workers the rabbi had never seen before.

"Abraham," said Rabbi Loew, "may I ask who those two gentlemen are?"

"Why, they're goyim from outside the ghetto. I made sure they had no leaven anywhere on them. But my regular bakers have become ill, and I need to prepare a great deal of matzoh in a very short time."

"Abraham, these men are plotting something. Perhaps they did smuggle some leavening in with them to ruin our seder."

Abraham called the two men over, and instantly, Joseph pointed accusingly at them. He towered over the two men, and after only the slightest questioning, with Joseph thrusting a handful of balled flour in their faces, they blurted out the entire story. They had brought poison into the bakery and were going to contaminate all the matzoh. They'd seen Joseph nearby as they talked about it on their way to the bakery, after having sickened the regular workers, but they hadn't believed the dumb man could understand them.

Rabbi Loew stepped outside and ordered a young boy to fetch a watchman, and soon the men were carted off. It was a difficult Pesach the first few days, with not enough matzoh to satisfy the stomachs of those in the neighborhood, but Joseph had saved the people again. Rabbi Loew offered up his thanks to the Creator yet another time for his mercy in sending a golem to protect them.

The rabbi felt rather proud that it was his very own special friend who had performed such a good deed. Not pride over having created him but pride in Joseph himself. The rabbi sometimes called his special friend his husband in his private thoughts. But was it possible to have both a loving wife and a loving husband? Since Joseph was not truly alive, Rabbi Loew felt secure that he was not sinning with the man. Lying with Joseph instead elevated his soul. He felt grateful every week that God had provided a way to permit his heart to be full without degrading his body.

Their lovemaking would have been a sin had Joseph been a true man rather than a special creation. To his surprise, Rabbi Loew found himself becoming more tender toward his wife now that he had Joseph for himself. And he dedicated himself ever more to his studies and his rulings, so he could be worthy of such a profound gift.

Rabbi Loew's children were growing. He was able to marry off another daughter to the tailor's son and arrange a marriage between one of his sons to the butcher's daughter. Miriam and Isaac now had two children of their own. They lived with Rabbi Loew and his wife, but the other married children had moved into their own abodes. Still, Joseph continued to sleep in the study, and Rabbi Loew continued to linger late with him one evening a week.

Joseph shoveled snow and helped stack firewood in the winter. He helped repair roofs and build carts any time of year he was needed. Joseph helped hang signs and sweep trash in front of the people's shops. Rabbi Loew forbid anyone to pay Joseph for his work.

The rabbi felt that since the golem was sent as a gift from God, he was to be used to help all Jews equally whenever possible, in whichever way he could. Rabbi Loew in turn felt it his personal obligation to provide for the creature. Even though Joseph was not technically alive, he did eat a great deal to support his large frame. Rabbi Loew sometimes wondered at that, but he supposed this was simply a minor trial to remind him of the great blessings which had been bestowed upon him.

One afternoon a few years later, seven years after the golem had first come to life, Joseph created another commotion. After the miraculous deliverances during the two Passovers, Rabbi Loew was quick to understand that something was amiss, especially since it was only a day before Yom Kippur.

Joseph took several books from the rabbi's library and carried them to the kitchen. He put three books standing on end and then placed a single book flat on top as if to make a roof. He pointed to the flame Pearl was using to cook with and then pointed to the little structure on the table. Next, Joseph opened one of the books and pointed to the Hebrew letters and then toward the door.

Joseph grasped Rabbi Loew by the hand and pulled him down the street to the synagogue. He pointed at the building and then waved his fingers upward.

"Is someone going to burn the synagogue?"

Joseph nodded.

"Can you find the man?"

Joseph looked uncertain and then shook his head.

Rabbi Loew quickly called ten men from the congregation and posted them at different locations in and around the synagogue, telling them they might need to wait many hours before anyone approached, and they must remain alert.

Rabbi Loew was grateful Joseph was such a fixture in the community. The rabbi had at first found Joseph's silence a difficulty, but he realized yet again that this was indeed a blessing, that people forgot the golem was nearby observing everything. It was what enabled him to serve so faithfully.

Late in the night, Yudl saw two Gentiles enter the synagogue, and he called out an alarm. The other men all rushed over and captured the two criminals. As before, the Jews were fortunate to have a watchman respond who believed their tale. The synagogue was saved, and though the ten men who'd stood watch were exhausted as well as famished because of their fasting for the Day of Atonement, when the congregation heard what had transpired, everyone dedicated themselves to becoming more observant and faithful in their prayers and commitments.

That evening, when Rabbi Loew brought Joseph to the study, he could barely keep his eyes open. He knelt beside the golem to kiss him good night and fell down right on top of the creature, immediately deep in sleep. He did not feel the golem stroking his hair gently during the succeeding hour.

When Rabbi Loew awoke in the morning, he realized that Joseph's arms were locked across his back as he lay on top of the man. When the rabbi began to stir, Joseph opened his eyes and smiled brightly. He raised his head and kissed Rabbi Loew on the lips. Rabbi Loew wondered how he would ever be able to sleep in his own bed after this.

"It must have been very uncomfortable for you last night," said the rabbi.

Joseph continued smiling and shook his head. He held Rabbi Loew tight against him for a moment and kissed him another time. Then he stroked the rabbi's cheek softly.

"Joseph, would it displease you if I stayed with you again some night?"

Joseph shook his head.

"Can I stay with you this evening?"

Joseph nodded.

Just then, the rabbi had a terrible thought. "Joseph, how long will you be mine?"

Joseph put his right finger on his left shoulder and slowly drew his finger the length of his arm to his fingertips. Rabbi Loew wasn't quite sure what that meant, but it seemed to signify something good and bountiful.

From that night on, Rabbi Loew began sleeping in the study with Joseph. Pearl never made a comment, and Isaac never spoke a word regarding the new arrangement. Rabbi Loew could not understand why it had taken him seven years to begin comforting Joseph through the night. He sensed that perhaps it was because Jacob had been required to work seven years for Leah, and so the rabbi needed seven years of anticipation as well.

Despite his weekly mikvah and special sessions with Joseph, staying the full night with him was an entirely different experience. After they retired for the evening, Rabbi Loew spoke to Joseph at length of his boyhood, his studies, his ponderings about God and the Torah, and of his feelings for Joseph.

When he looked at Joseph's face while he spoke, he realized that Joseph was communicating with him fully every day. The rabbi knew completely what Joseph was thinking. It was because their two souls could speak to each other in the realm of spirits.

But one day as Rabbi Loew was contemplating his blessings, he experienced a sudden, terrifying thought. If the golem had no soul, what would happen when Rabbi Loew died? Would the creature "live" indefinitely and continue to assist the Jews of Prague throughout time? Or would Joseph cease to exist?

Rabbi Loew was not certain what the world to come might offer, but he desired to be with Joseph in the next life as well. Yet if Joseph had no soul to cross over into that next world, would Rabbi Loew ever see him again? Would they be separated eternally?

This idea was too much to bear, and Rabbi Loew began fasting one day each week, beseeching God to impart Joseph a soul. The rabbi realized that if this request were granted, he would no longer be able to spend the evenings with Joseph. Their lovemaking would then become a sin.

Would it still be possible to love so fully, so completely, if they were never allowed to express their love in its entirety? Was the choice before Rabbi Loew that he either give up the man he loved or give up love itself? He now understood what his forefather Abraham must have felt when asked to kill the son who was to beget him multitudes of descendants. Yet God had provided an escape then. Perhaps he would do so again now.

Surely, if loving a soulless creature could be so rewarding, loving a man filled with a rich, deep soul would be even more beautiful. The Torah said differently, and the Torah was God's word. But Rabbi Loew wondered.

Rabbi Loew did not let his worries hinder his happiness. He was nearing sixty, yet when he was with Joseph, he felt as giddy as a schoolboy. His students often commented on how young he seemed. Joseph continued to serve, helping Chayim the woodworker construct furniture, and Elihu the tinsmith make kettles and cups.

Rabbi Loew sent the golem to assist any man in the neighborhood who was sick and needed a temporary helper, and he made sure to send Joseph to people in all parts of the ghetto, so no one would feel neglected, and everyone would be aware of God's love for them.

A few boys still tried to steal pears or plums, just to tease Joseph. But the months and years passed with no other grave threat to the community. The highlight of the week for Rabbi Loew continued to be immersing himself in the mikvah with Joseph. The golem's purity then seemed almost tangible.

One day, late in the fall of 1574, Rabbi Loew and Joseph hurried home after their purification and took off their heavy coats in the house. Pearl was sitting at the table alone.

"What is it, Pearl? You look unsettled."

"I have a pain in my arm," she said simply. "It runs to my chest. It makes me very tired."

"Shall I call for the doctor? Do you need attention?"

Pearl looked up at him sadly. "I no longer need attention. But I thank you for what you have been able to give me during our many years together. I might have desired more, but it has been sufficient." She grimaced and rubbed her chest.

"Oh, Pearl!"

"Do not worry, Judah. It has been a privilege to live in the same household with the chief rabbi. We have raised good children and grandchildren. I do not fear what lies ahead."

Rabbi Loew knelt beside her and held her hand tightly.

"I—I do not fully understand these things, though I am married to a learned man. But Judah…" She paused as another flash of pain streaked across her face. "Judah, you must ask Isaac and a few of your other trusted students. You must ask them…"

"Ask them what?"

"To hold the chuppah over you and Joseph. Once I have gone away, you must be joined together under the wedding canopy."

Rabbi Loew nodded. He thought he should feel ashamed that Pearl knew everything. Then he realized it was good that his wife knew his deepest secrets. It made him feel suddenly close to her, almost as close as he felt to Joseph.

"Yes, my wife, I will do as you say."

Joseph had been standing nearby silently, but now he knelt down as well and kissed Pearl on the forehead.

When he pulled away, Pearl's eyes were glazed and distant. Rabbi Loew wiped his face and tore the right side of his shirt. He hesitated a moment and then tore the right side of Joseph's shirt as well.

It was too late in the afternoon to bury Pearl that day, but the community buried her the next morning, and Rabbi Loew's son said the kaddish. The rabbi and Joseph and Isaac and Miriam and the other children removed their leather shoes during the week of mourning, wearing simple cloth slippers. Joseph seemed to want to comfort Rabbi Loew, but the rabbi knew he must abstain from his usual marital relationships during shiva.

How odd, he thought, to consider such a thing while mourning his wife. He was too humble to think he might be worthy of polygamy like some of his esteemed ancestors. The idea did cross his mind at one point that he was not truly polygamous. He only had one wife, after all. It was simply that he also had one husband. It seemed to him exactly the finest way to live, and he forgot at times that had Joseph been human, it would have been forbidden.

It struck the rabbi that Pearl had died seven years after he had begun spending the nights with Joseph. Was this God's way of denying him Pearl, the way Jacob had been denied Rachel for so long? Was the rabbi being punished for not appreciating his Leah enough? Or was this God's way of giving Joseph to him fully, the way Rachel had finally become Jacob's after fourteen long years?

Perhaps Pearl was being rewarded for her own faithfulness and love.

After the week of mourning, Rabbi Loew had a difficult decision to make. Did he dare, as Pearl had suggested, ask his most devoted students to marry him and Joseph? Was it even acceptable to marry a golem, even if it weren't a man?

Rabbi Loew knew that Isaac had long ago assumed the truth. Yet to act blatantly might bring disaster.

And would marriage make a difference in the eyes of God? Rabbi Loew was already quite certain he was not sinning. So what did it matter that he and Joseph did not legally belong to one another? Once Rabbi Loew died, the marriage would be null and void in any case.

Yet somehow, somehow, marriage *felt* like an eternal commitment, and Rabbi Loew wanted some small hope that he would be with Joseph forever.

"Joseph," the rabbi asked one night in their study, "would you like to wed?"

Joseph looked at Rabbi Loew blankly.

"Would you like to be mine in the world to come?"

Joseph pointed to the yellow circle on his shoulder, tracing the circle with his finger over and over. He stopped with his finger at one point on the circle, shook his head and frowned, and then moved his finger further along and stopped again. He again shook his head, and then he moved his finger round and round the circle several more times, nodding and smiling. Rabbi Loew understood.

"Eternity has no beginning and no end. You are wise, Joseph."

Joseph smiled and pointed to Rabbi Loew and then touched the rabbi's head and the rabbi's chest over his heart.

"We will wait until a month has passed, and then I will say something to Isaac." They couldn't participate in any events with music for thirty days after Pearl's death. Rabbi Loew wasn't sure if there would be any music for himself and Joseph, even if Isaac and the others to whom he might reveal his secret would agree to a private ceremony. But waiting at least thirty days seemed prudent in any event.

"Joseph, I asked God to bring you to me, and He did. I cannot believe He will forbid us from revealing His miraculous mercy to the most dedicated of my students. It is only in this way that we can pass God's wisdom along to future generations. After I am gone, they will be able to speak freely of God's compassion."

Joseph pulled Rabbi Loew to the cot, and they made love slowly and with deep consideration for one another.

It was the last evening, however, they were ever to spend together as one. The next day, around midmorning, Chayim the woodworker came running up to the rabbi.

"Rabbi Loew! Rabbi Loew!"

"What is it, Chayim?"

"Someone has stolen all the oil for Hanukkah! The three barrels are missing! The first night of the festival is this evening! Whatever shall we do?"

"Do you know where Joseph can be found?"

"I saw him leaving the ghetto as I made my way here."

"Let us see if we can find him," Rabbi Loew said calmly. Joseph had saved them in the past, and though there was no physical danger this time, only inconvenience, the rabbi was again amazed at how the hatred of the Gentiles would lead them to disrupt even a minor holiday. He smiled, thinking about how much the Gentiles were unknowingly devoting themselves to the study of Judaism, just so they could keep up with the various Jewish festivals and holidays, even if simply to hinder them. Perhaps it was God's way of letting hatred serve at least some small beneficial purpose.

Rabbi Loew and the other men who followed him outside the ghetto asked at every corner if anyone had seen a large Jew hurrying by. Some people refused to answer and a few even spat at them, but most meekly offered whatever aid they could.

Within twenty minutes, the rabbi and the other men came upon Joseph beating against a heavy wooden door. Rabbi Loew put his hand on Joseph's shoulder, and he ceased pounding.

"Chayim, fetch a watchman."

The woodworker hurried off.

"Gentlemen," the rabbi called out loudly in the direction of the building. "A watchman is on the way. It would be best if you opened the door and let us retrieve what is rightly ours." He felt generous today and decided that if the men returned the oil willingly, he would not have them arrested. Perhaps they would understand then that the Jews were a good people and desist on their own from wreaking further havoc among them.

A moment later, the heavy door opened, and two men stepped out nervously. One of them motioned toward the open doorway, offering to allow Joseph to pass inside freely.

Rabbi Loew smiled. Hanukkah was a time to celebrate the fact that the ancient Jews had not assimilated into Greek culture. Even now, if worthy Jews resisted present-day "Greeks," they would continue to be preserved and blessed. The rabbi briefly wondered if the love he and Joseph shared was "Greek," but then shook his head. True love between souls was the most Jewish thing of all.

Yet Joseph didn't have a soul, so could their love be Jewish? Could their love be true? Now that Pearl was gone, Rabbi Loew would need to pursue these questions more fervently.

As soon as Joseph passed Rabbi Loew and entered the building, one of the goyim suddenly reached back and pulled the door shut and locked it with a key. Then both men quickly ran off.

How childish, thought Rabbi Loew. He sent Abraham the baker after the men so that the watchman would be able to apprehend them after all. Then he called out to Joseph. "Find the oil so we may depart as soon as aid arrives."

A moment later, however, someone in the gathering crowd shouted. "Look! There is smoke!"

Rabbi Loew turned. Out of the one tiny window in the building, smoke was starting to drift out. With a sudden, horrible realization, the rabbi understood what the treacherous men had done. "Yudl! Go fetch an axe! Quickly!"

Rabbi Loew pushed against the door without effect. He called the other Jews with him to help push on the heavy wood, but the door would not move.

"Good people!" shouted the rabbi to the crowd of Gentiles looking on. "Bring a heavy piece of furniture with which we can ram the door! Quickly! There is a man inside!"

No one in the crowd moved, and Rabbi Loew noticed with horror that smoke was now billowing forcefully out of the single small window. Joseph began pounding on the door from the inside.

Rabbi Loew's heart beat faster and harder. "Joseph! You are strong! You can break open the door!"

Rabbi Loew thought how reckless it was to start a fire anywhere in the city, one that might spread quickly to other structures. It seemed that Gentiles would even risk hurting themselves just for the opportunity to hurt Jews. But his only real concern now was for the golem.

There was a gasp from the crowd, and Rabbi Loew looked up to the window. Tiny flames were now reaching outward. The pounding from inside the building became louder.

"Joseph!"

The flames issuing from the window were now large and deafening. There was a tremendous roar coming from inside.

"Joseph!" The rabbi pulled against the door with all his might. "God in heaven! Please grant me strength! Joseph!"

There was a sickening squeal from inside, followed by a strangled cry, barely audible over the crash of the flames. "Judah!"

The rabbi stopped. Had Joseph spoken? He began pulling at the door frantically, clawing, punching, kicking, scratching. He lost the nails on two of his fingers, blood staining the door.

"Joseph!"

There was no longer any pounding on the other side of the door. Finally, townspeople began arriving with buckets of water. Three buildings burned to the ground before the flames were extinguished, but the city itself was spared. Rabbi Loew sat morosely in the street, watching the activity, feeling a great emptiness and wondering why God had not allowed the entire city to be reduced to ashes.

By late afternoon, the crowd had dispersed, but Rabbi Loew continued to sit in the street. He was motionless, staring at the blackened wood. Isaac stood near the rabbi, afraid to approach him.

After a very long while, Isaac touched his sleeve. Disconsolate, the rabbi turned his head upward to look at Isaac. He let out an agonized scream and tore his shirt on the right and also on the left. He pulled a handful of hairs out of his beard. He pulled a handful of hairs out of his head. He beat his chest with one fist, over and over.

"Come, father, we must return to the ghetto before sunset." He reached down and took Rabbi Loew by the arm. The rabbi rose slowly and trudged haltingly back to his home.

The one mirror would need to be covered again, but when Rabbi Loew saw it, he reached out and struck it with his fist, shattering it. Isaac tried to bind his bleeding knuckles.

There was talk all over the ghetto that evening about how the golem had been destroyed, and the people wondered if it was a punishment, if they had been too wicked and unfaithful. They prayed devoutly for forgiveness for whatever sins they might have committed. And though there was a severe shortage of oil, every single hanukiah burned continually for the next eight days.

"It is the golem who has done this for us," the people said. "It is a sign that God still loves us."

Rabbi Loew was the only Jew in the ghetto who did not light his menorah, but Isaac lit it for him.

As the days and months passed, the people quickly adjusted to life without the golem. They took it as a sign that they were no longer in danger. The Gentiles had been appeased and would no longer torment them. Life was good.

Rabbi Loew spent many hours alone in his study. He would pick up a book to read, put it down, and take up an article of Joseph's clothing. He would lift it to his lips and kiss it, raise it to his nose and inhale deeply.

He could not forget the anguished cry he'd heard at the end. Joseph had spoken. Did it mean he had finally been made human? Had Joseph died a real man and not a soulless creature? And was that a good thing? Had he become alive only to die a moment later in the most terrifying and brutal of ways?

Rabbi Loew awakened many nights with visions of flames before his eyes. He felt the flames in his heart. He felt the flames in his soul.

Had his love for Joseph been a sin, after all? Perhaps killing him was God's way of keeping the rabbi from following the ways of the goyim. The golem had been sent to save the Jews of Prague. Had he now been taken to save Rabbi Loew's soul?

Rabbi Loew knew he'd willingly face an eternity in the flames which had taken Joseph, if only he could have the golem with him a few hours longer. He tried to bargain with God, day after day after day, pleading for damnation, if only it would bring the man back.

Eventually, however, Rabbi Loew resumed his duties as chief rabbi. He taught his students, he led the prayers, he offered rulings on disputes, and he performed weddings and wrote learned tracts.

Whenever he saw a chuppah, though, he struggled mightily to smile and be happy for the young couples.

Rabbi Loew fell asleep on his knees in his study, night after night, but there was never another dream telling him to go to the river. He went anyway many times, but the banks were always deserted.

Miriam took over the cooking, and her children were now almost grown and becoming fine young men and women. Isaac was becoming a great leader in his own right.

Rabbi Loew smiled at Sabbath meals and on holidays, and he continued to study the Talmud and go to the mikvah. He persisted in doing these things for many, many years, and all the Jews of Prague loved and respected him more every day. The people talked continually of what a great scholar the rabbi was, how wonderful it must feel to be such a righteous man.

Rabbi Loew smiled when he heard these things and bowed his head politely.

Then he would return to his study and sit by himself for many hours in the empty room, for the next seven years, the next fourteen, for the rest of his life, patiently waiting for a morning when he would not awaken, but would find himself again in Joseph's arms.

Books by Johnny Townsend

Thanks for reading! If you enjoyed this book, could you please take a few minutes to write a review online? Reviews are helpful both to me as an author and to other readers, so we'd all sincerely appreciate your writing one! And if you did enjoy the book, here are some others I've written you might want to look up:

Mormon Underwear

Zombies for Jesus

A Gay Mormon Missionary in Pompeii

The Golem of Rabbi Loew

Marginal Mormons

Gay Bumper Sticker Theology

Going-Out-Of-Religion Sale

Escape from Zion

Gayrabian Nights

Missionaries Make the Best Companions

Invasion of the Spirit Snatchers

Gay Gaslighting

Sins of the Saints

Out of the Missionary's Closet

Breaking the Promise of the Promised Land

I Will, Through the Veil

Am I My Planet's Keeper?

Have Your Cum and Eat It, Too

Strangers with Benefits

Constructing Equity

Wake Up and Smell the Missionaries

Racism by Proxy

Orgy at the STD Clinic

Life Is Better with Love

Please Evacuate

Recommended Daily Humanity

The Camper Killings

Kinky Quilts: Patchwork Designs for Gay Men

Inferno in the French Quarter: The UpStairs Lounge Fire

Latter-Gay Saints: An Anthology of Gay Mormon Fiction (co-editor)

Available from your favorite online or neighborhood bookstore.

Wondering what some of those other books are about? Read on!

Invasion of the Spirit Snatchers

During the Apocalypse, a group of Mormon survivors in Hurricane, Utah gather in the home of the Relief Society president, telling stories to pass the time as they ration their food storage and await the Second Coming. But this is no ordinary group of Mormons—or perhaps it is. They are the faithful, feminist, gay, apostate, and repentant, all working together to help each other through the darkest days any of them have yet seen.

Gayrabian Nights

Gayrabian Nights is a twist on the well-known classic, *1001 Arabian Nights*, in which Scheherazade, under the threat of death if she ceases to captivate King Shahryar's attention, enchants him through a series of mysterious, adventurous, and romantic tales.

In this variation, a male escort, invited to the hotel room of a closeted, homophobic Mormon senator, learns that the man is poised to vote on a piece of anti-gay legislation the following morning. To prevent him from sleeping, so that the exhausted senator will miss casting his vote on the Senate floor, the escort entertains him with stories of homophobia, celibacy, mixed orientation marriages, reparative therapy, coming out, first love, gay marriage, and long-term successful gay relationships. The escort crafts the stories to give the senator a crash course in gay culture and sensibilities, hoping to bring the man closer to accepting his own sexual orientation.

Inferno in the French Quarter: The UpStairs Lounge Fire

On Gay Pride Day in 1973, someone set the entrance to a French Quarter gay bar on fire. In the terrible inferno that followed, thirty-two people lost their lives, including a third of the local congregation of the Metropolitan Community Church, their pastor burning to death halfway out a second-story window as he tried to claw his way to freedom. A mother who'd gone to the bar with her two gay sons died alongside them. A man who'd helped his friend escape first was found dead near the fire escape. Two children waited outside a movie theater across town for a father and step-father who would never pick them up. During this era of rampant homophobia, several families refused to claim the bodies, and many churches refused to bury the dead. Author Johnny Townsend pored through old records and tracked down survivors of the fire as well as relatives and friends of those killed to compile this fascinating account of a forgotten moment in gay history.

A Gay Mormon Missionary in Pompeii

What is a gay Mormon missionary doing in Italy? He is trying to save his own soul as well as the souls of others. In these tales chronicling the two-year mission of Robert Anderson, we see a young man tormented by his inability to be the man the Church says he should be. In addition to his personal hell, Anderson faces a major earthquake, organized crime, a serious bus accident, and much more. He copes with horrendous mission leaders and his own suicidal tendencies. But one day, he meets another missionary who loves him, and his world changes forever.

Am I My Planet's Keeper?

Global Warming. Climate Change. Climate Crisis. Climate Emergency. Whatever label we use, we are facing one of the greatest challenges to the survival of life as we know it.

But while addressing greenhouse gases is perhaps our most urgent need, it's not our only task. We must also address toxic waste, pollution, habitat destruction, and our other contributions to the world's sixth mass extinction event.

In order to do that, we must simultaneously address the unmet human needs that keep us distracted from deeper engagement in stabilizing our climate: moderating economic inequality, guaranteeing healthcare to all, and ensuring education for everyone.

And to accomplish *that*, we must unite to combat the monied forces that use fear, prejudice, and misinformation to manipulate us.

It's a daunting task. But success is our only option.

Wake Up and Smell the Missionaries

Two Mormon missionaries in Italy discover they share the same rare ability—both can emit pheromones on demand. At first, they playfully compete in the hills of Frascati to see who can tempt "investigators" most. But soon they're targeting each other non-stop.

Can two immature young men learn to control their "superpower" to live a normal life…and develop genuine love? Even as their relationship is threatened by the attentions of another man?

They seem just on the verge of success when a massive earthquake leaves them trapped under the rubble of their apartment in Castellammare.

With night falling and temperatures dropping, can they dig themselves out in time to save themselves? And will their injuries destroy the ability that brought them together in the first place?

Orgy at the STD Clinic

Todd Tillotson is struggling to move on after his husband is killed in a hit and run attack a year earlier during a Black Lives Matter protest in Seattle.

In this novel set entirely on public transportation, we watch as Todd, isolated throughout the pandemic, battles desperation in his attempt to safely reconnect with the world.

Will he find love again, even casual friendship, or will he simply end up another crazy old man on the bus?

Things don't look good until a man whose face he can't even see sits down beside him despite the raging variants.

And asks him a question that will change his life.

Please Evacuate

A gay, partygoing New Yorker unconcerned about the future or the unsustainability of capitalism is hit by a truck and thrust into a straight man's body half a continent away. As Hunter tries to figure out what's happening, he's caught up in another disaster, a wildfire sweeping through a Colorado community, the flames overtaking him and several schoolchildren as they flee.

When he awakens, Hunter finds himself in the body of yet another man, this time in northern Italy, a former missionary about to marry a young Mormon woman. Still piecing together this new reality, and beginning to embrace his latest identity, Hunter fights for his life in a devastating flash flood along with his wife *and* his new husband.

He's an aging worker in drought-stricken Texas, a nurse at an assisted living facility in the direct path of a hurricane, an advocate for the unhoused during a freak Seattle blizzard.

We watch as Hunter is plunged into life after life, finally recognizing the futility of only looking out for #1 and understanding the part he must play in addressing the global climate crisis…if he ever gets another chance.

Recommended Daily Humanity

A checklist of human rights must include basic housing, universal healthcare, equitable funding for public schools, and tuition-free college and vocational training.

In addition to the basics, though, we need much more to fully thrive. Subsidized childcare, universal pre-K, a universal basic income, subsidized high-speed internet, net neutrality, fare-free public transit (plus *more* public transit), and medically assisted death for the terminally ill who want it.

None of this will matter, though, if we neglect to address the rapidly worsening climate crisis.

Sound expensive? It is.

But not as expensive as refusing to implement these changes. The cost of climate disasters each year has grown to staggering figures. And the cost of social and political upheaval from not meeting the needs of suffering workers, families, and individuals may surpass even that.

It's best we understand that the vast sums required to enact meaningful change are an investment which will pay off not only in some indeterminate future but in fact almost immediately. And without these adjustments to our lifestyles and values, there may very well not be a future capable of sustaining freedom and democracy...or even civilization itself.

The Camper Killings

When a homeless man is found murdered a few blocks from Morgan Beylerian's house in south Seattle, everyone seems to consider the body just so much additional trash to be cleared from the neighborhood. But Morgan liked the guy. They used to chat when Morgan brought Nick groceries once a week.

And the brutal way the man was killed reminds Morgan of their shared Mormon heritage, back when the faithful agreed to have their throats slit if they ever revealed temple secrets.

Did Nick's former wife take action when her ex-husband refused to grant a temple divorce? Did his murder have something to do with the public accusations that brought an end to his promising career?

Morgan does his best to investigate when no one else seems to care, but it isn't easy as a man living paycheck to paycheck himself, only able to pursue his investigation via public transit.

As he continues his search for the killer, Morgan's friends withdraw and his husband threatens to leave. When another homeless man is killed and Morgan is accused of the crime, things look even bleaker.

But his troubles aren't over yet.

Will Morgan find the killer before the killer finds him?

What Readers Have Said

Townsend's stories are "a gay *Portnoy's Complaint* of Mormonism. Salacious, sweet, sad, insightful, insulting, religiously ethnic, quirky-faithful, and funny."

D. Michael Quinn, author of *The Mormon Hierarchy: Origins of Power*

"Told from a believably conversational first-person perspective, [*A Gay Mormon Missionary in Pompeii*'s] novelistic focus on Anderson's journey to thoughtful self-acceptance allows for greater character development than often seen in short stories, which makes this well-paced work rich and satisfying, and one of Townsend's strongest. An extremely important contribution to the field of Mormon fiction." Named to Kirkus Reviews' Best of 2011.

Kirkus Reviews

"The thirteen stories in *Mormon Underwear* capture this struggle [between Mormonism and homosexuality] with humor, sadness, insight, and sometimes shocking details....*Mormon Underwear* provides compelling stories, literally from the inside-out."

Niki D'Andrea, *Phoenix New Times*

"Townsend's lively writing style and engaging characters [in *Zombies for Jesus*] make for stories which force us to wake up, smell the (prohibited) coffee, and review our attitudes with regard to reading dogma so doggedly. These are tales which revel in the individual tics and quirks which make us human, Mormon or not, gay or not…"

A.J. Kirby, *The Short Review*

"The Rift," from *A Gay Mormon Missionary in Pompeii*, is a "fascinating tale of an untenable situation…a *tour de force*."

David Lenson, editor, *The Massachusetts Review*

The Circumcision of God is "a collection of short stories that consider the imperfect, silenced majority of Mormons, who may in fact be [the Church's] best hope….[The book leaves] readers regretting the church's willingness to marginalize those who best exemplify its ideals: those who love fiercely despite all obstacles, who brave challenges at great personal risk and who always choose the hard, higher road."

Kirkus Reviews

In *Mormon Fairy Tales*, Johnny Townsend displays "both a wicked sense of irony and a deep well of compassion."

Kel Munger, *Sacramento News and Review*

Zombies for Jesus is "eerie, erotic, and magical."

Publishers Weekly

"While [Townsend's] many touching vignettes draw deeply from Mormon mythology, history, spirituality and culture, [*Mormon Fairy Tales*] is neither a gaudy act of proselytism nor angry protest literature from an ex-believer. Like all good fiction, his stories are simply about the joys, the hopes and the sorrows of people."

Kirkus Reviews

"In *Inferno in the French Quarter* author Johnny Townsend restores this tragic event [the UpStairs Lounge fire] to its proper place in LGBT history and reminds us that the victims of the blaze were not just 'statistics,' but real people with real lives, families, and friends."

Jesse Monteagudo, *The Bilerico Project*

In *Inferno in the French Quarter*, "Townsend's heart-rending descriptions of the victims…seem to [make them] come alive once more."

Kit Van Cleave, *OutSmart Magazine*

Marginal Mormons is "an irreverent, honest look at life outside the mainstream Mormon Church….Throughout his musings on sin and forgiveness, Townsend beautifully demonstrates his characters' internal, perhaps irreconcilable struggles….Rather than anger and disdain, he offers an honest portrayal of people searching for meaning and community in their lives, regardless of their life choices or secrets." Named to Kirkus Reviews' Best of 2012.

Kirkus Reviews

The stories in *The Mormon Victorian Society* "register the new openness and confidence of gay life in the age of same-sex marriage….What hasn't changed is Townsend's wry, conversational prose, his subtle evocations of character and social dynamics, and his deadpan humor. His warm empathy still glows in this intimate yet clear-eyed engagement with Mormon theology and folkways. Funny, shrewd and finely wrought dissections of the awkward contradictions—and surprising harmonies—between conscience and desire." Named to Kirkus Reviews' Best of 2013.

Kirkus Reviews

"This collection of short stories [*The Mormon Victorian Society*] featuring gay Mormon characters slammed [me] in the face from the first page, wrestled my heart and mind to the floor, and left me panting and wanting more by the end. Johnny Townsend has created so many memorable characters in such few pages. I went weeks thinking about this book. It truly touched me."

Tom Webb, *A Bear on Books*

Dragons of the Book of Mormon is an "entertaining collection….Townsend's prose is sharp, clear, and easy to read, and his characters are well rendered…"

Publishers Weekly

"The pre-eminent documenter of alternative Mormon lifestyles…Townsend has a deep understanding of his characters, and his limpid prose, dry humor and well-grounded (occasionally magical) realism make their spiritual conundrums both compelling and entertaining. [*Dragons of the Book of Mormon* is] [a]nother of Townsend's critical but affectionate and absorbing tours of Mormon discontent." Named to Kirkus Reviews' Best of 2014.

Kirkus Reviews

In *Gayrabian Nights*, "Townsend's prose is always limpid and evocative, and…he finds real drama and emotional depth in the most ordinary of lives."

Kirkus Reviews

Gayrabian Nights is a "complex revelation of how seriously soul damaging the denial of the true self can be."

Ryan Rhodes, author of *Free Electricity*

Gayrabian Nights "was easily the most original book I've read all year. Funny, touching, topical, and thoroughly enjoyable."

Rainbow Awards

Lying for the Lord is "one of the most gripping books that I've picked up for quite a while. I love the author's writing style, alternately cynical, humorous, biting, scathing, poignant, and touching…. This is the third book of his that I've read, and all are equally engaging. These are stories that need to be told, and the author does it in just the right way."

Heidi Alsop, *Ex-Mormon Foundation Board Member*

In *Lying for the Lord*, Townsend "gets under the skin of his characters to reveal their complexity and conflicts….shrewd, evocative [and] wryly humorous."

Kirkus Reviews

In *Missionaries Make the Best Companions*, "the author treats the clash between religious dogma and liberal humanism with vivid realism, sly humor, and subtle feeling as his characters try to figure out their true missions in life. Another of Townsend's rich dissections of Mormon failures and uncertainties…" Named to Kirkus Reviews' Best of 2015.

Kirkus Reviews

In *Invasion of the Spirit Snatchers*, "Townsend, a confident and practiced storyteller, skewers the hypocrisies and eccentricities of his characters with precision and affection. The outlandish framing narrative is the most consistent source of shock and humor, but the stories do much to ground the reader in the world—or former world—of the characters....A funny, charming tale about a group of Mormons facing the end of the world."

Kirkus Reviews

"Townsend's collection [*The Washing of Brains*] once again displays his limpid, naturalistic prose, skillful narrative chops, and his subtle insights into psychology...Well-crafted dispatches on the clash between religion and self-fulfillment..."

Kirkus Reviews

"While the author is generally at his best when working as a satirist, there are some fine, understated touches in these tales [*The Last Days Linger*] that will likely affect readers in subtle ways....readers should come away impressed by the deep empathy he shows for all his characters—even the homophobic ones."

Kirkus Reviews

"Written in a conversational style that often uses stories and personal anecdotes to reveal larger truths, this immensely approachable book [*Racism by Proxy*] skillfully serves its intended audience of White readers grappling with complex questions regarding race, history, and identity. The author's frequent references to the Church of Jesus Christ of Latter-day Saints may be too niche for readers unfamiliar with its idiosyncrasies, but Townsend generally strikes a perfect balance of humor, introspection, and reasoned arguments that will engage even skeptical readers."

Kirkus Reviews

Orgy at the STD Clinic portrays "an all-too real scenario that Townsend skewers to wincingly accurate proportions…[with] instant classic moments courtesy of his punchy, sassy, sexy lead character…"

Jim Piechota, *Bay Area Reporter*

Orgy at the STD Clinic is "…a triumph of humane sensibility. A richly textured saga that brilliantly captures the fraying social fabric of contemporary life." Named to Kirkus Reviews' Best Indie Books of 2022.

Kirkus Reviews

Selling the City of Enoch is "sharply intelligent…pleasingly complex…The stories are full of…doubters, but there's no vindictiveness in these pages; the characters continuously poke holes in Mormonism's more extravagant absurdities, but they take very little pleasure in doing so….Many of Townsend's stories…have a provocative edge to them, but this [book] displays a great deal of insight as well…a playful, biting and surprisingly warm collection."

Kirkus Reviews

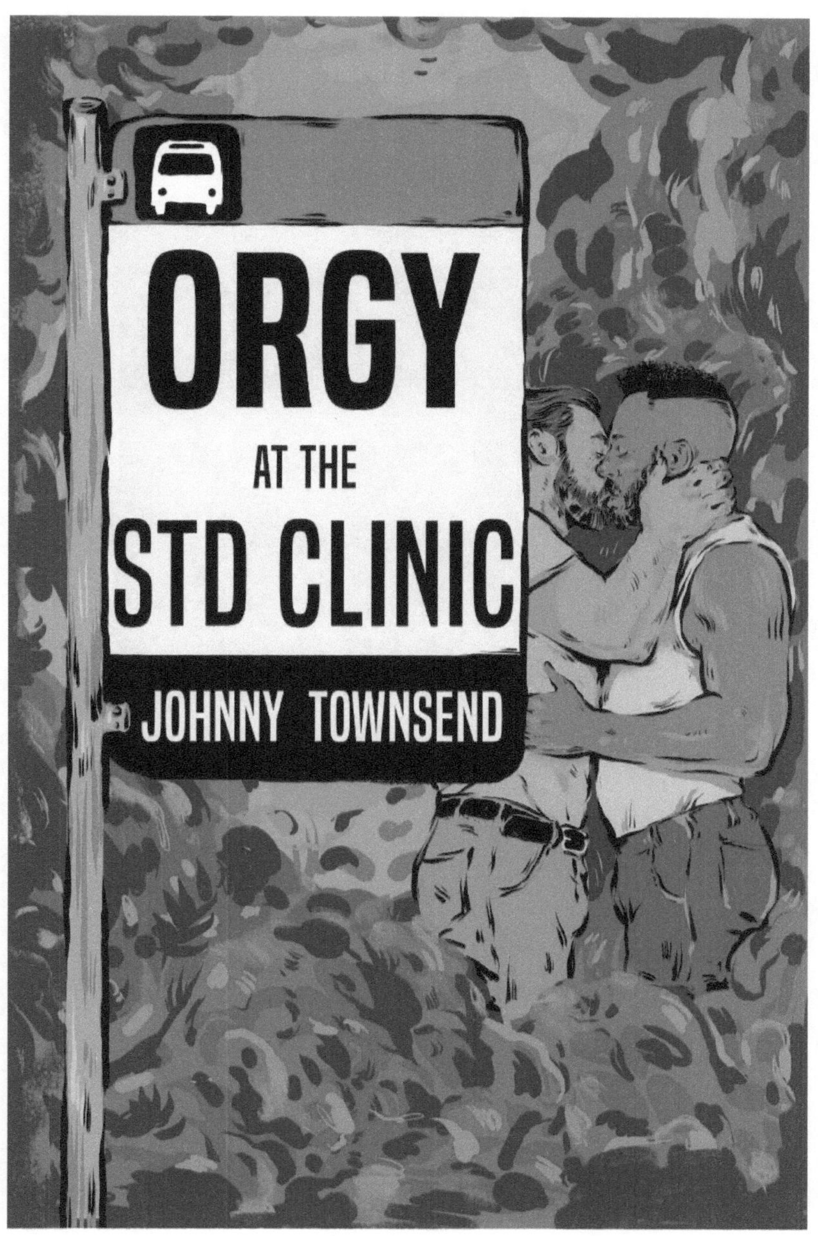
ORGY
AT THE
STD CLINIC
JOHNNY TOWNSEND

HAVE YOUR CUM AND EAT IT, TOO
JOHNNY TOWNSEND

Going-Out-Of-
Religion Sale
JOHNNY TOWNSEND

JOHNNY TOWNSEND
PLEASE
EVACUATE
AGAIN

www.ingramcontent.com/pod-product-compliance
Lightning Source LLC
Chambersburg PA
CBHW022023310726
48972CB00006B/1785